# A Murder in the Village

### And Other Mystical Tales of the Ouachita Mountains

by

## Evelyn Klebert

**A Murder in the Village**
*And Other Mystical Tales of the Ouachita Mountains*
By Evelyn Klebert

A Cornerstone Book
Published by Cornerstone Book Publishers

First Cornerstone Edition – 2025

Cornerstone Book Publishers
Hot Springs Village, AR
www.cornerstonepublishers.com

ISBN 978-1-61342-459-9

# Dedication

For Matt and Jenny,

Thanks for your continued inspiration.

I am more than proud and happy that I get to be your Aunt.

Love Aunt Eve

# Table of Contents

# A Murder in the Village

### And Other
### Mystical Tales
### of the
### Ouachita Mountains

# Missing: The Case of Elena Lora

*A night flower beckons*
*Calls me beyond*
*If I were different*
*I would know.*

With a deep sigh, he silently flipped through the impatiently written journal. Poetry wasn't his area of interest. The script that he'd labeled impatient was, in reality, pretty messy. Not on purpose, he could see some effort in it, curves and some letters more dramatic than needed for common consumption. But it felt painful. Holding the pen in the hand was painful. Either it was trembling or cramping.

*I never knew I would feel this lost.*

One line, set apart, full stop.

"Zeke, found anything?" His partner, Dylan Greg, called from the bedroom.

"Nothing," he lied, slipping the small handwritten journal into a coat pocket. He'd found it rummaging between sofa cushions, stuffed down deep near some crumbled saltines, not big on housework, this one.

But it felt like something. It had tingled in his palms, a flicker of creativity. Hope within the hopelessness, he thought with bemusement.

Dylan strode out of her bedroom. Her name was Elena. He knew that before he stepped into her cottage on the edge of the Ouachita Mountains. It was a rental for a month: January—the month of new things or tying up old ones. And he also knew it from the journal, the first page.

She'd written: *"This is the book of Elena, not a New Testament but more of an accounting."*

He could feel the sarcasm in her pen strokes as she dashed it off as an afterthought. She didn't know what it would be, just that she should write. And when she did this, her hand wasn't hurting.

"I don't see evidence of foul play, though I found her purse. Most chicks take their purse everywhere." Dylan was young, twenty-eight years young, and irreverent.

"How do you know she's a chick?"

He pulled a driver's license out of his pocket. "Let's see. She's thirty-five, didn't take her suitcase, still in the closet, didn't take her make-up, still in the bathroom. Was supposed to give a poetry reading at the local library in Hot Springs yesterday, never showed." Young indeed, but a decent detective.

"Yep," Zeke looked around and felt something glittering in the small vacation house. It was a secluded, rustic, large one-bedroom house with a massive stone fireplace in the den. "She's gone," he murmured.

"Sure about that?" young Dylan asked.

He shook his head, feeling confusion. "No, not really."

❦

Ezekial Ash didn't live in the mountains. For him, there were too many doors. Living in an apartment on the periphery of Hot Springs suited him just fine. The group at the library had reported the missing woman. Evidently, they were more than a little ticked by her not showing up.

And then, after repeatedly trying to reach her, it became clear that something was amiss.

He scrolled slowly through her website, Elena Lora—Writer of Poetry and Prose. How the hell did one make a living that way?

There was her picture at a book signing, long, shoulder-length brown hair, thick hair, then another picture from the back of a book cover—pretty face but large, luminous, brown eyes that felt like they leapt off the computer screen.

*I never knew I would feel this lost.*

Oh, yeah, the journal. He reached over to an end table where he'd deposited it, next to a now-cooled cup of peppermint tea. It was his evening drink, more stimulating in coffee in some ways. As he grabbed the journal to open it, something shiny slid out of the pages. He picked up the teal-colored key, turned it about, then smiled, holding it in his palm.

"Feels like an invitation, Elena," he murmured, grasping his fingers around it.

He took a quick breath inward as he began to feel, feel so many things.

❦

Elena Lora's cottage was in the woods, but not exactly isolated. The houses were rustic though not quite close enough to be labeled a subdivision. He parked his Jeep down at the end of

Marbella Lane, a good block away from her place, and proceeded to hike in darkness back up the hill.

The report he and Dylan had turned in was nonconclusive, still under investigation. His boss wasn't convinced the lady hadn't just gone off somewhere, maybe with a friend, a lover, or on a lark. Of course, Dylan had a point about her—belongings untouched, driver's license not taken.

Zeke rounded the house broadly, hoping not to draw the attention of neighbors. But he did remember the back entrance beneath the wooden balcony.

Twigs and winter leaves crushed beneath his heavy boots as he trudged through the darkness. In the summer months, he wouldn't attempt such a thing, but much of the wildlife, the most dangerous kind, was still sleeping. Too bad that wasn't true of everything.

He used his cellphone light to find the doorknob and try the key. He had no reason to believe this would work except that it did, and the door eased open into the darkness.

*Things that are supposed to work often do*—was his adage.

He was careful not to switch on any lights, although the nearest neighbor was two lots down. There was another house a bit closer, diagonally across Marbella, but no car in the driveway. Many of these places were summer getaways, but apparently not for Elena Lora.

And he wondered for not the first time what exactly she was trying to get away from.

The shadowed room seemed to be some sort of den but largely empty, except for a desk and a futon against the wall.

Ezekial Ash took a breath, trying to sort out what he was feeling. As he found his way to the stairs, he thought once again—way too many doors here.

✴

*A night flower beckons,*

   *Calls me beyond.*

It was a flare-up of lupus. She stretched her fingers out, grimacing. It wouldn't do for a writer to have hands that don't want to work. She glanced over at the rustling sound outside her sliding glass door. It was partially open, and there was a breeze tonight, a chilly breeze, but Elena didn't care. She loved the sounds of the night from the forest.

They were calming, mesmerizing.

Yesterday, no, it was today, she'd followed a black cat that was slinking between the trees down the slope of the backyard into the woods behind the house. She'd actually slipped once on the leaves, falling backward on her butt, but she continued onward, content to go deeper and deeper into the forest, down the hill.

Every once in a while, when she was just winded enough to give up, the furry feline would poke its head around a tree trunk as if to say, "Are you coming with me?"

So, she followed. Once she found herself on level ground again, there was a stream at the bottom of the hill that she had no idea even existed. It wasn't very wide, but the water was active, bending around stacks of curious rock formations.

Pretty tired at that point, she simply sank to the ground, feeling content to watch the water, but then that cat appeared again.

Almost out of nowhere, she thought with amusement because she really hadn't seen where it came from. Suddenly, it was just there, eying her with its bright blue eyes, then curling up on the opposite bank of the creek.

When she'd finally gotten back to the house, it was nearly nightfall. It was surprising how much time had passed, four or five hours. So, she'd taken a shower and then settled down at the small kitchen table, trying to write.

She didn't hear him behind her, didn't hear him coming out of the hallway from the stairs.

Struggling to compose, she wrote in a penmanship that she despised because her hands refused to properly convey her thoughts to the page.

*If I were different*

*I would know.*

And then the last thing she penned before she looked up was,

*I never knew I would feel this lost.*

❦

The stairs were carpeted with a break halfway. As Ezekial turned the corner, he noted soft lights seeping into the hallway door.

He took a deliberate breath. There hadn't been any lights on when he'd approached from the road. But now—

He paused at the turn in the stairs. He'd left his gun in the Jeep. Truth was, he didn't always carry. He had a sense of these things, an instinct when he would need it. He didn't like guns, not at all. Odd for a police detective? Sure. But then again, he hadn't always been a detective.

He made his way up the carpeted stairway. He remembered the house's layout from earlier. While Dylan was rummaging through Elena's bedroom, he had familiarized himself with the place.

A right turn would lead to the den, and from the hallway, it was clear where the light emanated. He closed his eyes, using his senses. It wasn't dangerous exactly, but something else. He looked back and forth a bit in disbelief. It couldn't have been that seamless.

There were always signs, sometimes a smell like the embers of a fire that were dying down or acidity, and visuals as well—things just looking a little off, maybe even tilted. But not nothing. There were always signs.

Slowly, he made his way down the hallway as silently as he could manage.

The den where he'd found the journal was shadowed, but as he silently turned a right corner toward the kitchen, he hesitated. The light over the small wooden dining table was on, and the figure had her back to him, hunched over somewhat.

Standing there, waiting, the telltale dizziness finally passed through him, confirming exactly what he was dealing with.

"Elena Lora," he said softly.

The shoulders straightened at his words. He could feel total shock passing painfully through her body. Then she turned to face him, brown eyes wide with terror.

※

Thoughts raced through her mind. How quickly could she spring to the small galley kitchen and grab a knife from the block on the counter? Or maybe just put her hands on something large enough to fling at him. But then the stranger standing before her did something unexpected. He put his hands up in front of him.

"Elena, I promise you. I mean you no harm."

She stood up, violently pushing the chair behind her and stepping backward toward the kitchen. "How did you get in?" she nearly rasped.

Slowly, he put his hand into his jacket pocket and brought out a teal key that he held in front of him. She recognized it from

7

the color, the backup key the realtor had given her, the one that had gone missing.

"Where did you get that?" she said harshly, struggling not to let the overwhelming fear that threatened to overtake her creep into her voice.

"I found it," he said quietly.

She stared at the key in his hand, feeling the trembling in her legs. Making a decision, in a leap, she sprang into the kitchen and grabbed the largest knife she could put her hands on, spinning around and putting it in front of her. And good thing she had because he'd moved directly behind her.

She gestured toward him with the knife. "Now, I want you out," she said with as much malice as she could muster.

He stared at her without expression, still holding the key in his hand but not in front of him anymore. "Don't you want to know where I got it?" he murmured in a curiously flat voice.

"I must have dropped it somewhere."

"No," the dark-haired intruder said. "I found it in your journal."

Her eyes widened. "My journal?"

"Yeah, you know the this is the book of Elena, not a New Testament but more of an accounting journal."

"What—" she sputtered in confusion. "My journal is sitting on the kitchen table."

He didn't even turn around to the table, just put the key on a nearby cabinet, and rubbed his beard a bit thoughtfully with his hand. "Yeah, let's see. A night flower beckons, calls me beyond. If I were different, I would know."

She glanced over to the table to find the book she'd just been writing in, but her eyes widened as she saw it had vanished.

Accusingly, she looked up at him, "What did you do with my book?"

Again, he reached into his pocket and, this time brought the small journal out. If she hadn't still been holding the kitchen knife in front of her, she would have snatched it away. But she was still afraid. "You must have picked it up when I turned around," she muttered shakily.

He shrugged a little, not much, just enough that it was noticeable. "And had time to read it?"

She opened her mouth but had no explanation. Maybe she was losing it. Maybe all of this wasn't happening, a hallucination of some sort.

"Now, don't jump to conclusions, Miss Lora," and then he frowned as though something distasteful had crossed his mind. "Lora? That's not your name, is it?"

Disbelief, she stared at him in complete disbelief. "Laura was my middle name. I changed it to the last."

He nodded, "Elena Laura, nice. My name is Ash, Ezekial Ash. I was wondering if you've lost some time lately."

It took a beat for his odd words to penetrate.

"What? Time?" she answered in complete confusion.

"Yeah, lost track of time in the last few days."

Her head had begun to throb oddly. Then she remembered the cat, the cat by the stream. How long had she sat there across from it? "Yes," she whispered, remembering. "There was a cat."

Again, he nodded slowly. "Animals, they do tend to travel. Well, maybe we should sit down and talk a bit. Is it all right if I call you Elena?"

"I-I don't know why you're here."

"Yeah, right, well, actually, I'm a detective. People have been looking for you."

"Looking? Why? I've been right here." And then Detective Ezekial Ash smiled at her, smiled at her in a way that made her feel silly to be still holding the kitchen knife threateningly in front of her.

"So, Elena. You wouldn't happen to have tea, would you?"

"Tea? Yes, I have tea," she murmured hesitantly.

"So, how about you sit down, and I'll make us both a cup of tea, and we'll try to sort through this." She glanced at the table, wondering exactly what she should do. And then he added reassuringly, "You can keep the knife, if it makes you feel better."

Absurd, that was what this felt like, completely absurd. "Okay," she answered shakily, moving cautiously to sit at the table and placing the knife blade down flat while still keeping her fingertips on the handle.

⚘

He'd noticed back home when flipping through the journal that more had been written.

*When do the tangled threads of life*

*Become compelling enough again?*

*To warrant notice, enthusiasm, or*

*Even an obligation to start over.*

He pondered her words for some time. When, indeed, was it time to try to start over? That was not a train of thought that he was wholly unfamiliar with. Ezekial had considered, in fact, often contemplated pulling up stakes again and starting over, elsewhere. He knew his family would be happy to have him back—mother, father, a sister, and brother, if he could even find them now.

He seldom looked in the mirror because, as his mother had always said, it reflected far too many things. But he'd done it tonight before he came to explore Elena's cottage. He'd looked closely and methodically at the face staring back at him from the bathroom mirror. The face was a bit grizzled, dark beard unkempt, but still clearly reflecting a man just in his forties.

Yet he had not seen his birth family for nearly two hundred years.

*"If you live there, you won't age the same as they do."* His mother had warned him. And as with most things, she was right.

*"But why, Ezekial, why would you even want to live there?"*

He had no answer.

**I never knew I would feel this lost.**

Her words, not his, the journal nearly burned a hole in his jacket pocket as though it were alive. Such was the kinetic energy of creativity, easier to sense in some places than others.

She hadn't even noticed that he hadn't given it back to her. And he was grateful because the truth was that he wasn't ready to give it back. He busied himself in the kitchen, arranging two mugs of mint tea and waiting for the kettle to heat up on the stove.

He didn't even have to turn around to see her.

In his mind, crisply, he could see her sitting at the table. Her eyes nearly bored into his back with intensity. He took a breath and rubbed his face. She, well, was really something.

He'd begun to feel it acutely, touching her things, feeling her energy, and then the writing. It made him drunk, nearly as if he'd uncorked a bottle of bourbon and was downing it unceasingly.

He shook his head. Of course, to do what she had, even if she had no idea what she was doing, should have tipped him off.

"*What are you looking for?*" His mother had asked.

"I don't know, something," and that was true. There was a restlessness, a need, a pull so profound to something.

"*Or someone?*" His mother observed, as she could easily see his thoughts where they were.

The tea kettle whistled jarringly, shaking him back to the present. He poured the hot water into the mugs and put them down, turning to face her. She was thin and hadn't been eating properly. In fact, she would sometimes completely forget. That made her dark eyes seem larger, large enough to devour, he thought with distraction.

"Are you okay?" he asked.

"Who is looking for me?" she responded quietly.

"Oh, the ladies down at the public library, it seems. You missed an event."

The eyebrows darted together slightly, "The reading? That's not for another week."

"Nope, two days ago. Seems you lost some time, Elena. Maybe with the cat."

She looked at him blankly. "What does that even mean, with the cat? It was just a cat."

"Yeah, well, maybe, but cats travel all night long. They travel into all kinds of places, have great adventures."

And then she frowned, "Mr. Ash or Detective Ash, I am not a child. What are you trying to say?"

"What I'm trying to say, Miss Lora, you might not be ready to hear. That was why I suggested the tea."

She pulled her hand off the knife and put it on top of the other one on her lap. That, he noted, though he doubted she'd even realized she'd done it. "You're wasting my time," she murmured.

"Am I?" he said. He'd tried to buy time, to send her calming energy that could make her more receptive, but she was obstinate, strong mind, old soul. "Well, let me try again."

He noticed a slight raising of one of her eyebrows in response. He'd be lucky if he got anywhere at this rate, so he might as well go for broke. "You see, these mountains around us, the Ouachita, are filled with doors."

"Doors? What does that even mean?"

"Doors to other dimensions," he answered.

⚜

He, the detective or so he claimed, who was sitting across from her, didn't ask her how she liked her tea. Why hadn't she asked him for ID, a badge? She glanced at the kitchen knife still poised in front of her. What was the point? She knew, and evidently, he knew as well, that she wasn't going to use it.

She brought the hot mug of tea to her lips. Just a touch of sugar, exactly how she liked it.

"How did you know?"

He glanced over to her, and his dark green eyes canvassed her in a manner that felt unsettling yet not unpleasant. What a combination. "Know what?"

"How to fix my tea."

"Ah, well, I could say I have a sense of these things."

"But that would be a non-answer. Is that why you're here to give me non-answers, Ezekial Ash?" She used his name because she liked the sound of it on her lips. Of course, she hadn't ruled out the possibility that he was a crazy serial killer who had broken into her house. And her only weapon against him was still well within her reach, although she had already admitted to herself that she wouldn't be using it this evening. And then she glanced over to him, noting that he was intently watching her. "Are you going to answer me?"

"Sorry, I was waiting for your mind to quiet down. There are a lot of thoughts there."

She leaned back in her chair. He was crazy, no question. "What are you saying? You're reading my thoughts, some kind of psychic?"

A bit of a shrug, "No, not exactly Elena, more an opportunist," then he sipped his tea before putting it down on the table. "We were talking about the cat."

"The cat?"

"Yeah, as good a place as any to start. Are you aware of all the crazy night adventures feral cats have?"

"Really? Okay, fine, um, vaguely, I guess."

"Well, I saw a video once of someone putting a camera on one. This cat was awake all night, traveling from yard to yard, place to place, getting into fights, climbing trees, and making its way across rooftops, but strangely, it always seemed to know where it was. Had an inside navigation system, so it could return to the same spots every night."

She nodded, trying to follow this thread that seemed opaque. "You said something about dimensions. What did that mean?"

And then he smiled, "Well Elena, your cat, the black cat you followed, is like other cats in that it likes to travel, all over really, but then comes back. But this one, maybe because of where it lives or maybe because it's a bit different, finds the doors."

"Doors again, Detective Ash? What does that even mean?"

And then he rubbed his beard as though thinking, and she found it kind of endearing. "Elena, please call me Ezekial or Zeke if you'd rather, though I like the way you say Ezekial. Well, as I said, the Ouachita area is unique, permeable in some respects. Your cat evidently goes in and out of doors to other dimensions, and it seems as though you followed it."

"I-I did what?"

"You've been gone, Elena. There's a missing person's report for you on my desk. Where you are now, here, isn't where you rented your house or where you were supposed to give your poetry reading. Somehow, you passed through a door to another nearby dimension that looks very similar but isn't quite the same."

She stared at him blankly, "That's crazy."

"Yeah, I can see how you'd think so," he said a bit gruffly. "Have you been out the house since the cat episode?"

"I-no, I've been tired."

"Yeah, probably best. I imagine things might be a bit different out there."

Her eyes flew to the open sliding glass door. It was dark, so she couldn't really see but—but nothing, this was ridiculous. Abruptly, she stood up, "Look, whoever you are. I want you to get out of my house. What you're telling me isn't possible."

Then there was a frown, just a slight one, that told her distinctly that he wasn't surprised. "Why did you change it?"

"What?"

"Your name, you changed your last name."

"It's a pseudonym. That's all."

He nodded slowly but watched her calmly as though he was searching for something. "No, that's not all, is it? You wanted to be someone else, change who you were. Your poetry is filled with sadness, Elena."

She was struck inside somewhere, like someone had punched a hole in her. "I've barely written in that journal. You can't know that."

"Yeah, but the one I have is full, full of verses that you will write. Dimensional traveling does odd things to creative matters like writing and painting. My mother used to paint beautiful pictures. Some would just appear in the morning, though she had just begun them. It was because she was a traveler, like me."

"Like you? What does that mean, a traveler?"

"Elena, I'm not from your frame. That's what we call it, frames of existence. That's why I was able to find you. You're lost here in this little pocket, very close to your home, but different. So, the question becomes now, Elena Lora, what do we do about this?"

�҂

*"You won't age as they do."*

"I know," he'd answered.

*"When will our family see you again?"*

"I'm not sure."

*"That place, that frame. It's a difficult one. Many are confused there. They don't understand the true nature of things."*

"I know, but I feel something important. I feel a pull there."

*"Yes, I can see that."*

He could feel it when he touched the journal. Her creative energy was alive and seeking, just as if she'd reached out and touched him. But here, in this pocket dimension where she'd mistakenly stumbled into, he could feel it and see it even more intensely. Just sitting across from her, the colors of her aura were leaping around the room, seeking a place to affix to. *Kindred* was the whisper that permeated everything, but Elena resisted. She was still so wrapped in fear.

"This can't be true," she whispered.

"Why?" he asked solemnly. "Because you were taught differently, because you were taught to reject such possibilities?"

Then her wide, fearful eyes fixed on him, and he felt reverberations in his soul. Small steps, he schooled himself. "Are you going back?" she asked. And he found it surprising. Out of all the possible questions she could ask, this is the one she chose.

"No, I'm not going back for a while. I haven't seen my family for a long time. I've decided to go home."

She stared at him, and he could feel longing. "I don't really have family," she said, then glanced away, and he felt things wrap around him, things from her past that pained her greatly.

"Would you like to come with me?" he asked because he had to. He had spent an inordinate amount of time in that frame, looking or something. And until he'd touched her journal, he wasn't really sure why.

She stared at him without answering, then said softly, "Maybe, I don't have anything back there."

He took an inward breath, somewhat amazed. This was too easy, but then again, maybe things that were right were this easy. "Well, let's finish our tea, then we can talk about it."

"Won't people wonder what's happened to you?"

"Maybe," he replied. But then again, people vanished inexplicably every day, and he would just be one more.

# An Unexpected Danger

She breathed in the cool forest air that clung deep in her lungs as if it would never let go. Tomorrow was the first time after several days off that she would return to work at the restaurant. Thoroughly enjoying her holiday, and not unexpectedly, something inside her felt sluggish and resistant to going back. The job, while necessary, was also remarkably unfulfilling. It did, however, help her keep an eye on things surreptitiously. But she was young, and being young, she couldn't help but yearn for more.

Peering outward from her balcony across the landscape, with its varying autumn shades of green, gold, red, and orange, it sloped down to the winding road at the bottom of the well-forested, hilly terrain. And then she could see a car in the distance, actually a jeep, a white jeep with a black top. It was not unusual for vehicles to make this trek, but this one gave her pause. Undeniably, something felt different.

Abra pulled her light gray jacket tighter around her as her eyes watched the meandering car. Most sped along the path, but not this one. And there was more. Undeniably, something inside her prickled, her blood rushing to her temples, causing her eyes to narrow and focus more succinctly. She swallowed on a bone-dry throat. How extraordinary, after all these years, a legitimate threat had come to this haven.

⚜

This was an indulgence. He had impulsively decided to stay a while in the *New World* after his contentious encounter with his long-lost blood brother in New Orleans. Kian, his enduring and most loyal comrade, had opted to head back to Europe immediately. The former region of Lorraine in France was currently where their coven had called home for many years. But Lapetus had curiously felt a pull, a restlessness compelling him to further explore this country once his business was completed, at least for a little while. In his absence, he had designated Kian to act in his stead.

Renting a car, he had only been casually driving through the state of Arkansas when he felt a distinct and insistent stirring in his blood. In some respects, it felt strangely reminiscent of a long ago call to a hunt, but not exactly the same. It was then, just outside of Hot Springs, that he stumbled upon its source—a gated community, some 26,000 acres, that designated itself as the Village at the foothills of the Ouachita Mountains.

As there was no free access to these lands, and there was undeniably a distinct pull of a more than compelling variety, he stopped at a realtor just outside the gates. Without much fanfare, he rented a vacation house from a well-coiffed middle-aged blond woman in a startling bright pink dress.

"Do you want a condo or a house?"

"House."

"By the water?"

"More remote."

"Remote, hmm, trying to get away from it all?"

"Something like that."

She clicked her mouse, pursing her well-lip-sticked mouth a bit more intently, and Lapetus wondered if he'd made an error in judgment. What would he do in this remote setting for a week? He didn't particularly like the water and was certainly not a bird watcher.

"I have a lovely two-bedroom split-level place. Brand new kitchen, lovely scenic view of the surrounding forest."

He breathed in deeply. Maybe he should move on, drive into the Ozarks, and head north. But then again, there was that delicious frisson along his skin that he hadn't felt since, well, at least several hundred years.

"Yes, that sounds like the one."

And then she'd smiled broadly, pleased that she would be taking his money soon. And she added with animation that he did not find sincere, "Where are you from again? I can't quite place the accent."

"Andorra," he replied softly.

※

"Abra, how are the classes going?"

She smiled back at the younger girl, tying her apron while standing behind the register. Glancing briefly up at the wall, she took in the vintage Coca-Cola clock. The sad truth was the whole restaurant was strenuously filled with vintage Coke memorabilia, from the polar bears perched on the partition walls to an old-fashioned cooler next to the register. "Okay, though studying online is tough for me. I'm more of a visual learner."

Young Lacey, just taking a part-time job here, just worked the weekends. She was a senior in high school and clearly, judging from her expression, had no idea what Abra was talking about. "Cool," she murmured with little interest. "I hope it's not busy today. I was up late last night."

Abra nodded with comprehension—no doubt partying in Hot Springs proper. Her head was pounding a bit this morning, as she was up late as well. But it wasn't from partying. She'd spent a good part of the evening yesterday with her grandmother, discussing the disturbing vibe she'd picked up from the Jeep traveling that winding road not far from her home.

Her Gran had been stoic, but then again, she was ninety-three. "It might just be someone passing through," she'd said softly. "This time of year draws a lot of vacationers to the Village. But they leave after a short time."

Abra sat on the stone fireplace mantle next to her rocking chair. Her Gran, Michaela Jensen, who lived in the small cottage near the edge of the Village with Abra's aunt, looked forward with bright green eyes that reflected little expression. "I suppose that could be true."

And then the old woman focused on her. "But you feel different?"

"I don't know. It's been so long since anything has happened here. But I did feel some sort of elusive threat."

The silver-haired woman pulled her heavy woolen shawl more tightly around her despite the room being warm. "Yes, well, then, do not ignore your feelings. After all, this is on your shoulders."

Abra shook her head, trying to focus on the task at hand. It was five to seven. She just had to get through the breakfast and lunch shift and then head home. It was undoubtedly just as her Gran had said, someone passing through, someone with an energy spectrum that sent chills to her heart.

❦

He didn't really have to eat, not like other people. In fact, he remembered once he hadn't eaten for an entire month. But energy renewal, well, that was another matter. Over the many, many, and yes, he could comfortably add one more many years, he had unraveled numerous methods of energy renewal. In the old days, hunting and consuming near-living flesh had been the optimum choice of renewal. Then, later, other methods were discovered that might be considered as some to be a bit less violent or grisly.

But it did call to him at times, the old lust for flesh, blood, and the challenge of facing off against a prey or perhaps even against a worthy opponent. But today, he just wanted breakfast. It slumbered, the hungry one, and he was taken by the quaint little restaurant called *Esme's*, tucked away in this vast scope of land they'd named the Village.

The draw he'd felt initially here had faded into obscurity. Maybe it was an element that had departed from this place, or perhaps an element that sought to disguise itself. Now, that could be interesting.

Lapetus had dressed in casual wear today, wearing khaki pants and a long-sleeved black shirt. Casual seemed the standard in this particular province. The house he'd rented for the week was comfortable enough, fully furnished, and oddly, it had a vast, open den stretching upward to skylights and rustic ceiling beams. Downstairs, there was an equally large bedroom, and a second smaller one, which oddly felt like a waste of space, but then again, he was used to accommodations in the old country. Admittedly, he was beginning to feel homesick for it. His nature was not to be a wanderer. He had roots and did not desire to be away from them for too long a stretch.

As he entered the doorway of *Esme's*, he was questioning his choice in renting that house. He was questioning his idea to explore this *New World*. And just as he walked into this cozy and bright restaurant, a young waitress approached him.

"Can I seat you, sir?" she said with a light, soft voice that sort of curled around his senses. He was close enough to her that he smelled the scent of violets on her skin. Though she held a menu in her delicate hand, his eyes were drawn to hers. These eyes were wide and flawlessly green and undeniably filled with the slightest tinge of alarm that she masked well.

And then, Lapetus allowed all his qualms to melt away. Ah, yes, this, she, was unquestionably why he was here.

❦

She steeled herself as she led him toward a corner table against the back wall of the small restaurant. "Is this all right for you?" she asked.

"Secluded," he noted.

"If you'd prefer up front—"

"This will be fine," and then he tacked on, "Abra."

An unwelcome chill traveled up her spine at his casual use of her name. But then again, it was plastered boldly on the plastic name tag affixed to her red t-shirt. "So, what can I get you to start, some coffee, tea, or something else?" she said lightly.

"How is the coffee here at *Esme's*?" She'd purposefully tried to avoid his gaze, but it was difficult, difficult not to engage with a customer when you are a waitress.

She smiled, staring directly into his eyes. They were such an odd color, light but not blue, instead a pale gray that contrasted with his well-tanned skin. Her Gran would call him Mediter-ranean in appearance, which his unusual enunciation supported. No, then again, swarthy was the term her Gran might use. And his hair was black, nearly blue-black, thick, with a well-clipped

23

beard and mustache affixed on a chiseled face, strong bone structure—undeniably foreign, unmistakably, but compelling, nonetheless. "It's good, and Clara has just brewed a fresh pot." Keep it light and bubbly: Waitress 101. That way, all of this might just blow over, and he'll never know.

"That sounds good, Abra. And if I might see a menu." She glanced down. Damn, it was still in her hand, and she hadn't even noticed.

"Oh, sorry," she replied smoothly, handing it to him. But then, when he took it from her, everything shifted. It felt like a shock or rather a bolt of some kind reverberating through the plastic-coated menu straight into her hand. "So, if you have any questions—" Her voice sort of trailed off because he wasn't looking at the menu at all. He was looking at her intently, and it felt somehow as if he was pinning her to the wall behind her with his eyes.

Mesmerism? Some creatures were undoubtedly capable of it. Mentally, she strengthened the energy shield she'd placed around her once she'd felt him approaching the restaurant, doubling down on it once he'd parked in the lot, and even more so when he took his first steps inside. It should have been enough. With every other creature of the diabolical variety, it had been. Again, she bared down, completely closing herself off from any interference.

Then, he allowed the menu to slip onto the tablecloth from his fingertips. He leaned back in his chair, a slow smile spreading across his face. "Yes, well, Abra. I will let you know if I have any questions."

And then she nodded and wordlessly turned around, heading back toward the kitchen.

⚜

Perhaps it was foolish, perhaps it was giving herself away, but she was in a panic. She'd never met a being quite like this before, with this level of—And there was that as well. How did she describe it? Power was the word that rose to her consciousness, but it felt like something well beyond that.

Clara, in the kitchen, and then Joe Monroe at the register, the couple who owned *Esme's*, seemed shocked when she simply dumped her customer on Lacey. She'd abruptly declared she was nauseous and would be barfing all over the customers if she didn't go home. Consciously or not, it had been deliberate, her seating him to the back of *Esme's* just in case, just in case she needed to run.

Her heart was hammering as she jumped into her off-white Volkswagen and made a beeline out of the parking lot. It was pointless anyway to continue a charade that she knew in her skin, her very essence, had failed. All she would do by staying would be to give him more information about her, and he, whoever and whatever he was, knew too much already.

❦

Lacey, the new waitress, was a redhead and precisely what she appeared to be—a very young woman looking for a good tip. And Lapetus, admittedly, was a bit disappointed when she brought him his coffee instead of the *other one*. Disappointed yet intrigued.

"What happened to Abra?" he asked casually, perusing the well-used menu.

"She wasn't feeling well, so she left. Anything I can help you with?"

He frowned, quickly canvassing the relatively short menu because, in truth, it was the first time he'd really looked at it. "How are your omelets?" he asked with little interest.

"Demon?"

She flopped down on the short sofa in the den of her Aunt Jolene and Gran's house with exasperation. "I don't know."

Her Gran wrinkled her already well-wrinkled face. She was bundled up in her heavy shawl over a long-sleeved duster that seemed like her requisite wardrobe these days. "Now calm down, Abra. You're much too agitated. You've encountered mystical and even dark-tempered entities before."

"Yes, yes, I have. But this, this is different. He felt so—" Good lord, how could she even begin to describe this? "I felt like I was drowning just being near him."

"Come here," the old woman commanded with a rough voice, in the way that had told Abra succinctly that she meant business. Abra stood up and walked over to her grandmother's rocking chair that was always positioned close enough to the plate glass window in the small cottage, so that she always had a view of the lush forest outside their home. "Now, give me your hand."

With some despondency, Abra put her hand in her grandmother's which she took in hers, none too lightly. "Now, clear your mind and focus, focus on this powerful man of yours."

She heard her Gran breathing deeply as she closed her eyes, visualizing the dark-haired man she'd seated at *Esme's* just an hour before. Vaguely, she wondered if he'd finished his breakfast and what he'd ended up ordering. "Focus on the energy," Michaela Jensen said gruffly.

She tried, tried to calm herself and let herself simply open to the vibrations of energy. It was so odd. In her mind, she could see herself in the restaurant again, standing in the center of *Esme's*, feeling an absolute cyclone of divergent energy bands circling.

"Shapeshifter," her Gran murmured.

"I've encountered shapeshifters before. They're easy enough to run off."

She heard her Gran's breathing beside her. "No, he's old, very old, my child. He won't be run off. But it doesn't appear he's on the hunt."

"The hunt?" Abra said with question, opening her eyes.

And then her Gran opened hers as well, those pure green wizened eyes. "Yes, lucky for you, he's not on the hunt. This one is a werewolf."

It shook her, what her Gran had said. "Are you sure? I mean, I thought most of those—"

"Were gone?" The old woman shook her head, almost as though she were thinking aloud to herself. "Yes, it does seem rare these days. Though I have heard there are still covens, very old ones in Europe."

"Have you—" Why were the words choking in Abra's throat? "I mean, during your time as the Protector, did you ever run across one?"

Her Gran's eyes fixed on her with concern. "You're afraid, child."

Was she? Perhaps it was the unknown that frightened her. This, without question, was an unknown quantity. "I don't really understand what I'm dealing with. This isn't just black magic or opportunists drawn to the area."

"No, no, this is something altogether different."

Abra nodded and smiled at her Grandmother Michaela. She was such a strong, wise woman. Surely, they could figure this out. "All right, Gran, I'll make us both a cup of tea, and then I want you to tell me every scrap of information you know about this sort of beast."

"Yes, yes, I will." And then she closed her eyes, and Abra could feel through her skin that the older woman was not sleeping, but communing with other spirits, attempting to draw in help and advice for her granddaughter.

❧

When Lapetus left *Esme's,* he went for a drive, a long drive through the area, hoping, well, hoping he could find her again. Even though his exposure to her had been brief, he was drawn, curious, and eminently aware that this indulgence could be profoundly dangerous for him. But the truth was that he didn't really care. Unexpectedly, his time in New Orleans had given birth to a recklessness in him, a stirring of embers that had been ignited by Abra, Abra Jensen.

The new waitress, the one who had taken Abra's place, Lacey was her name, had brought his coffee, smiling brightly. "Cream or sugar?" she'd asked.

"No, just black," he'd answered softly.

"Well, your omelet won't be long."

At that, he reached out, grabbed her hand, and then looked into her startled cornflower-blue eyes. "Why don't you sit for a moment, Lacey?"

He could tell by the expression of confusion on her face that she had no idea what to do. When his influence was exerted, it hit everyone differently. But oddly, the other one, Abra, seemed to elude it quite easily. "Maybe just a moment."

And then she sank into the chair across from him. She glanced down at the hand he continued to hold. "I was wondering if you might tell me something about your friend."

"Friend?" she repeated, now clearly in a state of mesmerization.

28

"Yes, Abra."

"Abra?"

"Yes, I'd like you to tell me everything you know about her. But most particularly where she lives."

⁂

Deliberately, he didn't want to go near her house. He didn't want to tip her off, not yet. So, instead, he canvassed the area casually, driving and feeling, seeing if he could pick up any sense of her that was not cloaked. But so far, there was nothing, as though she were a mirage. He smiled. How fascinating, and why indeed would she feel the need to shield herself so extensively?

⁂

"The original ones, the old ones, were largely beasts, bitten by wolf creatures and transformed into monsters controlled by the phases of the moon. They would stay in the man/wolf mode for three nights of the month, then appear as normal the rest of the time. Though some were solitary, they largely moved in packs or clans, which have evolved into covens."

"Like witches?" Abra offered, then took a sip of her black tea, which today tasted strongly of licorice. It was fine, though. She needed something to stimulate her mind.

Her Gran's eyes were closed, and Abra understood that she was almost in a state of channeling. "Not exactly. Witches often aspire to power and develop their craft, though yes, some are born more inclined to it. But the beasts, the werewolf covens are tied together because they are of a like mind and live a similar existence."

"Okay," she murmured, taking another sip of tea, not really knowing how helpful this was.

"Initially, the old ones would consume flesh, often human, to devour the spirit, or rather, the energy force of its prey. Energy is a key component in their survival."

"You said used to."

"Yes, some have evolved from this baser nature, have become more attuned to power points on the earth, and can draw and reenergize without the need to kill."

"What about this one?"

"It's unknown, Abra. It is clear he is very old and also clear that you've been marked."

"Marked? What does that mean?"

"As far as can be told, he is aware of you."

※

Lapetus pulled into a small boat launch near a lake. He didn't know how far he had driven, but it was quite a distance from *Esme's*. He closed his eyes for a moment, sinking, sinking deeply into an instinctual place where he could see. Things shifted in his mind as he began to access the wolf. If he wanted to, he could transform here, now, by sheer will, but there was no point in that. But the vision, yes, that was what he was after.

※

"Is there anything else?" Abra asked with a shakiness in her voice. "Anything I can use?"

Her grandmother swallowed, and her chin was lifted, although her eyes were still closed, as though she was determined to find answers for her. "The old ones, some have come to the point where they can transform by will."

"By will? Like a shapeshifter, you mean."

30

"It's different. It takes tremendous determination and power to harness the wolf within."

"I see," she murmured, feeling despondent. "I'm not sure what I can do here."

Her Gran slowly opened her eyes and peered directly at Abra. "He's near."

"What?" Abra stood up abruptly, spilling some of her tea onto the polished wooden floor in her Gran's den.

"Be easy, child. Don't let him smell fear."

She swallowed on a parched and constricted throat. "What does he want?"

Her Gran expelled a breath. "All I can sense is curiosity. It's not impossible that he might just pass through with no significant trouble."

"Significant? What does that mean?"

But there was no answer, just her Gran leaning back, settling again comfortably in her rocking chair and sipping her tea as though nothing of particular consequence was happening.

❧

When he opened his eyes this time, he could see through the wolf. Now it was easy, across the lake on the other side, a house, a small house just spilling forth with energy.

❧

"Have you heard of the Snawfus?"

Abra looked at her blankly. "The what?"

"The Howler?"

31

She took a deep breath, her eyes passing over her mother, who was quietly sitting in a chair some yards away from this interrogation. "Is that some kind of a mixed drink?" she murmured lightly.

The woman, dressed in black, frowned, which created a disturbing effect, given that her foundation was a light, pasty color and her lipstick a dark burgundy that was difficult to imagine looking good on anyone. "No," she said with a definitiveness that should have curled the young fifteen-year-old's toes. But it didn't. As her Gran had always said, young Abra Jensen had hutzpah.

"The Gollywog?"

Abra felt a slight smile threatening to make its way out. Really, was the old hag making this stuff up?

"The Woozer?"

She shook her head with no sound as she was sure it wouldn't due to giggle just now.

"The Whistling Wampus?"

"I've heard of Ewoks. Any of those about?" She asked with the softest lilt in her voice.

The woman, with jet-black hair, which was way too severe for her advanced age, and the oh-so-badly chosen shade of lipstick turned to her Gran, who was sitting next to her with an expressionless face. "Michaela, did you teach her nothing?"

"No, Elliana, her mother forbade it. She wasn't sure her child would be capable of taking up the mantle."

Abra frowned. Not capable? That wasn't very generous, even though she was largely clueless as to what this was all about. "Yes," her mother, Sarah Jensen, spoke from her spot across the room. "That is correct. I have not indoctrinated Abra into our ways. But it was not that I felt her incapable; instead, I wanted to give her the option of choosing another kind of life if she wished."

"And you would leave this Ouachita Valley without a protector?"

Her mother was silent. And Abra found that odd, just about as odd as she had always found the fact that the Jensen women did not marry. Back several generations before her mother, all the women in her family had remained single, yet each had one daughter out of wedlock. She'd asked about the strange coincidence more than once but was always met with noncommittal non-answers.

"The times are changing, Sister. I will not choose my only child's life for her. That must be her choice to make."

And then the strange woman who suddenly felt keenly like a pure rush of flame from their well-used fireplace peered at her with eyes almost the color of soot. "So, young one, if I offered you a genuine purpose in life, accompanied by a vast well of power and influence. Would you be willing to make the sacrifices to take on such a mantle?"

She frowned, glancing at her Gran's unreadable expression and then her mom with the concern marring her expression. And Abra had thought that perhaps, at that moment, her mother wished a different fate for her. But, as it was, it was all too late, and she felt the powerful call already deep within and the stirring of her blood. "Tell me more," was her reply.

⚜

"It's too late," her Gran said softly in her raspy voice. "He's marked the house."

Abra straightened up, feeling an awareness sweeping over her. "I have to lead him away."

Her grandmother reached out suddenly, grasping her with a strength she didn't suspect she had in that thin, bony arm. "Child, if you shift, you could make yourself vulnerable. His is a very old power."

She felt her mouth, throat, and, it seemed, her whole body go dry with fear. But she forced herself to calm and began to draw from the old magic of the forest that fed her being. "Trust me, Gran."

The old woman still wasn't looking directly at her, but she saw a slight nod as she released her. Abra moved toward the sliding back door of the cottage, pulling it open and feeling the energy of the forest sweep into her as she stepped onto the patio. She allowed it to flood her and strip away the spell of disguise that she had used in an attempt to shield her presence. It was important now that she be quite visible to those searching for her.

✴

*"You must not use your mind but allow the spirits around you to choose your form."*

Her mother began to train her after the first meeting with Sister Alliana. And she had met more Sisters from across the State, then from further away, and even some no longer of the flesh. And then, just three years into that training, her mother, Sarah Jensen, succumbed to an unexpected cancer that spread swiftly and aggressively throughout her body. For Abra, it was an ending and yet a beginning as well.

She felt the rush through her blood and the whispers in her ears as her body began to meld, rather fluidly, into a form that she was not unfamiliar with.

❋

To him, the energy emanating from the small house suddenly became a painful, blinding flash of white light that caused him to shut his eyes. He took a deep breath as it felt acutely like an ethereal attack, causing his head to throb painfully.

Slowly, opening his eyes, now back to conventional vision, he saw movement through the woods beside the cottage. Without consideration, he stepped out of the car and saw a quick fluttering along the side of the lake. Then it stopped. An animal was there now, staring right toward him. In fact, it was a stag, though a white one, the color of snow. It was motionless, eyes focused directly on him, then suddenly turning its head and beginning to run.

"Abra," he whispered, almost to himself. Then, he began to move without thought, almost without will, after it. And from without, the wolf within him took over as well.

❋

Moving through the forest was always dazzling. In this form, particularly in this one, there was peace and communion with everything about her. She did not exist separately. She existed as part of all: the wood, the trees, the earth, the water, and the sky.

*"It is truly being at peace, at one with everything."*

*"Yes, my child,"* her Gran had told her. *"But it will always keep you apart from one world, the human one."*

Her senses expanded as she led him away, away from her grandmother's cottage. But to where? Thought was so expanded. In her mind, she saw a vision of her own little house, perched atop the hill overlooking the forest, deep within the heart of the Village. But she was moving so quickly, and she could feel him, actually feel him behind her, gaining on her. Then, finally, the thought crystallized. He'd transformed and was now the wolf.

A bolt of fear shot through her as she clearly saw in her mind the great black wolf closely on her trail.

*"Never let negative emotions enter your sphere when you are in the sacred form."*

She brushed the terror aside, which was so much easier than when she was in human form. Here she was spirit, controlled, but wildly free. She called on the power around her that she easily accessed to canvas around the great dark wolf who seemed at least three times the size of an ordinary variety. Like a gentle net woven of energy, she envisioned the power rising out of the earth and softly encasing him, binding him softly, quietly, to slow his progress.

⚜

Lapetus was on her scent as she'd taken the form of a dazzling white stag. It was maddening, the blood lust he felt—the need to conquer this being. His essence had not been stirred this profoundly since he'd first made the transition, too far back to remember. It was as if all control had been stripped from him, and he only yearned, only lived in the need to absorb that power, that pure, untainted power.

And then, as he continued to run, leaping through the woods rampantly, he felt something else, something soft surrounding him like the gentlest rain falling or perhaps a soft snow. But that was impossible. He stopped, sensing it even stronger, a fog, mist surrounding him, soaking into him, dulling his senses and burying that wild instinctual drive, that insatiable need.

The witch—she had spun a spell around him was his very last thought as he fell into an unnatural slumber. *"Sleep now, Master Wolf."* He heard the softest voice as everything faded to black.

⚜

*"What about my clothes?"*

*"It is a mystical transition. They will return as you are reforming your physical form. It is not as you think."*

And much of it had not always been as she expected. She sighed deeply as she took out her spare key from its hidden spot under a heavy chunk of quartz outside in the garden and opened the back door to her house. Now that she was back to her usual self, Abra felt the fear coursing through her. Her head was throbbing and her stomach cold with the realization that she hadn't solved anything. She'd simply kicked the can down the road, and doubtless, when he awoke, this wolfman, he would be royally pissed.

She flopped down on her sofa, wondering distractedly how she would get her car back from her Gran's house. Maybe her aunt. But she was so tired and desperately needed a shower. She definitely had to think, had to try to think clearly, because the one thought that had crystallized while she was in the Snawfus form was that he knew. He knew exactly where she lived.

🦌

Once he returned to his car, he took a moment to consider. It would be easy enough to just drive over to Abra's place, as her waitress friend had so readily supplied the address. But there were realities to weigh. The chief concern was that, although he had learned long ago how to place a glamour around himself after the change to wolf form to avoid awkward encounters concerning his state of undress, the reality was that he did need to put on some new clothes, as his had been decimated during the transformation.

The truth was that he needed to think. What exactly did he want to do here? Just going in and destroying this fascinating creature was an option. There was no doubt he would be able to absorb untold amounts of energy from her. But then that would be it—experience finished. It was the alternatives that intrigued him, dangerous as all of that could be.

🌣

Sometime after lunch, Abra's Aunt Jolene showed up at her door unannounced.

"Aunt Jo, this might not be safe," Abra muttered, having just woken from a heavy nap after a shower.

"I brought your car, Abbie. Let me in and make me a cup of coffee. I have some ideas."

Her family, all her family, undeniably were amazing. It was all in the bloodline. Her Gran had told her this more often than not.

"How are you feeling, pumpkin?" Aunt Jo asked with concern, sitting at Abra's small bistro table in her kitchen.

"Like hell."

She nodded slowly, looking at her intently. Aunt Jo strongly resembled her mother, but she lacked those distinctive green eyes. Hers were more of a brownish-muddied hazel shade. It seemed that only the protectors possessed the purest green. "That makes sense. You've had quite the morning. I thought I might share some insights with you that could be useful."

Aunt Jo, though not a protector, was definitely a profound psychic and had quite a knack for reading Tarot cards. Abra shrugged, "Sure, I could use all the help I could get."

Jolene smiled, and with distraction, Abra wondered why she'd never left this place. Aunt Jolene wasn't obliged to stay, and she could have started her own family somewhere else. But then again, she did seem to be a fierce dedication in her family line, and her aunt had stepped in as a strong supporter and con-

38

fidante once her mother had passed away. "So, I've been focusing on this man. And I am sensing conflicting purposes."

Abra leaned back in her chair and sipped her coffee. "Conflicting? What does that mean?"

"It means rather than just using your usual tools for dealing with opposing forces, you might consider some other tools."

Now Abra deliberately frowned, "What does that mean? Other tools."

"I mean, it isn't out of the realm of possibility that this person, this man, is just on vacation."

She blinked her eyes, wondering if she needed to clean out her ears. Had she heard correctly? "Aunt Jo, he chased me through the forest. He was a huge, black, unnaturally sized wolf. It really doesn't seem like he's here for a few matches of pickleball."

And then her aunt sighed, "Well, yes, clearly, Abra, he's capable of causing great harm and is extremely dangerous, but I wonder if his heart is really in it."

"His heart?" she murmured, dumbfounded.

"Yes, dear, maybe you could just distract him, reason with him, use some of that famous Jensen charm on him."

"You can't be serious," she blurted out. She couldn't help it. "You want me to flirt with the werewolf!"

"Yes, well, honey, you might need to put aside your pride and your ego and consider my words. The reality is that he is very old, and if he overcomes his conflicts within, he will be formidable. And there is much concern, much doubt, I'm afraid, that you can prevail."

Aunt Jolene didn't stay long. Abra drove her back to Gran's cottage and then took some time riding around the Village to clear her mind. One could actually drive forever around here and still be inside the gated community. In modern times, the region had evolved into a more retirement-oriented settlement, while also serving as a major resort area during holidays and the summer. And of course, there were niches of all sorts of communities within as well, including her very own antiquated esoteric populace.

But Abra had no doubt that the area would evolve over time. It was the hope, however, that the forest would always remain largely untouched, though it was a hope rather than a foregone conclusion. When she finally came home, she fell asleep on the sofa in front of the fireplace. She felt like lighting a roaring fire, sprinkling it with white sage, and smoking the whole house. It would strip its energy, forcing everything to start over—and then she mused, perhaps even going back to when she was fifteen. This time, she might pause before answering Sister Elliana's question and deeply consider taking another path, another path where she belonged to herself rather than obligations.

With a discordant mind and heart, Abra fell into a deep sleep. She shifted restlessly, dreaming of traveling through a darkened night with the fullest moon brightly beaming overhead. Its illumination filled everything, every part of her, and she reveled in its power. And then she stopped by a glistening lake on the edge of the forest and sat beside it, drinking deep of its luminescent water.

*"It's a gift at times to be mindless."*

She shifted in her sleep restlessly. "Is it?"

*"Oh yes, a gift to be stripped free of the constraint of obligations to run wild with one's own passion."*

She opened her eyes in the darkness of the room, though she felt sure she'd left some of the lights on. Across from the sofa near the fireplace, there was a pine rocking chair that had belonged to her mother. She sat up slowly, still peering through the shadows at the figure clearly sitting in it.

"How did you get in?" She asked of the darkness.

"It's foolish, Abra Jensen, to leave a key beneath such a prominent stone in your garden. It is so careless that it could be easily regarded as an invitation." His voice was so smooth and filled with almost a teasing, sarcastic timber.

And then he switched on a standing lamp that stood nearest to the rocker. It softly illuminated a portion of the room largely couched in shadows. She sat up cautiously, her eyes falling to the clock on the wall, seven-thirty in the evening. She'd been asleep for so long. As she came to a sitting position, she stared with restrained emotion at the stranger sitting in her den, the same man she had waited on at *Esme's* just that morning. "So, do you intend to murder me, whoever you are?"

"My name is Lapetus," he said quietly with that odd accent of his. But who was she to talk with her light Arkansas drawl?

"Okay, again, you haven't answered my question. I don't like suspense."

"Pity, suspense is one of life's pleasures that should be savored."

She straightened up. "Shouldn't you have to be invited to enter someone's home?"

And then he smiled, oh, how wonderful, she amused him. "I'm not a vampire, Abra."

"No, you're not. You're a werewolf, evidently a very old one."

"Yes, and you, my dear, are clearly a witch."

"Not exactly," she murmured.

"No, well, I'm more than sure you wove an incantation around me out in the forest. But you're not the only one with such skills. Aren't you curious why you slept so deeply while I entered your home, as you say, uninvited?"

She took in a deep breath. This was bothersome, and she was impatient. "Fine, you have a few tricks up your sleeve, as do I. But you still haven't said what it is you want."

He leaned forward a bit. She focused on him clearly now. He was dressed entirely in black, a black shirt, and black jeans. No wonder he melded in so well with the shadows. "Abra, it's clear you're a shapeshifter of a kind—the white stag. Why? What is your purpose here?"

"Why should I answer your questions?"

"You're brittle, tired, and impatient. Do you desire an end to something, dear Abra? Am I feeling that within you?"

Her eyes widened in surprise. "Of course not. Why would you think?" And then she stopped. He was reading her emotions and thoughts. There was more to this man, if she could really call him that, than met the eye.

"You are not careful. You are brazen, even though you confront someone who might easily destroy you."

"You seem very confident."

And then he leaned back. "No, more than that, I am intrigued. So, let's talk more."

Then, the image of Aunt Jo crossed her mind. *"You might consider some other tools."*

She sighed inwardly. So, maybe time to break out a softer arsenal. "I haven't eaten. How about some nachos and a margarita?"

And then Lapetus, the werewolf, smiled at her with genuine amusement. "That sounds difficult to resist."

꙳

It wasn't especially cold, but Abra lit the fireplace and threw some dried rosemary on it, not sage. As she'd been told long ago, sage smudging and smoke destroy all energy, while rosemary only destroys the negative variety. She didn't know if that would make her uninvited guest uncomfortable, but it made her feel more secure. Though the truth was that the vibrations she felt from Lapetus were undeniably mixed. Eclectic, actually, was a better description.

"Do you drink alone?" he asked from across her bistro table.

"Sometimes," she murmured, taking a bite out of the plate of nachos she prepared for them not long ago. Her guest had seemed content to quietly roam her rustic den and flip through her collection of books as she made them dinner.

"You?" she asked lightly.

"No, not often. Alcohol doesn't affect me the way it does others."

She smiled deliberately. "Pity," she echoed him, then took a deep sip of her margarita. Whether she was going to be killed or something else entirely, she preferred to be drunk.

"You seem very young, Abra."

"I'm twenty-two." She dug deep for some sort of name for him, "Pete."

"Pete?" he repeated with incredulity.

"Maybe, Peter, I can't seem to wrap my mind around Lapetus. It's so antiquated, speaking of," picking up another nacho and shoving it indecorously in her mouth, "how old are you?"

"Peter, if I have a choice, I would prefer Peter, and to you, I would say solemnly, my dear, closing in on a millennium."

Her throat went perceptively dry, closing in on a thousand years. "Wow, what do you do, living that long? I mean, how do you keep yourself interested in living without being—"

"Being what exactly?" he asked, casually picking up his margarita. "Finish your thought, please."

"Well, without being bored."

He nodded slowly as though considering. "Yes, well, I continually look for things that intrigue me."

Ah, and then her stomach sank. Evidently, that was her now, something to intrigue him, something to toy with until, well, until he was finished with her.

🜨

Sometimes, he felt like an old man. He'd been alive so long, maybe too long. And sometimes, he felt as though he simply lived outside of life, didn't really participate, just marked its passage. Some in his clan had taken a mate, a partner to walk their peculiar path with. It was a select few. Most beings of modern times lacked the physical stamina and constitution to make the transition. To put it plainly, modern man was of a weaker stock. And ultimately, in his estimation, that would make his kind a dying breed because the gift of immortality was no assurance one would live forever. One might not age, but all sorts of things could kill you, apathy amongst many. Finding a new and hopefully scintillating reason to be alive was always important.

The young brunette in front of him took a large sip from her oversized margarita glass, and he vaguely wondered if she was trying to get drunk. Alcohol, as a rule, didn't do much for him. But then again, his blood wasn't exactly what one would consider normal by any stretch of the imagination.

And then she focused on him, and he felt a frisson along his spine. Those eyes, green eyes so wide and penetrating, just like

44

the lightest touch of fingertips brushing along his skin. "Do you want dessert?" she asked cautiously.

He sighed inwardly, deeply because he didn't want her to know how oddly and comfortingly confounding he found this situation. What was it about this slight little girl, this woman, that made him so captivated? Maybe he was just tired of what he expected. And then she leaned her head to the side ever so slightly as though she was actively trying to understand what he was thinking. Could she glean thoughts? Could this be another gift of hers?

"I'm trying to entertain you," she murmured.

"And why is that exactly, Abra Jensen? You found me in your house uninvited, a predator no less."

"Are you?" she asked softly. "A predator?"

He breathed in a bit, "At times, yes, of course."

She just continued to stare at him speculatively. "What about this time?"

"This time?" he echoed. Was it a spell? Was she weaving a spell, or had he been alone too long? Unloved for too long?

"I was wondering if I had anything to fear from you, My Lord Werewolf."

And then he smiled. Actually, he couldn't help it. She, this shapeshifter, was an odd little thing. "Curious title."

"Curious circumstance," she said, placing her oversized glass on the table. And yes, she'd pretty much downed it. "Are you going to answer me?"

"As to my intentions?"

"Yes, that was essentially what I asked. You'll find that I'm not a very complicated individual, Peter. I like to get things out on the table, so I know what I'm dealing with."

"I'm not sure I like Peter."

"Well, answer my question, and I'll give you another name."

"Impatient one. And if I answer, how will you know I'm sincere?"

"I'll know," she said softly, and for some reason, he believed her. Something about her eyes seemed steady and unflinching at the proclamation. Perhaps that was one of her gifts.

"What else do you transform into? Other than the white stag?"

"The Snawfus, that's what they call it around here."

He considered for a moment. "Not really?"

"Oh yes, really," she said, reaching for her margarita glass, then seeming disappointed that it was empty."

"Do you want mine?"

She wrinkled her pert little nose, and he was overcome with a curious impulse to kiss it. Good lord, was he actually attracted to this creature? This was not like him at all. "Probably shouldn't, until I know what I'm dealing with. So, Peter," he noted that she said that name with emphasis. Did she have no clue who exactly she was dealing with? "How about a game?"

"A game? I'm listening."

"Yes, well, I'll answer a question of yours, and you'll answer a question of mine."

He leaned back in his chair, deliberately taking a sip of his margarita, not because he particularly liked it but because he knew she wanted it. "Intriguing, but how will I know, Abra Jensen, that you are telling me the truth?"

Those beautiful green eyes narrowed just a notch as she focused on him. "All right, I'll swear on the souls of my ancestors."

He lifted his eyebrow because, frankly, he couldn't help it. "The souls of your ancestors?"

"Yes," she looked back at him with a bit of disdain. Had he ruffled her lovely feathers? And would he like to ruffle a few more? "That is a very solemn and binding promise amongst my kind."

"And what kind is that exactly, Abra?"

"No, not yet. You haven't agreed to the game. Once you do, then I'll answer." And then she pursed her lips, and Lapetus recognized with some surprise that he did actually very much want to kiss those lips, those lovely little pouty lips. Had he decided not to kill her? Maybe all of this was just too compelling. "All right, I agree."

⚜

Abra swallowed on a dry throat. She really wanted another margarita, though she might already be a bit tipsy because she was finding the werewolf fellow kind of hot. On the one hand, he seemed distant, rather cold, with his dark eyes and black hair that was long enough to curl around the top of his collar. And his skin was that swarthy, olive sort of tone. But there was something wild about him, too, just brimming beneath the surface, sizzling—

"What did you say?" She had to ask because, in the midst of this strange muddle, she really had no idea.

"I said I'll agree to your game." He answered rather languidly.

"Oh, okay, so who goes first?"

"First, you take your oath." And then she smiled because he was so handsome, and it was clear he wouldn't let her get away with anything.

"Of course," she said lightly. "I swear—"

"No," he said abruptly, cutting her off. "Don't you have some sort of holy book around here?"

"Holy book? Oh, you mean like a Bible."

"Whatever you find sacred."

"Sacred? That's a tall order. Well, Peter, I can't claim to be much of a churchgoer, but my mom was. And it did belong to her." Quite smoothly, she stood up and strolled as casually as she could manage over to the bookshelf built into the wall near the fireplace. Her head spun a bit, and she understood at that moment that it wasn't the liquor, not at all. She was in the company of powerful magic. She had a built-in radar for sensing this. Then, the random thought crossed her mind. Maybe it was just who he was. He was the powerful magic. She grasped the old book in her hands. It had belonged to many Protectors before her mother and had been passed into her hands at her mother's death.

As she settled back into her seat at the small table facing the incomprehensibly old werewolf, she asked herself if she was going to do this. Was she really going to make herself this vulnerable to this very, very dangerous man? Was this in any way wise, or was this incredibly foolish?

And then she plopped the book a little irreverently down on the table in front of her. Yes, in answer to all those questions, it did seem as though she would be doing this. Some might say it was a rash decision. Some might say it was an unwarranted gamble. But a fierce recklessness inside of her was driving her toward the edge of this particular cliff.

She placed her left palm face down on the cover.

"Wait," Lapetus again interrupted her.

She glanced up, a little annoyed. "Yes."

"Which hand do you correspond with?"

"Which hand?" somewhat confused. "Oh, oh, I'm right-handed."

He nodded, "Then use that hand. It will make the oath more powerful."

She took a deep breath. Undeniably, he was a man of details. So, she switched hands, then focused, saying aloud. "I, Abra Mera Jensen, do swear on the souls of all my ancestors to tell Peter—"

"Iapetus," he corrected.

"Iapetus, the truth during our game of question and answer." And then she glanced up at him, smiling prettily. "Will that do?"

He stared at her oddly, intently, as though trying to see something that probably wasn't there at all. "Yes, I suppose it will have to do. And would you have me swear as well, Abra Mera Jensen?"

"No," she said flatly, removing her hand from the good book. "I will know if you are lying."

And then he smiled, but not in a warm way, in a calculated way that sent an undeniable shiver right up her spine. "All right, then let's begin."

But before they began this wonderful game that had been her brainchild, Abra went into the refrigerator and brought out a half-eaten key lime pie. It had been her mother's favorite, and she had many fond memories of them curled up on this sofa in this house, watching the flames jumping around the fireplace as they ate key lime pie. She didn't ask. She simply put out a piece in front of her remarkably quiet guest. After her first rather tart bite, she looked at him and commented abruptly, "You go first."

"Why?" he asked.

"Do you want that to count as your first question?" She said, taking an overly large bite, but then again, she loved this stuff.

He frowned a bit, and it made her smile. He didn't like being ruffled. "Quite the stickler, no."

She licked the fork with relish, then realized that maybe she shouldn't be doing this in front of such unpredictable company. "Because you're the guest, and I'm trying to be polite."

He nodded begrudgingly, she thought. Then again, maybe not, though she did feel as though she was getting the vibe of this fellow. He eyed the pie suspiciously, then used his fork to take a tiny bite. Maybe he thought she was trying to poison him, an idea that oddly hadn't even crossed her mind until this very moment. "Why this pie?" he asked smoothly.

"This pie?" she repeated, looking at him quizzically. Of all the things he could ask.

"Yes," he said, scooping up an even bigger bite. "It seems to have some significance for you."

Her eyes widened. He'd picked that up, more intuitive than she'd expected from a centuries-old lycanthrope. "Yes, it was my mother's favorite. We used to—" Then her voice tapered off. She wondered if perhaps she should keep these true confessions short and sweet.

"Used to—" he prodded in a low voice that felt oddly like it was skimming along her skin.

"That very well could qualify as a compound question."

And then he focused on her with his dark eyes. Did she mention that they were sexy, dark eyes? Maybe she was just starved for male companionship, and he wasn't nearly as sexy as she believed him to be. "And here I was hoping for just a friendly conversation with a new acquaintance."

"Oh, are we pretending, Peter? Are we pretending that we are just acquaintances, and you did not just chase me through the woods as a vicious beast ready to tear me apart."

"Vicious? Determined, yes. And to be succinct, I was chasing a stag, a snowy white stag that seemed somehow unearthly."

"Snawfus," she said softly.

He looked at her oddly, but then again, he had been looking at her oddly ever since she'd laid eyes on him. But this time, he did not speak. He just took another bite of the slice of key lime pie, in fact, a rather large bite. From where she was sitting, it did seem her mother's favorite pie was half gone from his plate. "So, you've said," finally, he spoke. "And that is your only alternate form, this Snawfus?"

She hesitated, damn that oath. "No," she answered.

"Ah, then what—"

"And now I think, Peter or Lapetus, if you prefer, it must be my turn by now." Then she smiled back at him, almost teasingly, "Don't you think?"

And he smiled back in response, but slowly, as though with genuine thoughtfulness. "Of course, proceed."

She nodded, gathering her thoughts. Best to make it count, as this whole situation was feeling remarkably unstable. "I would very much like to know what brings you to this area. You must be very far from your home."

"Yes, that is true," he said slowly. "Traveling, I suppose. I had business in the south of your country in the city of New Orleans, and I decided to take a little time to explore the New World before I returned home."

"The New World? Is this your first time in the United States?"

"To the United States? Yes, but not to this land. The last time I was here was well before the birth of this country, and things, well, I have to say, were markedly different, more primitive, more natural."

"I see," she said, clearly now seeing it, concrete images as the memories passed through his mind. "And so, you weren't looking for anything—"

"For anything in particular? No, not initially. But there does seem to be powerful energy here in this community, in this land. I sensed it immediately. That was why I stopped."

"Yes, the area is very old, filled with mystical energy."

"And you are part of all of that, Abra," he said her name in a way that felt almost like a caress.

"Not Abra Jensen?"

"Who are you, Abra?" he asked slowly, but his dark eyes were foraging, almost foraging in her mind, or so it felt.

"I—" she hesitated, not at all sure why. "I am the protector here, as was my mother and as were her ancestors."

"Protector? From what exactly, my dear?"

"From any who would cause harm in this sacred region."

There was a hesitation, and then he nodded slowly, his eyes settling on her in a most profound way. "And you are wondering if I am such a threat."

"Of course," she murmured, feeling it might be impossible to look away from his gaze. Hypnotic? Was he indeed casting a spell?

And then he reached across her small bistro table and took her hand in his. And she felt the power surging through the contact with his skin, a cataclysm of ancient power coursing through this being, connected to so much. "And I can tell you now, Abra, I've decided perhaps in just this moment that I am not a threat to this protected place of yours."

"You're not?" she murmured distractedly because he'd risen to his feet and was now standing beside her, grasping both her hands and drawing her to a standing position.

"No," he murmured. "But most especially, I am not a threat to you."

She nodded slowly, mesmerized, and completely and unexpectedly falling into those eyes that seemed to go on forever. "I'm not sure about that," she whispered huskily because in the next moment he'd bent in and had begun kissing her.

⚘

"Why did you do that?"

There was something odd in his dark eyes, sparkling with amusement. Was this all just a game to this centuries-old lycanthrope? And she, a distraction to toy with? "No," he murmured softly, continuing to hold her arms with his hands, continuing to peruse her face, her lips with his gaze, telling her in no uncertain terms that he'd like nothing better than to kiss her again.

"No?" she questioned, stepping back and forcing him to drop his embrace.

"No, you are not something to toy with, Abra."

She drew in a sharp breath because she was definitely feeling it, drawn, mesmerized, as if in some sort of hazy web. "Are you hypnotizing me with that werewolf thing?"

An eyebrow rose, "Are you always this suspicious when someone kisses you?"

She frowned, not really wanting to admit how seldom that happened. "No," she murmured. "But when someone kisses me, someone who was quite a formidable threat not very many minutes ago, I have to wonder."

"Good point," he whispered in a low, throaty voice.

"So, this isn't like an I'll do this for you, you do this for me thing."

"Quid pro quo. And no," suddenly pulling her against him. "You really have to stop all of this, Abra."

His arms were around her now, and she was in a close, dizzying embrace. Undeniably, she didn't feel like herself anymore but someone else, something else, unencumbered. "Stop what?"

"Thinking so much," he murmured just before he kissed her again, and this time, she kissed him back.

꒰

Lapetus wandered through the small mountain home of Abra Jensen. It was still dark outside, but the time eluded him. Last night had an unmistakably unreal quality, and more than that, it felt like a spell. But a spell he had no desire to resist.

He'd been in love once, long ago, before he became who and what he was.

The girl was a childhood friend in his village, and her parents and his expected a marriage. But once he'd taken a midnight walk along a lake on a restless night, everything changed.

His family, everyone he knew, believed he'd died from his wounds after the savage attack from a beast—a beast no one really saw. But he hadn't died, and he returned to her late one night, telling her what happened, how he was now transformed. But she, Aelynn, the girl of his childhood dreams, saw only a demon. He recalled how part of him was tempted to crush her for her scathing words and rejection. But he didn't. He showed restraint, a restraint that, oddly enough, he'd found none of the night before. It wasn't like him being so out of control, making him very suspicious.

Lapetus had cultivated governing his impulses and his emotions through many lifetimes. Nothing he did was spontaneous, without thought, without calculation. But last night, a desire, a riotous, overwhelming force swept over him. And he didn't really understand why.

He stared out Abra's back sliding glass door into the darkness of the forest. It felt like something beyond passion to him. It felt like manipulation.

He heard a rustling noise behind him. If he was not mistaken, it was the sound of her bare feet on the cool wooden floor. Slowly, he turned around. Abra looked thoroughly disheveled. She wore a short, silky robe over her T-shirt. Her dark hair was strewn rather wildly around her shoulders, and her face was beautifully flushed.

"I thought you might have left," she whispered softly. She was looking at him a bit wide-eyed and as confused as he felt on a level, though admittedly, he didn't seem as vulnerable as she did to him at the moment. Was this slip of a girl indeed the so-called protector of this realm?

She frowned. "Now, that's just insulting."

He walked over to her, lightly touching her face with his fingertips. He was drawn, still drawn, and not sated in his need for her. "Now you're reading my mind."

She took a quick breath. "Did I? I didn't realize—" A lovely blush cascaded across her pale skin at his words, acknowledging her innocence, at least her innocence, until last night. "Um, yeah, things got a little crazy."

He nodded slowly at her understatement. "Yes, I would agree."

She glanced around as if in a sort of confusion. "Yeah, I was going to get some water. Want some?" she asked awkwardly.

"No," Lapetus said softly. "But I would like to ask you something." Her eyes widened, but she said nothing. "I know you are a shapeshifter, but are you also a witch, my dear?

"A witch?" she repeated, seeming genuinely confused.

"Yes," he said softly. "Because without doubt, I sense an incantation in the air."

⚜

"What?" she whispered with a measure of disbelief.

Madness, all of this felt like madness. Talk about sleeping with the enemy, and she had done that, not once, but several times. And it felt clearly as though she couldn't help herself. There was a need for him, this werewolf, a crazy, unstoppable need, and now he was staring her down, accusing her of using witchcraft to bewitch him while she should be the one accusing him.

"You heard me."

His hands were on her, but now he was holding her arms just as he did at the beginning of this craziness. "You're accusing me of putting some sort of spell on you. Well, I think you put some sort of strange werewolf fugue on me because this, what happened, is not at all like me."

He frowned, pulling her closer and looking her over with those dark, sexy eyes as though he were truly peering into her soul. "You're telling the truth, aren't you?"

"Yes, yes, I am telling the truth, Lapetus, Peter, whatever we decided to call you. I can't remember."

"Lapetus will do. So, you do not claim to be a witch, though I remember a spell when I was in the wolf form. Someone lulled me into sleep."

Her eyes widened. "I called on the powers of the earth to aid me. That wasn't a spell. That was bubble wrap." The quizzical eyebrow went up, an expression she was getting oddly fond of. "I am the protector of these sacred lands, the Ouachita Valley. I can assume the form of the snawfus, the woozer, and a wampus cat, but I am not a witch."

He frowned explicitly. "What's a woozer and a wampus cat?" he said a little dryly.

"A woozer is a panther and a wampus cat a bobcat," she mumbled, feeling more than a bit deflated.

"And you do battle as these creatures, Abra?"

"Usually, I just scare away anything that is potentially a threat."

"Unless it won't scare."

She sighed deeply, "Yes, unless it won't scare, like you." And then she pulled away abruptly. "Look, I'm a modern girl. If you want, you can go on your way, and we can chalk this whole confusing night up to too many margaritas."

He was still staring at her in a way that felt as though he was boring right into her skin. "There was a spell."

She pulled her silky robe more tightly around her. "Yes, yes, of course it must be a spell. Why else would you want to sleep with me?"

"No, it's just not my nature to jump into something unthinkingly."

She shook out her hair, suddenly deciding she'd had enough of this odd inquisition. "So, I'm going back to bed. You do what you want, Lapetus."

He took a deep breath. "It's three in the morning."

She glanced at the clock, frowning. Three o'clock? What had her aunt said about three o'clock, a strong time for the spiritual world? "Yeah, or you could just stay over, I guess."

He nodded slowly, now gazing at her in a way that made her feel tingly all over. "Yes, that is an option." And then he reached out, taking her hand and quite expertly pulling her toward him. He put his arm around her, and at that moment, she decided she quite liked the snuggly feel of being next to him. "Would that be acceptable to you?"

She smiled, that strange magnetic pull, not sure if it was wise, not sure if she cared. "Maybe," she said lightly as he softly kissed her again, knowing it was more than acceptable.

🜏

The old woman drew in a sharp breath that seemed to rattle throughout her frail body. Jolene felt her mother squeeze her hands more tightly, painfully. But then Michaela Jensen exhaled softly and leaned back in the rocking chair, loosening her grip on her daughter. "Enough," her voice rasped with exhaustion.

"Do you think the spell was strong enough?" Jolene asked in confusion. All of this felt strangely chaotic to her.

Slowly, her mother opened her eyes. There was a foggy quality to them that made her daughter uncomfortable. She was too old for such incantations any longer. They took too much out of her. "They're together. I can see them. The spell we wove was largely unnecessary. There was already an attraction, a draw. We just needed to give them a push."

Jolene nodded silently, trying to rub her hands together discreetly. She didn't want her mother to know how much she'd hurt her. She bent to blow out the white candle positioned between them on the small table. "No," Michaela said with a voice filled with fatigue. "Let it burn down."

Jolene nodded. "I hope Abra won't regret, well, anything."

Michaela sighed deeply, closing her eyes again. "It is the way it has always been. With me, with her mother, and all those before."

"Yes, I suppose," Jolene murmured. "She's just different, you know."

"Yes, I know."

⚜

Abra opened her eyes slowly. The light was streaming into her bedroom, and the spot beside her was empty. She sat up, pulling the sheets up to her neck and glancing at the clock. It was already nine. If she had been working today, she would already be several hours late. Thankfully, it was her day off.

Her hand drifted to the spot beside her that not so very long ago had been occupied by a very handsome werewolf—one who also happened to be a passionate lover. The memories flooded in with an intensity she was overwhelmed by, but then again, she literally had nothing to compare it to.

She wondered if he was still in the house or if he'd left.

She wondered if she should look for a note or if she'd simply never see him again. Her hand drifted to the spot he had occupied on the bed. It was still warm, so he hadn't left long ago. They hadn't used birth control. She wondered if she should be worried. She wondered if she should stop wondering so much. There were so many things to consider, and she was still tired. Much went on the night before, but sleep hadn't played a large part in that.

But as much as she would have liked to stay in bed and sleep the morning away, she was not one to dodge whatever was coming. So, Abra pulled on a pair of denim shorts and a pink t-shirt and brushed out her hair. By the time she entered the kitchen, she was more than convinced she was in the house alone. But

59

sitting right at her tiny dinette table was the man in question, sipping what she assumed was a cup of coffee.

"I didn't want to wake you," he said softly. "You seemed very tired."

"Yeah," she smiled awkwardly because this morning-after thing was a first for her as well. "I thought you might have left."

And he was looking at her intensely, or maybe she wasn't awake enough to assess anything accurately. "That would have been rude."

"And hunting down your prey in a wolf form isn't?"

He took another sip from his cup and then asked smoothly, "Do you want some. I made a pot?" Evidently, not wanting to address her barbed observation. He was dressed as he had been the night before, in black jeans and a button down shirt, and looked remarkably unruffled considering what had gone on last night.

"Oh, yeah, but I'll get it." She wandered over to the counter, slowly taking a mug out of the cabinet and pouring the coffee while trying to figure out where they go from here. In the harsh light of day, a few realities had filtered in, like the fact that this man, who seemed like such a threat maybe a day ago, she'd spent an intense night making love with. She didn't know how the other Protectors of the Sacred Valley conducted themselves, but she may have just slightly wandered outside the job description.

She felt his hands slip around her waist. "Are you all right, Abra? You seem quite out of sorts this morning."

"Oh, I don't know," she murmured as she stirred the sugar in her coffee. Now he was leaning against her, reminding her of that electrical, crazy attraction she felt for this man.

"I know how innocent you were, and I wanted to make sure you're well."

"Yeah," she murmured, wondering vaguely how exactly she would get the milk out of the fridge if he continued to hold her this way. "I'm good."

And then he straightened up and stepped away from her. She smiled at him a little awkwardly as she moved to retrieve the milk from the refrigerator and then pour it into her coffee. "I'm not sure what we have around here for breakfast. We might have a few bagels."

Quite oddly, he took the milk carton from her hands and returned it to the refrigerator. "What is it?" he asked, staring at her intently again.

"I-I'm not sure. I guess I haven't processed things yet. I didn't expect last night to go the way it did—"

He nodded slowly as though considering thoughtfully. "Yes, yes, it was unexpected."

"Yes, and I wasn't really prepared."

She found herself leaning with her back against the fridge while he canvassed her face, looking, it seemed, for something. "We, my kind, don't procreate in the ordinary way," he murmured distractedly.

She frowned, trying to piece that statement together when it dawned on her. "Oh, okay, well, so I shouldn't be concerned about, well, about—"

"No," he cut her off abruptly, though an odd, somewhat unreadable expression crossed his face. "No, you shouldn't be concerned."

She nodded, smiling but still feeling something unspoken in the air. She took a sip of her coffee, realizing she'd put way too much sugar in it—not all that unexpected, considering the circumstances.

And then she felt his fingertips lightly brushing her cheek. "There is something, though, Abra."

It wasn't an unfamiliar feeling, as she'd experienced this more than once in her life. It seemed acutely as though the other shoe was getting ready to drop. "What?" she said, straightening up with the recognition she was still leaning back against her fridge.

"I asked you about an incantation last night."

She drew in a breath, trying to think. After everything that had happened, it took her a moment to sift back to that particular conversation. "Yeah, you accused me of putting a spell on you. I didn't, you know."

His fingertips brushed her cheek. How could such an innocuous gesture feel so erotic? Of course, the truth was that just about everything about him felt that way right now. "Yes, I know that. But the problem is, there was a spell, an incantation, that drew us together last night. To be blunt, I have an acute sense of smell and could smell magic."

"So, you don't mean that metaphorically. You actually could smell an incantation. So, us being together last night—"

And then he bent in and kissed her softly on the lips. "Was wonderful, unexpected but lovely, Abra. Don't misunderstand me."

"But—" she murmured.

"But I am certain it was orchestrated. Something or someone very much wanted us to be together."

✷

Lapetus knew some things.

He knew, staring into Abra's wide green eyes, that she was telling him the truth, but he also knew deep down, in his flesh,

62

his very old bones, and in his blood, that she wasn't entirely clueless as to what he was speaking about. Quite smoothly and methodically, he took the cup of coffee she'd just poured out of her hands and placed it on the counter beside them. Then he pushed her backward so that she was ostensibly pinned between him and the refrigerator as he pressed his lips against hers, kissing her deeply, thoroughly, passionately so that she could be more than convinced that now there was no incantation coercing him.

Then suddenly, and somewhat unexpectedly, she broke the kiss, looking at him with wide, confused eyes. "What are you doing?"

And then he smiled and softly said. "I'm kissing you because I want to and because I want you."

Confusion marred her lovely features. But after a hesitation, she leaned in softly, kissing him back. It would wait. Unraveling things that might mar this lovely interlude would wait. And then he pulled her with intent securely into his arms.

✻

She was really hungry now. It was closing in on noon, and she hadn't eaten all day. Beside her, she could feel Peter, or hell, who was she kidding, Lapetus, trying to sleep but then waking and tossing restlessly. She thought about talking to him and discovering what was wrong, but part of her was afraid.

It felt like opening Pandora's box. Strangely, she felt guilty, as though she'd done something wrong, but she didn't know exactly what that could be.

"I'm awake," he murmured.

She smiled, turning toward him and putting on a light-hearted demeanor. "I thought you were tired."

He pulled her against him. "Sleep, I can always catch up on."

She laughed, feeling a curious joyfulness that was unfamiliar to her bubbling up within her. "Well, I have an idea. How about we pick up some food from *Esme's* for lunch and then sit outside by a lake? There are tons of them here."

"Would you like that, Abra?"

"Yeah," she whispered enthusiastically, "and *Esme's* makes incredible club sandwiches."

He nodded, twirling his fingertips in a tendril of her hair, "All right, but let's run to my place first so I can get a change of clothes."

She smiled, feeling her mood perceptibly lighten. "Sounds good. I'd love to see where you're ensconced."

⚘

Abra had grabbed a granola bar just to quell the headache threatening to overcome her from lack of food. But her companion seemed less affected by a drop in blood sugar than she did. They took her car because, evidently, last night, Lapetus had traveled to her house on foot. She didn't want to ask if that was on two feet or four paws because, well, it wasn't as if she had room to talk. But she was curious about how he managed the clothes thing. With her, there was some magic contortion involved. Her mother called it dimension-tearing, where her clothing was stashed in a little dimensional pocket during the transformation and retrieved afterward. Like a handbag strategically stashed in an alternate reality. Somehow, she doubted her centuries-old werewolf boyfriend here managed things the same way. Boyfriend, wow, was he? No, werewolf lover seemed to suit him more. So complicated and confounding. Maybe she was just his vacation shape-shifting hook-up.

"On the left," he murmured.

He'd been quiet during most of the ride. "So, I've been meaning to ask you. How do you like the Village?" She said as she maneuvered her Volkswagen into the driveway behind the black and white Jeep. The house, as much as she could see of it, was one of those vacation types, octagonal in shape and well-hidden in the surrounding forest.

"Is that really what you've been meaning to ask me?"

Good point, she thought reflectively. "Well, you have to admit we haven't had much time for small talk. I was just curious. You've been around, I mean, seen a lot of places. I was just wondering what your impression is of it—" She murmured, now, actually feeling rather foolish for having brought up the question.

They were sitting in the driveway, and she was struck again by the awkwardness. After all, her life experience was so narrow, and his, well—"It's very picturesque," he commented flatly.

"Oh, yeah, I suppose," she said half-heartedly.

"But there is an energy here, an undeniable power, very old. I could feel it immediately once I came into the area."

She breathed in deeply. "That's true. I guess I don't always think of that. I'm here all the time. It's just become—"

"Part of you," he finished her thought again.

"I suppose."

"You and this place are intertwined, Abra. Of that I have no doubt. But I wonder if you're happy here."

She sighed deeply. It was so hard, nearly impossible, keeping conversations light with this man. "I think I would have to say that's very complicated."

And then he smiled, but in a way that felt as though there were many layers of consideration going on behind his eyes. "Why don't we go inside?"

It was airy, a strange house. There was a huge den on the first floor, connected to an open kitchen, and lots of picture windows everywhere. "I'm assuming there's another floor," she murmured, canvassing the expansive space.

He smiled, sitting down casually on the long, beige L-shaped sofa, facing a brass-accented fireplace. "The bedroom is downstairs," he responded.

"I don't know," she said, sort of slowly spinning around, trying to soak it all in. "I would expect something a bit more gothic with you."

"Well, it was what was available, already decorated. But it does have its charms," he commented, holding out his hand for her.

He pulled her beside him on the couch, putting his arm around her. "I thought you needed to get a change of clothes."

"Having you here has made me rethink things. How about we have someone deliver lunch, and we relax for a while?"

She smiled, "Not many places deliver. Maybe Dominos."

"Pizza it is," he said softly, pulling her in for a kiss.

"All right, but you do have to feed me soon, you know."

"I know," he whispered huskily.

❦

It was like being caught up in a haze—a pleasurable, compelling, and comfortably tantalizing haze, but a haze nonetheless. Lapetus wandered up the curved staircase that led to the upstairs in the vacation house. He and Abra had indeed ordered pizza, eaten, and spent much of the rest of the afternoon in each other's arms. Something about her drew him fiercely, hypnotically, and it puzzled him.

In truth, he was usually a colder individual, more exacting and calculating; one might even say detached. But this girl, woman to be precise, had gotten beneath all that iciness. It was not just the fact that she was a shapeshifter, because shapeshifter or not, she was very young, twenty-two, to his over five-hundred-year-old self.

He slowly began to button the long-sleeved dark blue shirt he'd pulled out of the closet. He'd left her asleep in the king-sized bed in the master bedroom. Yes, moving in a haze was just how he'd describe it.

But it was late in the afternoon, and as much as he would love to go on spending days like this, it was best to try to piece together what was happening.

He finished buttoning the shirt and settled on the sofa, trying to clear his mind of the fog that seemed determined to cling to him.

⅔

"Don't be so nervous."

Jolene stared down at the collection of Tarot cards she'd spread out on the coffee table only moments before. "Things are in disruption."

"It only seems like that. This has always been the way this is done. A new guardian, a new protector of mystical origin, must be raised."

"But this figure at the center," Jolene eyed the card of the Magician with great trepidation. "He seems formidable."

"You're concerned about the lycanthrope," Michaela muttered. And Jolene noted how breathless her voice still sounded. She had yet to regain any of her strength after the spell was cast.

"Yes, I am, but the Priestess seems linked to him. Do you think Abra has fallen in love with the fellow?"

"Love? Lust, yes, but love? Seems unlikely. They barely know each other. Once the spell fades, he will move on and be long gone before—"

"Before they figure out what we've done." Jolene reluctantly completed the thought.

❧

Abra awoke with a start, though it took a few moments for her vision to clear. She was in a strange, remarkably spacious room, a ceiling fan slowly turning over the king-sized bed. She glanced beside her. The spot was empty. And she remembered, remembered the intense passion that had swept in whenever they touched, whenever it seemed they were near each other. She didn't know such a thing was possible, to feel—such a desperate yearning to be so close to another human being. But then again, he wasn't exactly an ordinary person, and she, well, she could very well say the same thing about herself.

She struggled to clear her mind as she retrieved her clothes from the floor where they'd ended up earlier. Lapetus, she turned the name over in her mind. Several times, he'd mentioned a spell being cast. She'd disregarded his assertion, but it was undeniable how altered she felt. Truthfully, though, she'd just attributed it to the intoxication of the new experience—passion, something she ostensibly had never encountered before.

She was groggy, and her mind didn't feel as sharp as it usually did. After pulling on her T-shirt, she sat for a moment on the edge of the bed, closing her eyes and clearing her thoughts.

She remembered so many times sitting next to her mother, attempting a meditation.

*"The most important thing you must do, Abra, is to be calm. It is not possible to connect with the Great Spirit if your mind is in turmoil,"* Sarah Jensen had coached her.

Abra cleared her mind and took more than a few deep breaths. Then, she opened herself to knowledge.

*Whispers, whispers*—she could hear them all around her as she began to feel herself softly pulled to another place.

Her head began to swirl with disorientation, but suddenly, she could begin to see again. Around her, things started to solidify. It was the den of her house, but not now, rather in the wintertime, with the fireplace lit and its flames jumping about zealously.

*"So, the child will never know?"* Her mother's voice was younger than she remembered. The figure was hazy, but she stood in front of the fireplace, her hand resting on the mantle as she stared into the flames.

"No, it is for the best." Now, it was her Gran's voice. She was sitting on the sofa, but the images were still unclear, out of focus in Abra's vision.

"And the father?" Sarah's voice again, and as she turned, Abra could see she was pregnant.

"The tea that you gave him made him forget."

Her mother turned back, staring a little sadly. Abra could now see her face as she stared into the mutating flames. "Forget me?"

"Forget you, forget this place, forget the time you were together."

And then her mother nodded and turned to look directly at Abra. And her Gran, Michaela, did the very same. The old woman spoke in a voice that was much younger and stronger than Abra could ever remember hearing before. "Welcome, my child. It's time we had a chat."

※

When Jolene drove up to Abra's house, it was just as Michaela had predicted. The car was gone. Evidently, the two of them were elsewhere. Nervously, she let herself inside with the spare key Abra had entrusted her with. *Trust,* that word chafed just at the moment. Moving into the kitchen, she opened one of the cabinets where Abra kept her coffee and tea. She pulled the small ceramic jar out of her pocket and placed it on the shelf, closing the cabinet door. Of course, Abra would have to choose to give him the tea, the tea that would make him forget her.

Jolene took a deep breath before she left the house. Her part was done. Regardless of how she ultimately felt about it, her part was indeed finished.

※

She felt solid here now, as though her body was with her.

"It's not," her Gran spoke again. "Just feels that way."

She turned to her mother, whose soft green eyes were fixed on her. "Are you really here?" Abra said, choking up with tears.

"I am, my dearest one." And then she lightly put a hand on her stomach. "And I am carrying you. My deepest blessing."

Abra smiled at her and then looked back at her Gran, whose face betrayed no emotion whatsoever. And in that, her heart sank. What had she heard?

Slowly, she turned to her mother again, a younger Sarah Jensen, who was still smiling at her. She took a deep breath before she asked the question she had been forbidden to ask all of her life. "Who was my father?"

70

✣

Lapetus focused, although it was a challenging prospect. It was as though the great well of old magic permeating the forests throughout the Village was conspiring against him, not really in a tangible, aggressive manner, but in a way that he could only describe as feminine. He smiled to himself, almost a seduction of sorts, soft, pervasive, distracting, so he could not see clearly, nor was he inclined to do so.

It would be easy, so simple, to let go and not concern himself with these intangibles. But it went against his grain. So, instead, he focused more deeply.

The face of Kian, his lieutenant, whom he had left in charge of the coven during his absence, rose in his mind.

"Brother," Kian sent the thought forward. Lapetus had spent much time training his kin in the arts of thought transference and meditative skills.

"Yes," he answered.

"Are you well? I haven't been able to contact you."

Lapetus thought about the cell phone he begrudgingly carried with him. Part of him always resisted the modern ways. "Yes, is there a problem?"

"No, no, some of us were concerned. That is all. We worried for your well-being. It's not like you to be out of contact for so long."

"I've been distracted. That is all. I'm not sure when I will return."

"Yes, all is good here, my friend. Be well."

"You also, Kian." And then the image faded from his mind. He'd checked the phone not long ago. There were no messages or missed calls, almost as though things in this mystical valley were somehow being blocked. His mind wandered to Abra again. He could feel her downstairs in the bedroom, but in a quiet state.

He concentrated further, more deeply, and then took in a breath. Her body was indeed there, but her spirit was traveling. He leaned back, now completely zeroing in on following her to wherever she might be.

⚘

Her mother looked at her with genuine distress in her eyes at Abra's question. "I know you told me not to ask, but I feel as though—"

"Yes, indeed, it is time," her Gran said, coming to her feet. Seeing her this way was so strange, so much more vital and alert than she was now. These days, when she spoke to Michaela Jensen, she often sensed that she was in two places at once—her body still in the present, but her mind frequently already having moved on to the next plane.

Abra's eyes settled on her Gran. "So," she said softly.

And Michaela smiled broadly at Abra's spunkiness at such a moment. "Sarah," she instructed expectantly.

"Your father," her mother's voice sounded shaky. "I didn't know him very long. He was visiting this place, drawn here."

"Drawn?" Abra questioned, feeling a haunting familiarity.

"Yes, my dear," her Gran said.

"Who was he?" Abra asked.

"But my dearest, is that the proper question?" Her Gran injected roughly, which, even in this astral state, Abra was beginning to find rather irritating.

"What does that mean?"

And then the old woman, who wasn't quite as old anymore, moved right in front of her. "It means perhaps the question is not who he was, but what he was."

She drew in a quick breath as something hit her, actually hitting her right between the eyes. And all she could think of just now was Lapetus.

⚹

There was a block, or rather a fog, around the place that Abra Jensen had traveled to, and he found that more than disconcerting. No doubt some sort of strong magic barred him from seeing, but Lapetus was not without his own arsenal.

He sank deeper, deeper into his meditative state until he found himself in a place where he'd spent some time long ago. It was in Prague under the tutelage of a sorcerer named Cyprian. The face of his old Master materialized before him.

Of course, Lapetus' friend had moved on from this earth centuries ago, but he was still in contact with him occasionally, dropping in ostensibly on the past when he required guidance.

Now, he found himself in a very cold chamber, which he remembered well, a basement beneath a stone building. Here was where Cyprian often dabbled in alchemy. The old man was bent over a table, presently seeming to be chiseling stones that, if Lapetus was not mistaken, were made of obsidian. "Master Cyprian," he said softly.

The white-haired, slight fellow dressed in a long red cloak looked up, his eyes as black as the gems he'd been working on. Of course, Lapetus was aware that he'd just connected with his body in that time frame, which was the simplest method of communication at this juncture. After all, given his longevity, it was the same body he existed in at present, whereas Cyprian was no longer of the flesh. "Lapetus," he said in his rich Slovak accent. "Ahoj," and then he frowned, staring at him with confusion. As if

73

focusing intently, he spoke again slowly. "I will speak in your present language. You are in another time."

"I am, my friend."

The old man grimaced, and Lapetus felt him intently canvassing his mind. "I wouldn't have thought it of you."

"Nor I, my master, at this point I, would think myself well past such things."

And then his former Master smiled. "We're never past love, old friend."

He felt uncomfortable hearing it phrased in such a way. "Is that what this is? Love?"

"I see. It's been so very long for you, and such an occurrence is unrecognizable."

And then he nodded. At this moment in his history, Lapetus wore a hooded robe as well, but his was purple, not matching his Master's. Cyprian was fond of bold colors. "Well, my concern at present is more selective. There's magic."

And the old man leaned in, lightly touching his shoulder. "Yes, I can feel that about you. The old and powerful magic of the earth, those who wield it seem formidable within their sphere."

"Yes, as I thought, a narrow scope."

"Very narrow, it seems. And the one, the woman that binds you, is she a part of this?"

Lapetus sighed deeply. What a good question, a question, at present, he couldn't answer. "Limited is what I believe. I have felt and touched her thoughts, and—"

"And she seems genuine to you."

"I would have used the word innocent."

"Innocent?" Cyprian murmured. "A state that is most difficult to hold onto."

74

Abra stared blankly at both her mother and Gran, who seemed rather stoic in the moment. "What the hell does that mean? What he is?"

Her Gran from the past frowned at her in disapproval. "Show a little respect, child."

"Answer me," she demanded with so much irritation that she wanted to smack the old woman's face.

And then she felt her mother reaching out and gently touching her arm. "Calm yourself, Abra. I know this is difficult. It was difficult for me. It is the way, the way it has always been."

"What does that mean? The way it has always been. What has been?"

And then the stern voice of her Gran cut in. "Your father was a traveler, one from another dimension, an elemental. He was drawn here by the old magics, stayed long enough to conceive you, then left."

Abra's eyes widened at this bizarre pronouncement. "What? Why would he—"

"Your grandfather was a vampire from Albania. Your great-grandfather was a shapeshifter from England; before him was a warlock from Greenland."

"Greenland? What, and they all just dropped in, hooked up, and left?"

Her mother backed away, head bent, as though she couldn't look Abra in the eyes anymore. Her Gran peered at her sternly, an expression she remembered well from childhood. "No, Abra, these magical beings sired the Guardians of this sacred valley. And then were made to forget."

She stood there, feeling her head swirling in dizziness. "A spell," she whispered. "Lapetus said there was some sort of enchantment."

"Yes," her mother said softly. "To bring you two together."

And then Abra looked at them both as a creeping sort of horror took hold of her. She'd been manipulated and lied to. "He can't have children," she whispered.

"This is a sacred place, strong in ancient magic. What is not possible becomes possible here," her Gran stated emphatically.

"No," she said, feeling herself trembling with rage.

And then her mother's hands again, her mother who had died, the mother who, in this vision or whatever the hell it was, was now pregnant with her. She held both of Abra's arms. "You must be calm, my daughter. You have a child to think of now."

※

"There are a number of powerful energy points within the Northern Continent that will be known as The New World."

"You can foresee this?" Lapetus asked Cyprian.

"Of course, you are not the only one who can traverse time." Roughly, his old Master picked up a handful of obsidian stones on which he had carved archaic symbols and spread them out on the table before them. He lightly touched several of the stones, never manipulating their position. "It is an old coven if they can even be designated as such."

"Then they're not witches?"

"Not exactly," Cyprian muttered. "It is more of a calling that binds them rather than personal advancement. They adhere to old ways and are led by the spirits of the land."

"Guardians, protectors," Lapetus murmured.

"Yes, yes, it seems so, and this—what was her name again?"

"Abra."

"Ah, yes, Abra seems to be at the center of it. Always female, not the longest lifespan, but protectors of the old magic."

"Yes, that is what she claimed."

"And you doubt her?"

"No, no, actually, I don't. I just don't know what part I could possibly play in this."

She wondered if she should take a moment to scoop her jaw off the floor because she certainly felt as though it was down there somewhere. "What did you say?"

"You heard your mother. You are with child."

"That's not true," she stammered. However, her mind was now flipping back frantically through all the times in the last several days that she and Lapetus had made love with zero birth control. But then again, he had told her this was impossible.

"Not impossible here," her Gran said flatly.

"Stop reading my mind," she snapped out harshly.

"Abra, my dear. I know it is a shock," her mother said.

And then she abruptly pulled out of her deceased mother's grasp. "Ya think?"

"This is how the guardians have always been conceived."

She stepped back further in recoil from both women. "How could you do this? How could you use me like this?"

And then her mother looked at her with deep upset in her green eyes. "You mustn't look at it like this, Abra. It's a blessing."

77

"And Lapetus, you're just going to cast a spell on him so he forgets all about me and never knows he has a child."

"A daughter who will be a guardian like you," her Gran explained.

"No, no," she snapped. "I won't force this on her."

"It wasn't forced on you, Abra." Her Gran said somewhat harshly. "If you remember, you freely chose to stay here, chose to learn, and to become the protector of these sacred lands."

"Did I?" she said shakily as unwanted tears began to slip down her face. "Or was it all some enchantment to make me believe there was a choice?"

"Of course, there is a choice, Abra," her mother's voice, so soft, so filled with anguish at her daughter's upset. "I almost decided not to. I was quite young but was rejecting everything."

Her Gran stared at her with a stony face. "Yes, that is true. The elders compelled me to have another child because it seemed your mother would never accept her calling."

"Aunt Jo?"

"Yes," Sarah murmured. "She would have been the protector if I had chosen not to. But I realized it was my burden and also my gift to serve."

Abra stared at both women, dumbfounded. How could she not have known this was coming? But she never thought of it and wondered if that, too, was an enchantment placed upon her so she wouldn't think clearly.

"Well, ladies, I have to admit this has been enlightening." It was a voice, an unexpected intrusion. Abra felt her head absolutely swirl as Lapetus seemingly materialized out of a shadow from a far corner of the room.

"You cannot be here," Michaela Jensen nearly screeched. "This is a protected space."

"Yes, well, every spell has its flaws, I'm afraid. Even yours, it seems."

⚜

Cyprian's focus remained glued to the stones as though they were opening visions within him. "And what precisely do you require of me, old friend?"

Lapetus lightly tapped his fingers on the wooden table where Cyprian was now seated. "Yes, it seems my lady has gone traveling."

"Traveling?" Cyprian glanced up at him with confusion on his face.

"Out of body, some sort of meditation that I am barred from."

"Ah," the old man said as though he'd quickly gleaned the situation. "And some sort of spell is keeping you from following her."

"Yes, it appears there is more calculation here than meets the eye."

Cyprian nodded slowly as though intently concentrating. "I can see this," he murmured, pausing as though contemplating matters. "But I might ask you, my friend, if you're quite sure you want to continue on this path. There is a window here I see, a possibility now to simply go and return to your old life and not embroil yourself in these domestic matters."

"Domestic?"

"Oh, do not misread me. The events unfolding in your present time frame are of paramount importance to many, but they don't necessarily have to be to you. You can walk away, forget the woman, and disengage yourself."

There was a hesitation in Lapetus as his old Master's words soaked in. "And if I don't?"

79

Cyprian sighed with gravity. "If you don't, it seems your presence will shift the course of things, more particularly your life."

Lapetus considered, considered the very long and largely uneventful nature of his life as of late. Did he indeed want to return to such an existence, or did he want to explore a divergent path?

"It is something that should be seriously weighed. Your next move will change much, and not just for you. However, in response to your request, yes, I can assist you. The enchantment is not that strong. Its strength lies in its secrecy, which, as of now, has been effectively breached. So, take a moment before you choose, Lapetus."

⚹

Michaela Jensen stepped forward in front of Abra and her daughter, Sarah, in a stance that Lapetus could only interpret as fiercely protective. Once he'd used Cyprian's counter spell to breach the fog surrounding this gathering, it had been quite easy to follow the path that Abra's spirit had taken here. "This is a private matter," the woman rasped. "You must not interfere. It does not concern you."

He raised an eyebrow and was more than deeply angered at this woman's audacity. "This does not concern me? I believe you have just declared that it is my child that Abra is now carrying."

"The child belongs to these lands, this earth. This sacred magic allowed her to be conceived," she stated with rage in her voice. "You cannot interfere with our ways. They are ancient and sacred."

"And I am just the facilitator for this miracle?" Lapetus asked, his voice dripping with sarcasm. If she actually had a physical body at the moment, he would have propelled the old witch right through her lovely plate-glass window for daring to speak to him this way.

"Mother," Sarah said, moving from behind Michaela. "Lapetus has a stake in what's happening here. You can't disregard him this way."

"No, no," Michaela said angrily. "We can't disregard the old ways. The old ways are—"

"Old," Abra stated flatly. Quietly, she walked around the two women and stood directly in front of Lapetus, her eyes filled with unshed tears. She reached out, took his hand, and said softly, "I am so sorry. I didn't know. I didn't know we were being manipulated. I should have seen, but—"

Lightly, he put his fingertips on her lips to stop her from talking. "No, not your fault, my dear. Come with me, and we will decide what happens next."

She grasped his hand firmly and moved beside him, but just then, the grandmother said harshly. "You should know, this child you carry, Abra, will not survive away from this place. Any more than you or your mother or any of us could survive for a prolonged period. The magic here helped create life, and its absence will take it away."

※

By the time she returned to her body, Abra's head was pounding unmercifully. It was too much, too much to take in, too much to absorb. All of it, it felt as though the whole fabric of her life, of everything she'd always believed, had been ripped away from her. Choice? Choice in anything? The mere suggestion of that was laughable. When had she ever had a choice?

*"You should know, this child you carry, Abra, will not survive away from this place. Any more than you or your mother or any of us*

81

*could survive for a prolonged period. The magic here helped create life, and its absence will take it away.*"

That had come from her Gran, her beloved Gran who had been a mentor to her, a confidante, and now seemed like an adversary. Maybe she should just leave, pack her bags and test out their theory.

She had stared at her grandmother in total disbelief, caught somewhere between outrage and pain. How dare she? How dare they, all of them, keep so much from her, use her like some puppet, and now drag an innocent child into this, if indeed it was true at all that she was really pregnant. At this point, she doubted just about everything.

"What did you say?" she uttered in no less than total shock. And then her Gran's face had frozen as though she suddenly realized the news she'd delivered and exactly how heartlessly she had done so.

"Abra, I am sorry. I am sorry to have told you this in such a way. But it is the truth. The Guardians are created here. We are magical beings who draw our strength and power from this earth. If you leave, if your child does so, it will become ill, weak, and eventually die."

"Abra, darling, I'm so sorry," her mother's voice, her sweet voice that would be no more once she left this place.

"Is that why you stayed?" She asked her.

But her mother looked down and covered her mouth, indicating she was too overwhelmed to answer.

"Abra, much rests on your shoulders," her Gran said sternly.

And then she turned back to her, filled with fury. "And you are a bitch. I hate you for this."

But she never flinched, just stared at her with no expression. "Yes, I imagine you do."

She couldn't remember leaving, only a great swell of dizziness and now nausea as she sat at the foot of the bed in Lapetus' rental home. Nausea, good lord, it couldn't be that quick.

"Are you all right?"

She looked up, somewhat surprised and not surprised to see him standing in the doorway. "Oh, me? I'm delightful."

And then he smiled grimly, walking into the room and quietly sitting beside her on the bed. "I'm sorry."

She nodded slowly, "Which part? There seems to be a lot of regret to go around just now."

And then he took her hand gently. "Not sorry about meeting you."

She sighed, feeling the heavy weight of desolation washing over her. "Maybe sorry about rushing into things, though."

With his other hand, he gently touched her on the stomach, closing his eyes. It was an odd feeling. She could sense a sort of tingling in the contact. Slowly, he opened his eyes, his hand dropping away.

"So?" she asked.

"It seems there is indeed a child."

She nodded, "Yep, well, what do you want to do about it?"

Her eyes were so enormous, filled with fear, with pain, and with shadows. That, more than anything, he didn't like. What was it Cyprian had said about innocence being so hard to hold onto?

He put his arm around her, pulling her close. Whatever spell had been placed on him and Abra at the outset, what was clear was that his draw to her had not diminished one bit, only become somewhat more complicated. "You've had a very upsetting time of it. You should rest."

She leaned against him, laying her head on his shoulder. "You can't possibly already be acting like a protective father," she said.

"I am protective of you," he murmured.

"Maybe we can leave together. I can go with you back to Europe, and we can have the baby there."

He lightly touched her arm, stroking it gently. He didn't want to say the obvious, though what Abra's grandmother had said about the magic of this valley fueling this impossible conception did resonate with him. "This place has become so tainted for you?"

"I-I don't know. I feel like I can't trust anyone. People that I thought I could depend on, who I thought were on my side, were just manipulating me."

"And you're sure you can trust me, Abra?" he murmured.

And then she sort of stilled, straightening up. "I-I don't know. Can I?"

He squeezed her hand, which he still held. It was quite the situation for him. His traditional tactic in most things was to find a way to gain the upper hand, but here, in this place, he'd been a different sort of individual and, oddly enough, wasn't in a great rush to return to who he had been before. "Yes, yes, you can, my dear. And in that spirit, I will tell you something that might change everything."

He felt her draw in a breath, a sharp, fearful breath that he could sense acutely as the side of her slight body was pressed right against his own. "What is it?" she whispered.

"When I placed my hand on you, I felt something."

"The baby?"

"Yes, but not one baby. I felt two. I could sense a boy and a girl."

She turned to him, her green eyes filled with confusion. "I don't understand. It's always supposed to be just a girl. That's what they said."

"Yes, but evidently, things are changing here in the Ouachita Valley."

※

They didn't speak of it much the rest of the day—these great matters. Closing in on the evening, they picked up food from an Italian restaurant in the Village and returned to Abra's house. She'd thought to suggest getting a bottle of wine, but she didn't. Already, things were changing in her life. She had a child, no, two children to consider. And a great part of her wanted very much to leave this place now. It had changed for her, or rather, something inside her had changed.

"Do you like working at the restaurant?" Lapetus asked out of the blue.

"Not really," she murmured.

She was curled up on the sofa in the house with his arm around her. She dearly wished it were Winter, and they could light the fireplace to warm a chilled room. That was her favorite season here. "Have you thought of doing something else?"

"I'm taking classes at an online college. And thought maybe one day I might open some sort of a shop here in the Village, gift shop or something like that. I don't know."

"Do you still want to do that?"

She snuggled closer to him. "I did. I don't know what I want now."

He leaned over, kissing her softly. "Let things settle."

"You don't think I should leave."

He seemed to hesitate before he answered. "I tend to believe the veracity of what your grandmother said. What's happened, well, I did not believe was possible."

She nodded. "Yeah, I know. I just don't want to do this alone."

He held her closely, "You mean you don't want me to leave and forget you and our children?"

"No, I don't want that."

"Neither do I," he said softly. "I can't be here all the time. I have obligations as well. But I do want to watch our children grow, and I want to be beside their mother."

She smiled, feeling a warmth spread about her heart. "I want that too, Lapetus."

"So, tomorrow I'll find you a ring to hold the place of the one I will have made for you back home."

She smiled at the prospect, "A ring?"

"Yes, of course," he murmured. "An engagement ring."

Again, she smiled. She was going to be Mrs. Werewolf. "You know, I don't even know your last name."

"There have been many."

"Well, you'll have to settle on one."

"Understood," he said softly, kissing her again.

"You know, Aunt Jo left some tea in the cabinet that is supposed to make you forget me."

"Really? What are you going to do with it?"

"I thought I might flush it down the toilet. What do you think?"

"I think that's an excellent plan, my dear one," he said softly.

# Kylie

"I'm worried about what will happen to Luna."

"She'll be fine."

"Do you think so?"

"Animals have a purpose, a path, if you will, just like people."

She nodded and wandered to the fireplace. She always moved around better, hell, felt better when he was around. And he had shown up—when exactly?

"It's been several months, Ky."

That's what he called her, Ky, short for Kylie James. James was her maiden name. She'd been married once to Derek Ross but had dropped his name when they divorced as there were no children.

"Would you have liked to have had children?"

She considered and sipped her tea watching the flames leaping around in her fireplace. It was one of those ignitable logs she'd had sent from Walmart. Of course, he'd helped her light it. He helped around the house with a lot of things lately as she wasn't feeling very energetic, to say the least.

She glanced over at him. He was sitting in the rocking chair across the den. He knew she liked to curl up in the lazy boy with a blanket atop her and sleep. Now what had he asked, oh yeah, children. That was the thing about him. He asked a lot of questions.

"I don't know. I didn't really think about it much."

"Even when you were married to Derek?"

She sipped the tea again. It was warm and comforting and made her feel cozy—cinnamon, maybe. He did like to probe, make her reflect, as though it was the price she paid for him hanging around.

"Will Luna have a new family?"

"Maybe," he answered. "Would that be okay with you?"

She took a deep breath that reverberated through her weary frame. "Sure, I'd like her to be happy."

"She will be."

She nodded and sat down in the lazy boy. "Do you want to watch a movie tonight?"

"If you like."

"Maybe a mystery, nothing bloody, a cerebral mystery."

There was silence. He wasn't pushy, but she knew, somehow in her skin. He was still waiting for an answer and would do so until she gave him one. "It was difficult to think about having children with Derek. I wasn't happy."

"Why? Why weren't you happy, Ky?"

She sighed. What was this, like sorting through old things, putting things in order before the end? "Am I dead already?"

"Dead isn't a good word, Ky. Crossing over, transitioning are more appropriate descriptions. And no, not yet."

"Why can't it just happen? And I'll be done with it."

"Everything in its proper time. You can't rush things. When it's time, well, then it will happen."

She sighed, feeling impatient. She didn't like all this drama. Everyone who looked at her, spoke to her, very well knew she was on the way out. And she was pragmatic. She wanted things settled. But there was silence, something, oh yeah, his question again—"The relationship, the marriage, wasn't what I thought it would be."

"What did you think?"

"I thought," and she tried to remember because now it seemed like eons ago, "I thought I wouldn't be lonely anymore."

"And you were?"

"It was worse than when I was actually all alone. I never understood why."

"He wasn't right for you. You know there are right and wrong people for you in the world. That doesn't make them bad, just not right for you, not kindred. And it creates a disturbing situation where they always want you to connect with them in a way you simply cannot. And the same for them."

"So, I shouldn't have married him, you're saying."

"Not necessarily. Every relationship you have, everything that happens to you, is meant to be learned from, good or bad. Do you see?"

"No," she laughed softly. "But I guess I'll just have to take your word for it."

✵

How could she explain? She couldn't. It's always best to start a story at the beginning, but her beginning, well, she didn't find it all that remarkable. So, here we were, ostensibly at the end.

But then Dax did tell her it wasn't the end, just a change, a new beginning.

Who is Dax?

That one is tougher.

❧

Are you a doctor? She'd asked.

She'd been sitting on her sofa, and the pain came over her in a rush. It was so quick and acute that it seemed as though she'd passed out for a while. When she awoke to a nudge on her arm, he was bent over her with a glass of water and a pill in his hand. "Take this. It will help," he said to her softly.

She sat up, still so dizzy and hurting everywhere.

"Are you a doctor?" Because she didn't know, didn't really know where she was in the moment and who this stranger was.

"Of a sort," he replied.

But she took the pill, and he put a pillow under her head so she could sleep.

She noticed Luna nosing her feet at the other end of the couch. But she seemed undisturbed by the mysterious doctor, so that was good enough for her.

❧

"Do you regret your divorce from Derek?"

She glanced over to Dax, sitting in the rocking chair watching the episode of Poirot she'd put on. "No," she said.

He'd moved in, though she didn't know exactly where he slept. He just sort of appeared here and there when she wasn't paying attention. Sometimes she thought he was a hallucination from the strong painkillers she was on. But he was very tactile for a hallucination.

"Why did you marry him?" She picked up the remote and paused the program on the TV. Dax did like to pepper her with questions.

She looked over at him, explicitly frowning. "How could that possibly matter now?"

He was gazing at her with that warm, inscrutable expression. "It will make things easier for you. To sort through important decisions, like cleaning out old things."

Dax was what she considered a handsome man, around her age, which was late forties, blondish, with kind blue eyes but also the sort that seemed to be able to sift through anyone's bullshit, which of course given their living arrangement, was mostly hers.

Quite clearly in her mind, she could see Derek's eyes—dark, furtive at times, concealed. They'd married when she was thirty-five. And what was the question again, the one attempting to clear out old forgotten cobwebs? Oh, yes, why did she marry him?

She took a deep breath. They'd dated on and off for two years, and if she hadn't married him, he would have moved on. "He wanted me to."

"Really? Is that the reason, Ky?"

She considered. Was it? She could see Derek now, standing right in front of her chair, frowning. "Is this real?" she murmured.

"Yes, it's real, but not the reality you're used to dealing with."

She straightened up, noticing that her usual aches and pains weren't present. Derek, the Derek from about ten years ago, continued to stare at her but said nothing, which for him was quite extraordinary.

"He liked to talk?"

"More than anything, he liked to hear himself talk." She hadn't acknowledged the fact that Dax had responded to her thoughts. In fact, she hadn't thought about that for some time. This wasn't an unusual occurrence. "What do you mean by not the reality you're used to dealing with?"

"That means you're existing between, Ky. So much more is possible here."

⚘

"Kylie," she raised her eyes. Every day she would walk outside, using a crutch of course to help support herself. But it was important to keep things moving, even though—

The blond plump woman walked up to her from where she'd parked her car on the side of the road. She wasn't actually plump. It's just that she was so thin herself. Everyone seemed that way to her.

"I was worried about you. I hadn't heard from you, so I thought I'd drop by."

Marilyn was her cousin, who had let her stay in the rental house when she became ill. She was a good ten years her senior but face blooming with health. "Luna," she called. "Sit." The large golden retriever who'd been wandering at least a yard ahead came dutifully back to sit beside her. Such a good sport, though she did look forward to her one walk a day. "Sorry Marilyn, I've had an off week."

Marilyn had a lovely round cherubic face that reflected genuine concern. "Can I help?"

"No, no, it's business as usual. Do you want to come in for some coffee?"

"No, actually, I'm on my way out of the Village to run errands. Is there anything I can get for you while I'm out?"

She smiled. "No, I have things delivered, so I'm good."

She nodded enthusiastically. "Ok, well, give me a call now and then just to let me know things are all right."

"I will, thanks."

Kylie watched her walk away. Marilyn didn't like coming into the house. A woman dropped by once a week to help with the cleaning, so it wasn't that.

※

"She's uncomfortable here," she said to Dax who was sitting at her small kitchen table sipping a cup of tea.

"It's the unknown. She feels it here. It frightens her."

"You're sure it's not the smell of death," she quipped dubiously.

"Death doesn't smell like anything. Fear does though. People fear death because they don't understand it. They can't control it, and that frightens them."

"You make it sound like I'm already gone."

"Are you hungry?"

"A little."

Then he smiled that warm smile of his. "Then you're still here. How about I get us some lunch?"

※

"So—"

93

"So?" she echoed him, still observing the figure of Derek standing directly in front of her lazy boy chair, blocking her view of the television.

"We were talking about why you married Derek. Did you love him?"

She drew in a breath. "Just a bit off the course, why is he in my living room?"

"That's how things work here. Thoughts manifest easily. It's the same way in the other reality, but it takes longer. Thought is a creative force. That's why it's very important not to concentrate on negative things. You will pull them to you."

"Is that why I got sick because I concentrated too much on negative things?"

"Of course not, you chose the illness when you charted your path before this life. It was something to learn from as was your relationship with Derek."

"Funny how you dovetailed that in."

He shrugged, "Not my first rodeo."

"Okay, but then if I answer, can we make him go away?"

"He makes you uncomfortable?"

"Well, yeah, he was kind of a jerk."

Dax smiled gently. "So then why—"

"Okay, okay, why did I marry him?" It was difficult turning back, sort of like opening a locked room that she just didn't want to go into. She remembered when they first met. She was working as a paralegal in a law office and Derek was a young attorney just starting out. And she was surprised when he asked her out. The support staff at the firm, well, was just like wallpaper to a lot of the attorneys. But he was different, energetic, enthusiastic, and interested in her. "He paid me attention, I suppose, initially. I was used to people disregarding me. At first, he made me feel important."

"I see why that would draw you."

"Yeah well, it's not like most women get to pick who they date. At least, I didn't. I waited, waited for someone to pick me."

"You said at first," he reminded her calmly.

She sighed. It hurt, actually still hurt inside to talk about any of this. "Yeah, I guess that was his technique to pull people in. Make them feel important and then—"

She stopped, looking around. Derek had vanished. "Where did he go?"

"You weren't putting any energy into the creation. By airing out your old feelings, it began to diminish his importance— healing in a way. If you do more, it will help."

"Why didn't you say that to begin with?"

Then he looked at her with that elusive compassionate expression she was becoming very familiar with. "Because I'm here to help guide you, Ky, not do your work for you. So, what else?"

She looked around somewhat befuddled. It did feel a bit lighter here, so odd. "Um, well, we moved in together. And his career was stalling, so I was paying for a lot of things."

"I see."

"Yeah, I guess that was one reason I agreed to marry him. It would have been messy to break up and separate everything after living together. And he depended on me or at least my income. You see they asked him to leave the firm. He wasn't bringing in enough business."

"But you stayed there."

"Yeah, for the money. But I left later, after he was doing better, after we were married."

"Were you close?"

She took a breath that felt like an emotional stab around her heart. "Why does this still hurt so much?"

"Unresolved emotion, powerful stuff."

"Emotion and thought. I never thought they were much of anything."

"They carry a lot of significant energy. That's why they shouldn't be allowed to run rampant unconsciously. It's like knowing what's in your pantry or your fridge. If you don't look at it occasionally, there is no telling what you'll find growing in there in six months."

"That's vivid. I'm not sure I like your analogies, and I may not be here in six months anyway."

"Or you may. That's unknown. Best to clean out the pantries while you're here."

She frowned at him. He had such an unruffled demeanor. Not at all cold but more serene. "And what would happen if I don't?"

"If you don't deal with it now, you will later. Nobody gets a free pass. If there is a mess you must sort through and clean it up, one way or another. It's just easier to move on when you don't have old things weighing you down."

※

Maybe it was madness, hallucination, dementia brought on by her illness. Because how could Dax be real? How could that apparition, or whatever one might call it, of Derek be real?

But she was too tired to consider any of this too much. After all, at this point in her life, did it really matter if she was losing her marbles on top of everything else? And what if she was just talking to herself instead of the nice-looking gentleman who was now approaching her patio table? Isn't that what old people did? But she wasn't really old, just sick. Maybe that's what sick people did.

"You're in a bleak mood this morning." Her porch overlooked a sloping forested field, trees, so many trees that were now losing their leaves. It was the beginning of autumn and, evidently, she was losing her leaves as well. Dax had seated himself beside her at the small wooden patio table.

"The birds aren't coming around. I haven't filled the bird feeders in so long," she murmured.

"Would you like me to do that for you?" he asked in his cordial manner.

"No, it's best they find food elsewhere. I don't know how long—" Then she stopped, oddly not wanting to voice the words, though it didn't usually bother her doing so.

"No one knows how long they have on this earth. You could live another twenty years, Ky."

"Not according to my doctors," she answered somberly.

Dax lightly tapped his fingers on the table. It was a habit of his she'd noticed, this tapping thing. "Modern man is so convinced he has things figured out."

She couldn't help but smile a bit, "And you're saying he doesn't."

He shrugged, "I'm saying there's a lot more mystery to life than anyone feels comfortable acknowledging."

"Why, why do you think that is?" She asked because she did honestly want to understand things.

And then he looked at her directly. "Because they can't stand feeling they have no control."

She took a breath and deliberately let that thought slowly sink in. Is that where the fear came in, loss of control? "Maybe," she murmured.

"What has you sad today?"

She frowned. Could he really be this obtuse? "I don't know, maybe the prospect of dying soon. It tends to put a damper on things."

And then he smiled. He had a handsome face, and undeniably it was even more handsome when he smiled. "It doesn't have to. Death isn't an end, just a change, moving onto the next phase of your existence, like walking into another room."

"But won't I be either cast into hell or lifted into eternal peace in heaven?"

He laughed softly, and she wondered how that laughter might be received at some of the local churches around the Village. "Well, what you describe does suggest a measure of finality."

"In English, please."

"Sorry, it suggests that you've finished your work, all you need to accomplish. So, tell me, Kylie James, do you feel complete as a human being?"

"Complete?"

"That you've learned all you need to know, experienced everything that is of use to you. Done everything you've wanted to?"

She stared at him a bit shocked, and it took a lot to shock her these days. "No," she whispered.

He nodded. "Yes, then I would say you don't qualify for eternal retirement of any sort."

"Don't you think you're being a little crass?" She said sharply because she did have a sharp tongue. In fact, that had often been a complaint of Derek's what a sharp, caustic way she had of speaking when, well, she was displeased. And with Derek, especially toward the end, that was often.

"Well, I'm sorry, Ky. I thought since you are on death's door as you so often tell me, you might prefer plain talk."

She took in a breath that felt like pure tears, tears that wanted to come out, wanted to weep at the unfairness of it all, but that her pride never allowed to escape. "Fine, talk plain. Explain to me what that means."

He watched her, and she did see the compassion in his blue eyes. It was just that he usually handled her more carefully. "Why are you upset?"

"I told you—"

"Yes, you told me because you are dying. But be more specific. If you weren't dying, what would you do?"

"What would I do? I'd live, live more," she tacked on in a murmur.

"And do what exactly?"

She took a breath and, it was painful. Not because of the illness but because of the pent-up emotion. And then suddenly on the empty bird feeder not far from the table a small blue bird landed, a red-breasted bluebird. "I never see those around here," she said, somewhat in astonishment. "They were my mother's favorite."

"Yes, her favorite," he said echoing her. "She sent it to you. She wants you to be calm and not be so afraid."

And then she looked at him strangely, "How could you know that?"

He nodded. "We'll get there. It's important you try to answer my questions, Ky. What would you do with more time here?"

"I-I don't know. I'd travel and meet people. I wouldn't be so closed off. I might meet someone, maybe get married again."

"Did you like being married?"

Then she frowned, "Maybe marry someone nice."

"Someone kindred?"

"Kindred? What does that mean?"

"It has to do with spirits. On this earth, people are convinced they are bodies, and satisfying the body's wants and desires is what is most important."

"And you're telling me it's not." She glanced over and noted that the bluebird was still with them, just seeming content to sit by and watch.

"I am telling you that the body is an instrument for the spirit, an instrument the spirit uses to evolve and learn with."

"Learn?"

He nodded, seeming undaunted by her questioning. "Yes, learn. The spirit chooses to incarnate on the earth in a body and sets forth a path to learn from before birth. If you look around the world, Ky, you'll see everyone doing something else, living a different sort of life. That is because they have all mapped out a different path filled with learning."

"But if we're all learning different lessons doesn't that mean we're evolving in different ways?"

"Of course, and that is why the spirit lives many, many lives in many, many different situations. And in each life, it chooses relationships and situations to learn from. And illnesses as well."

She stared at him blankly then at the bluebird who at present seemed to be fluffing up its feathers. "What are you saying, that I chose to be sick?"

"I'm saying your spirit chose it. It chose your body that en-cases your soul and spirit and chose to experience this for the purpose of growth."

She stood up abruptly. "That's a bit of a hard sell, Dax."

And he stared at her unmoving, his eyes never leaving her face. "I think you need to get out for a bit, Ky. How about a drive?"

She frowned. "You know I'm not driving anymore."

He nodded, "Yes, of course, I know. I'll drive. Just give me the keys."

✻

"Where are we going?"

"Out the village, to get some ice cream."

"Seems a little cold for that."

He smiled, "Not really, we're still in autumn. Winter hasn't kicked in yet. And besides, Luna wants some."

She frowned. "She told you, did she?" Glancing toward the back seat, she could see Luna absolutely mesmerized, looking out the window at the passing scenery. Poor thing, she couldn't remember the last time she had taken Luna for a ride anywhere.

"Dogs communicate with images. If you concentrate on an image, then send it to them, they'll often understand."

"Telepathy for dogs?"

"Animals are very sensitive, Ky. They see a lot more than people allow themselves to. They see energy, spirits, all sorts of things. We don't give them enough credit."

She glanced over at Dax in the driver's seat of her little red sports car. It was her last indulgence before she got sick, and before all the medical bills started pouring in ripping through

101

her savings. She could have sold it, she supposed, but she didn't have the heart to part with it. Not that she used it often.

"You should relax and enjoy the outing. Don't focus on things that upset you."

"How do you know I'm focusing on things that upset me?"

He shrugged. "Let's just say you're easy for me to read. I've been in your proximity for a bit now, and I can see the energy of your emotions. Negative ones put out darker colors, reds, browns, orange at times, sometimes just muddied. But happier emotions put out blues and greens, white sometimes, generally more vibrant, lighter colors."

"You see emotions?"

"I see energy, Ky. You could too if you tried."

She silently slumped a bit in the seat and looked out the window. Not long ago she was fairly convinced Dax was someone she conjured up in her mind, but here he was driving her bright red Mustang down the long stretch of Desoto Blvd. How often did a delusion do that?

"I don't think I have time to learn such a skill."

"Time is a peculiar construct. Haven't you noticed that sometimes things seem to stretch on at an interminably slow pace and at other times years fly by like minutes."

She smiled. It was difficult to remain dour around Dax. His upbeat outlook was undeniably infectious. "Your point?"

"My point is time can be whatever you want it to be. You can make time for anything."

She took a deep breath. "Okay Dax, you're overloading me a bit with this time thing and the dogs seeing ghosts and all that."

"Spirits, Ky. Big difference between a spirit and a ghost."

"Super, where is this ice cream place?"

"It's just outside of Hot Springs. Close your eyes for a while and rest. I'll wake you up when we're there."

And it was true. Suddenly, she was incredibly sleepy whereas a few moments before it hadn't been the case. "Okay," she whispered, leaning her head back and letting her eyes drift closed.

※

It was autumn, and then she remembered that it was indeed autumn, late October, and all the leaves crunching beneath her boots attested to that fact.

"Be careful," he said. "It's easy to slide. The hill is steeper than you think."

He was beside her, Dax, in a long-sleeved shirt and hiking boots. "What are we doing?" she murmured, taking in the fact that they were deep in a forest, in a forest whose trees were beginning to be divested of its leaves.

"I think there's a trail down there," he pointed forward. Curious shirt he was wearing, like a long-sleeved corduroy of some sort, dark brown.

A trail, she considered. There were trails all over the place. Hot Springs Village was known for its hiking trails. She'd always wanted to explore them but had put it off. Big mistake, now she didn't have the stamina to walk them.

He reached out grabbing her hand. His was warm in hers. It was the first time she could ever remember him touching her. "It's getting steep," he said. His breathing was deep. Evidently, she wasn't the only one getting winded by this excursion.

But that was the thing. She wasn't, not like she usually was. Usually, she would take a crutch with her just to check the mailbox, which was a short walk down the street from the house.

He stopped and looked around, surveying everything around them. "I think we can make it. It's somewhere down there at the base of this hill."

"Why are we going there?"

And then he looked at her with a smile. "Don't you like exploring, Ky?"

※

"We're here." She opened her eyes and looked around. It was true. They were parked right in front of a soft-serve ice cream stand just before entering the city. She was sure she'd seen it before, but in the clamor of events had forgotten about its existence.

She straightened up in the seat, the dream still clinging to her. "Oh, yeah."

"Okay Ky?" he asked with genuine concern.

"Yeah."

"Good," he said before he turned off the car.

※

They got their ice cream, then walked down the street to a small park not far away. Dax managed Luna on a leash and she walked, without her crutch. Just like in the peculiar dream, she felt stronger than she usually did. But then again, maybe all of this was just a dream. She sat on the edge of the bench by the table finishing her ice cream and watching as Dax held what remained of his ice cream cone for Luna to devour.

"I hope you didn't want any more of that."

"Nope, that's why I got an extra-large one. I thought I'd be sharing."

She nodded, looking away. It had been some time since she'd done this, just sat in a park. Not far from them, there was a little wooden bridge built over a rushing stream of water. "This is pretty," she said.

"Yeah, there is so much beauty around here. When you're up to it, we can explore some of the trails."

And then she looked at him with surprise. "I don't think I'm going to get better."

"Well, things unfold in curious ways. Sometimes what feels like an ending is only a beginning."

⚜

She lost track of time, and it was a delightful thing. After ice cream, they walked around, exploring the park—she, Luna, and Dax. And it felt like a curious family, bizarre and impossible as that seemed.

"I'll miss her. I mean wherever I end up, after—" Then she stopped. Why was it so difficult to talk about this, so taboo.

"Fear," he murmured. "People are so trained to be fearful of life as we know it ending. But I assure you, there is no ending. You don't stop being or being who you are when you leave this body. You in most ways become more of who you are. And as for Luna, she'll be with you."

"But she's not dying," she almost choked on the word dying. It was true. She was afraid, afraid of it, afraid of not knowing what was coming.

"I told you that time is a construct, Ky. It's used for putting our experience in the physical in some sort of perspective we can understand. Luna will be with you and also all those who are kindred will be around you."

"What about you?" She hadn't meant to ask, but it just came out.

They'd been slowly meandering around the perimeter of the park. And he stopped, then looked at her intently with a gentle expression that for the life of her she couldn't ever remember anyone looking at her with. "Of course, if that is what you want, Ky, I'll be with you. We've been together through many lifetimes. Our spirits are extremely close." And then he caught her by surprise and bent in softly kissing her. And Luna nuzzled her leg as he gently pulled her into his arms and kissed her much more.

※

There was a different mood when they drove back to the house. She felt calmer inside, not so worried about everything. It was a curious thing letting go of worry. In strange ways worry is a touchstone, a way that you believe you can will yourself to safety, to a shore that is recognizable.

But letting go, not clinging to those familiar shores that in some ways are so limiting and even damaging is a remarkable experience.

He grasped her hand in his. "How are you feeling, Kylie?" Kylie? She smiled. It had always been Ky.

"I feel better," she said.

"I'm glad." He responded with a sincerity she could feel.

And then as they pulled into the driveway of her house, she straightened up abruptly. It was jarring, shocking really. There was an ambulance in the driveway, and several police cars parked on the side of the road. "What's going on?" she rasped.

And then he grabbed her arm. "It's all right," he said calmly. "Just listen to me. Lean back and close your eyes. Try to clear your mind." She took a deep but jarring breath in. "Easy," he murmured. "Just be calm." She nodded and tried to follow his direction, but the anxiety was still there, the panic that had surged up at the sight of all of those emergency vehicles. "Okay Ky, now slowly open your eyes again."

She took one more breath before she did as he asked, slowly opening her eyes. Then in total astonishment, she looked around, taking in the fact that the ambulance and police cars had vanished. "I don't understand. Where did they go?"

"It seems things are changing around here, Ky. You're evolving and your time frames are already merging."

𝓎

She had no idea what he meant, time frames merging. But talk about throwing cold water all over the lovely mood she'd been in when they returned from the park. Dax walked out of the kitchen looking way too chipper for her mood. "I thought I could make us a salad for lunch."

"I thought Meals on Wheels was bringing things. But I haven't seen them for a while," she commented with distraction.

He stood in the middle of her den, looking at her intently. "Things have been changing a lot around here lately, Ky. You just haven't noticed everything."

She crossed her arms in front of her dimly recognizing the fact that her current attitude could be construed as backsliding. "That's just vague enough to tell me next to nothing, Dax."

And then infuriatingly he smiled, just a bit. "Yes, you never were the complacent sort. Well, let's eat then I'll try to explain things a bit more concretely. Deal?" he asked lightly.

"Fine," she said a bit sharply. Then he nodded amiably and returned to the kitchen. How she hated being handled. Derek had tried it occasionally, and how she detested it.

107

Silently, she wandered into the hallways connecting the two bedrooms in the small house. To the right was her bedroom and to the left was the spare bedroom that she had converted to a sort of office or as of late storage room that was largely unused. Strangely, still feeling somewhat disoriented, she felt drawn in that direction, pulled in a strange way.

The door was closed but she gingerly took the knob in her hand that felt unusually cold to her touch. As she silently pushed open the door, she stopped right in her tracks. It was different, completely different, decorated with pretty white furniture she didn't recognize—a dresser, a bookshelf, a computer desk against one wall, and against another wall was a white wrought iron day bed. And Kylie couldn't help but draw in a startled breath because seated on the edge of that bed was a girl, a teenage girl with long brown hair she'd never seen before dressed in blue jeans and a yellow pullover top. Suddenly the stranger looked in Kylie's direction. Tears were running down her face. Kylie felt the turbulent emotions rush out of the teenager and punch into her almost like a blow.

Abruptly she felt herself yanked into the hall and the door closed forcibly in front of her. "You're not ready for this," Dax whispered a little harshly.

"Who was that?" she sputtered.

"Her name is Maria. And she lives here."

⚜

She was sitting in her lazy boy chair staring at the television, though the tv wasn't on.

"Are you all right?" he asked from across the room.

She frowned. To begin to answer would open up a whole can of worms that she wasn't at all ready to unleash at present. "I'm sure all of this could seem overwhelming to you," he said softly.

"You think?" she murmured tearfully. Crap, she didn't want to start with the waterworks. There was too much, too much to weep over. Too many of *the way things should have been* floating about.

"Expectations are a dangerous commodity."

And at that, she turned to stare at him, wiping away a stray tear that had rebelliously crawled down her cheek. "I have no idea what that means."

He shrugged, "The primary source of unhappiness is expectation. We mentally decide what we expect, what our threshold is for contentment, for happiness. And then when things don't go just that way, we are unhappy, unsatisfied. And in the process, we miss much."

She stared at him blankly wondering precisely to what he was referring. "Who is that girl in my house?"

"She isn't exactly in your house. She moved in, well, after you'd left."

It took a moment for what he said to completely sink in. "After I left? You mean after I died? Does that make me a ghost?"

"No, of course not. Time as I've mentioned is all happening at once. And the truth is that no one really dies, Ky. Life does not end, change yes, of course, but not end." Drawing in a deep breath, her head spun a bit. "You're fighting things."

"Am I?" she asked slowly.

"Yes, you're trying to pin things down, hold onto life as you believe it should be while it is evolving miraculously all around you. Don't fight so hard, my dearest."

She took in another breath, a sharp one this time that felt distinctively like fear. "Am I fighting?" she whispered.

And then he was standing next to her. Did he move across the room? She hadn't seen him, hadn't noticed. His hand went on her shoulder, and it made her feel stronger. "A bit, but it's all right."

"Why is she so sad?"

"Marie?"

"Yes"

"Very difficult home life," he murmured.

"Oh, poor thing," she responded, understanding that all too well.

"Send her good thoughts. Being so close in proximity will help her."

She nodded, accepting on some level what he was telling her. Closing her eyes, she focused on the sad little face.

⚜

"Be careful," he said. "It's easy to slide. The hill is steeper than you think."

They were deep in a forest, in a forest whose trees were beginning to be divested of its leaves. Although she had been here before, it wasn't exactly as though she was reliving an event but rather expanding it.

*"That's it. Time is all happening at once."*

His voice was not external but rather internal. He was speaking directly to her mind.

*"Or maybe your spirit, Ky. We are not really of flesh. We are all spirit."*

She glanced to Dax beside her. Curious shirt he was wearing, like a long-sleeved corduroy of some sort, dark brown. Yes, that's right. She remembered.

He reached out and grasped her hand. And it felt like more, more than skin on skin, palm against palm. She could feel so much right now, feel right inside him.

He turned and smiled at her. *"It's getting steep."*

And then she smiled back, *"Let's see what's there."*

*And It Was Only The Beginning*

# Snow Moon

here are questions that persist, persist incessantly in one's mind. What is the nature of good, of evil, of self-serving action versus those who strive for selfless acts of good?

It was nerve-wracking, puzzling through these philosophical conundrums. But what was worse was entertaining such things as pragmatic concerns.

Madison Angleterre was such an old name for such a young woman. You'll grow into it, her mother had always said. But she wondered if indeed she'd live that long, long enough to grow into it.

Ostensibly, she was a witch, being hunted by witch hunters who didn't deal in philosophical abstracts but absolutes.

And as a consequence, she was in hiding, hiding behind the locked gates of a somewhat exclusive community as large as it was.

Some had called her a rogue witch, having ditched the coven that she was raised in as essentially a second family. She was initiated at the age of ten by her mother and aunt as a Wiccan. But then the coven had split when she was twenty, the young dividing from the old.

And, granted, everyone makes mistakes, particularly at twenty.

She'd made twenty-four a week ago. She celebrated alone. She couldn't be in contact with anyone. It was too dangerous. The coven that she'd called home for a number of years had been split asunder, like lightning splitting through a majestic tree.

*"Jayelle, you reach too high. It will not go unnoticed."*

How had she responded, their dynamic, red-headed leader? It was hard to remember. In her mind, it was so very difficult to recall.

The response, she believed, had been something like—*"Nonsense, nothing is out of my reach."* Had she actually said that? *"My reach?"* And the others heard her as well and did nothing? But now Jayelle was in a facility somewhere, her mind turned to mush. Was she pondering the nature of evil somewhere inside that tortured shell? No, it seemed not. From what Madison understood, she was not pondering anything, reduced to the mental capacity of an imbecile.

Her heart pounded wildly in her chest with fear. Her sensitivities were collapsing in on her. Why did she break with her mother's coven? She had thought them too inflexible, outdated, too adhered to the old ways. With one step forward was also a thousand reasons to step back, to be cautious, to be wary.

*"Remember the rule of three,"* her mother had counseled. It was always subject to interpretation, but the gist was that whatever energy you put out into the world, you receive it back threefold. She breathed in deeply. She had to focus, to concentrate. She looked out of the apartment over the lake outside. Just lie low, just for a bit, until the danger passed, then go home. After all, it wasn't as if she'd done anything directly to hurt anyone. She kept telling herself that, though it sounded remarkably unconvincing even in her own ears.

✴

He was certain of it. There were only three left now of the small covenant of nine. And this one, particularly gifted he felt, had broken off quickly, trying to melt into the Ouachita mountains.

"Certainly, we've broken their backs, their group, the leader is completely depowered."

He frowned. Curiously, there were three of them as well, at present working together. One was a former academic, one an ex-priest, and he, with his very checkered past.

"Depowered? That seems a rather innocuous description, Clarence."

The younger man, the ex-academic, philosophy was it, looked directly at him with eyes filled with regret. That was good. They hadn't lost their humanity, not yet anyway.

"I wasn't prepared, Brother. When she was confronted, I felt as though my thoughts were in a muddle. I literally couldn't remember who I was or why I was there. And then she fell upon me, putting her hand to my chest, ripping energy out of me increasingly. I-I wasn't prepared," he stammered.

"Yes," Lucas murmured. "She was apparently formidable."

"If Jackson hadn't shown up, I don't know what would have happened."

Their ebony-skinned Brother commented dryly. "I performed the ceremony quickly, more so to save Clarence, and well, she fought it, so I pressed too hard."

"And her mind snapped," Lucas said softly.

"Yes," Jackson replied, seeming much less concerned than his younger Brother. But then again, he was an older, well-seasoned man in his forties and had seen much of the world during his time serving the church.

"We should always approach with at least two," Clarence nearly whispered.

"That's not feasible. We are only three at present," Jackson stated flatly.

"Move on for now," Lucas murmured.

❦

An order, a sacred order, and a nearly extinct order.

*La Lumiere,* his father had inducted him into at twelve. And throughout its existence, its members had ebbed and flowed, always meeting in secret, in someone's basement on a stormy night, or perhaps in the back of an antique shop in the French Quarter.

And as many of the older members had died off, they found no need to try to find replacements. This particular variety of threats to the general populations, such as aberrant magical communities, had largely died off or perhaps just evolved into an underground, nearly unrecognizable state.

Many had become not as organized, but more self-serving and rogue covens, based on, admittedly, self-gratification.

"What does that mean, self-gratification?"

"The witches of old, many were a benefit to the community. They used their talents and gifts to help people, to bolster energy to protect. But sometimes, these modern ones, who have only half-learned from books, with partial information and flawed training, are in it for themselves. They consciously or not align themselves with low ones to get as much out of it as they can, using people like parasites."

He had frowned. He remembered that. "All?"

"No, not all, a faction."

"How does anyone combat that?"

115

"How? First learn their ways, then use it against them."

She'd taken out cash as she traveled, renting, trying to leave as little of a paper trail as possible. But were they following the paper trail?

Madison hadn't actually seen anyone, not even in her dreams. Since Jayelle's mental collapse, they'd returned. So odd, ever since she was a child, she would dream—not prophetic exactly—but largely dreams of information, guiding her and letting her see clearly the things she needed to know.

Somehow, though in all the hubbub and excitement of the new coven, she barely noticed how they'd slipped away. And with their absence, things she needed to know became opaque, unclear, and muddied.

*Jayelle*—the name whispered in her mind. She was a gray figure to her now, shrouded, but she would still feel her presence from time to time. There were things, suspected, ephemeral things that she could not allow herself to contemplate now.

It was February, offseason in the Village, so the room she took over the marina store was at a lesser rate, which was good for her.

Because the hard truth was she was running out of funds.

*"Maybe we could arrange a meeting."*

"A meeting?"

"With the ones tracking you all."

It had been the night before she'd gone on the run. She was in her mother's kitchen, her Aunt Delphine eying her dubiously while her mother spoke.

"I don't know if they can be reasoned with," she answered quietly.

"Then maybe just submit, what happened to Jayelle, it happened because she resisted."

"So, you want me to allow them to strip me of my gifts?"

Her mother spoke with grave concern. "Jayelle's coven tried to tamper with elemental energies when they should not have. My angel, that kind of meddling with natural forces comes with a price. The law of three."

"And those men are men you feel have the right to exhort that price?"

Her aunt frowned. She had always known Delphine, now in her fifties, to be a hard woman, not so kind, not so empathetic as her younger sister, Edira. "Well, they seem to think they do," she muttered.

"I will not allow them to take what is mine."

"That kind of thinking got you into this mess," Delphine snapped back. "Me, mine, not thinking of the whole, of what a black mark the covenant of Jayelle has become for all of us, just selfishness." The word she nearly spat out like it was something distasteful in her mouth.

And then her mother, Edira, the healer, had looked at her with eyes brimming with fear and sadness. "Without your gifts, you can live a normal life, my child. And you would not end up like Jayelle."

"But I'd be a shell," she whispered. "Not myself."

"When was the last time you were yourself, Madison?" Delphine asked with steel in her voice. "And not Jayelle's puppet?"

She remembered her mother's words, but Aunt Delphine's pierced her soul. *Selfishness,* the word hung over her like a dark cloud. Early in the morning, she got in her car and had left before dawn broke. As she drove off, she saw her aunt watching her from the upstairs bedroom window, but with no expression and evidently no desire to stop her.

She left her cell phone and bought a TracFone. Because it was very important that no one be able to reach her.

✣

"Are you sure this is best?" Jackson watched him with skepticism in his dark eyes, skepticism he understood well.

"Yes," he responded, zipping up his suitcase. "This one is different, I believe."

A studied eyebrow rose. "Are you certain? If you have miscalculated, there will be no one to back you up. The kid and I are headed out West."

Lucas softly patted Jackson on the arm. The stress and anxiety actively permeated from him. This whole business was proving too much for the three of them. What they needed was a break and some new recruits. "I'm certain, my friend. I have seen it."

There was something in Jackson's expression at that pronouncement. The two had worked together long enough for him to respect what Lucas had said. "Very well, God's speed, Brother."

"And to you as well, my Brother."

And three days later, and more driving than he'd anticipated, he found himself inside the gates of a secluded community. A forested community spanning 26,000 acres, one that he couldn't have managed to get inside without renting a property, even if it was only for a week.

If he couldn't accomplish what he'd come to do in a week, then he did not deserve the title of master of the order of La Lumiere, even if its active membership at present had only three.

118

He wondered dubiously how their senior members had allowed things to go dormant for so long. *"We didn't feel the need for recruitment. This manner of evil is archaic, largely snuffed out."*

But it wasn't, not really, just curiously camouflaged, until it wasn't.

The group the rogue coven had targeted was agitated to a state close to madness, inciting violence, and then the dark witches had drained their energy like wolves feeding on the carnage. If he didn't know they were vampires, he would liken them to such. That has been the account. Most covens, even the shadier ones, acted with more restraint. This one hadn't. It had been sloppy, driven by gluttony, and their own sense of entitlement. Essentially, acting with the belief that because they could do it, they should.

That incident in the French Quarter was the red flag that had brought this order out of dormancy. Three deaths, many injured, and the spiritual toll was indeed enormous. And here he was in his small, cozy vacation home nestled by a lake and within a forest, getting ready to take on one of the perpetrators—Madison Angleterre, who believed she was smarter than him.

꙰

It was foggy, and he was dressed in black. Appropriate, she supposed. His hair was long, dark, just brushing past the collar of his coal-colored trench coat. He was slim, his skin pale, not very tanned at all.

She saw him walking slowly through the woods, leaves crunching beneath, yes, black tennis shoes it seemed. Everything was black, even his cargo pants, which she assumed were because of the pockets that were that dusky coal color. Was it symbolic or deliberate?

And then he stopped and closed his eyes as though focusing. "I see," the man murmured as if to himself. "Not a meditation, a dream then."

Somewhere, wherever she was, she drew in a sharp breath. He was cognizant.

"You can call me Lucas," he spoke softly, deliberately. "It's not really fair, Madison, that you can see me, but I can't see you."

His words swept around her, feeling as though there was a power accompanying them here. And as it was, she felt the moistness of the forest touching her skin. She looked down. She wore the scarlet red ceremonial cloak that Jayelle had insisted they all dress in during ritualistic gatherings. After she broke from the coven, she'd burned it, but here it was covering her again with only a white slip beneath.

"Symbolic," he murmured. She looked up. He stood only yards away, leaning against a tree with mist and heavy fog all around them, permeating the forest.

She thought to speak but wondered if she was in jeopardy here. "It's alright. The fog protects you. I've just awakened myself in your dream."

"You are here in this place?"

"Not far. Your energy has a unique signature, Madison. How long have you had these revelatory dreams?" He asked quite calmly.

"Always," she answered, "but," then she stopped. Was it truly wise to freely give out information to this man?

"But you wanted to say, not lately."

"You're reading me?"

"I am, Madison." He straightened up and began to slowly move closer to her. "Why does your subconscious cling to relics from Jayelle's coven?" He lightly tapped the outside of the red cloak.

"I-I'm not sure."

She noticed he had light eyes, piercingly blue, that watched as though he were scrutinizing her. "I can still feel her energy influencing you."

She took a step backward but then hit the trunk of a broad tree behind her. "That's not possible. Her mind has been destroyed."

"Has it?" he whispered because he was directly in front of her now. "I always thought that was a bit easy." It was so odd how close he was, the witch hunter, his body nearly but not quite pressing her up against the tree. His finger grazed her cheek. "I think perhaps she only abandoned the shell."

"Abandoned? What does that mean?" She whispered anxiously, because she could feel his very breath against her skin.

And then ever so lightly he brushed his lips against hers. She was so cold. She didn't push him away, didn't feel repulsed, but instead succumbed to the warmth. And then he pulled back, looking at her oddly. "I still feel her tangled up in your mind, Madison. What has she done to you?"

⚜

Madison sat up in her bed, her breathing panicked. She picked up the cell phone on the nightstand. It was 3:00 AM.

She glanced around the shadowy bedroom. Dim, scattered light splattered across the rustic wooden floor. She was alone, but the dream still remained with her, as did the sensation and desire elicited with that kiss.

※

"I'm not sure what you're telling me," Jackson's voice seemed strained. Evidently, the road trip across several states with the youngster as a companion was beginning to wear on him. So odd, in truth, Clarence was just three years younger than him. But it didn't feel that way in experience, disposition, and emotional control.

"I've had contact with Miss Angleterre. I was able to get close enough to ascertain that she's been compromised by the dark witch."

"By Jayelle Simone? But surely all bonds were broken once I performed the binding ceremony, and she was," he hesitated. Clearly, he found it distasteful. "When she was ostensibly destroyed."

"Yes, on the surface it appears so. All I'm saying is approach with caution. Make sure they are separate, and before you separate them from their powers, be very sure they aren't being used by a very clever witch who may have puzzled out how to escape her fate."

※

Her head ached from a restless night. She dreamed, and she'd seen her foe. But it all felt so confused. She could see him in her mind, tall, slim, with dark hair, dressed in black. But where?

Where exactly had she seen him? It was very confusing, giving her a panicked impulse to flee. But she was still convinced it was best to wait, at least for a little while, until things became clearer.

It was a cool February morning, very cold, with temperatures just in the low 30s. So, to clear her head, she bundled up to take a walk on a foggy beach.

❦

*"Why did you target these people?"* Her mother's dark eyes were solemn, not judgmental, but also not in the least comforting.

"They're practitioners, dark practitioners," she'd stated without hesitation.

And she was so emphatic because she'd seen the evidence they'd uncovered often enough in her mind, in vivid, concrete memory.

There was uncertainty on Edira's face. "Are you certain, Made?" That was her mother's nickname for her.

"Yes, of course," she murmured, not allowing any hint of uncertainty to pierce her reply.

❦

As she silently walked the sandy shoreline of the lake near the marina where she'd rented her upstairs apartment, her mind settled for a moment.

"Don't forget the snow moon," she remembered Jayelle's words. "Its energy is powerful. Some say transforming," she'd said lightly.

Madison couldn't remember a full moon that the coven hadn't celebrated, always outside with ceremonies.

Some, admittedly, she found disturbing, definitely Pagan in flavor, with small sacrifices, cuttings on their arms, and ceremonies—always ceremonies to take advantage of the profound energy of the lunar event.

"Wherever you are, Madison, remember the snow moon."

She squirmed and pulled her short woolen coat more tightly about her and her tan slouch hat down around her ears. It was a bit too cold for such a walk, but she was beginning to climb the walls. Maybe she should move on. She'd been here nearly a week, and something about the place was starting to get under her skin and not in a pleasant way.

It was picturesque enough, but something near, just beneath the surface, was steadily beginning to chafe her. Positioned on the sandy beach were picnic tables and umbrellas, no doubt occupied during warmer weather but now desolate and abandoned, only mimicking what she was feeling inside. If she walked to the far end of the lake, she'd find a walking trail into the forest. This was something she discovered only several days earlier, but she was feeling too moody just now to explore it.

As she made the curve toward more picnic tables, she noticed that, surprisingly, one of them was occupied. A chilling breeze rose for a moment, and her vision blurred, then cleared again.

She stopped, wondering if she should turn back. The figure just sat beneath one of those huge umbrellas. From what she could see, it was an elderly woman bundled up and staring forward toward the lake.

She glanced at the parking lot on the other side. There was a lone car parked there, a white sedan.

She could easily retreat. She was some yards away from the figure, and if she walked past her, she could do so with no interaction.

The wind blew and chapped her face. She should decide quickly. She couldn't stay out here much longer.

She took in a deep breath. She needed some exercise. Down to the trail, then back to the marina store and to her apartment upstairs. Maybe tomorrow she'd make arrangements to leave. Maybe then, she repeated to herself reassuringly. So having decided, she bent her head, intent on passing by without engaging the old woman. Quickening her pace, Madison marched forward.

Everything would be alright, period, time would take care of everything, and these hunters would lose interest.

She purposefully didn't look forward or to the side as she walked by, just down. But as soon as she passed the figure, she felt a strange sense of relief that passed through her. Something, something was off. She slowed her pace slightly and then suddenly felt the oddest thing, like a tap on her back.

More than surprised, she stopped her trudge through the cold sandy beach and turned to look behind her.

An old, scraggly, wrinkled face met hers. But with strange eyes of the purest blue.

"What?" she began, but speech stuck in her throat as a bony hand shot out and grabbed her arm.

Madison yanked away, but the grip was like iron. And then she looked up again, as that old face literally melted away and was replaced by a familiar one, one she'd seen in a dream.

"Nooo," she screeched, struggling against his unforgiving grip, but then he pulled her harshly forward, covering her mouth and nose with a towel.

So strong was the medicinal smell that she felt herself too quickly dropping into a drugged state of unconsciousness.

🪓

She seemed young to him and when he touched her, touched her actual skin, he didn't feel what he'd expected to.

One that readily embraces evil has a corruption to their energy, almost like a cancer that has infected the body. Unchecked and well-fed, corruption grows and spreads, engulfing healthy flesh, or in this case, the healthy spirit.

But what he felt from Madison Angleterre was different. He could feel degradation within her as manifestations of extreme stress, like a pure piece of paper singed on its edges by contact with a flame but still intact.

In short, he suspected she'd been duped and was foolish, very foolish.

※

She fidgeted uncomfortably in the upholstered armchair he'd deposited her in. There was no doubt it would be uncomfortable, but there was no other choice. He needed some answers, and she would give them to him.

Slowly, she shifted in her sleep, then suddenly straightened up, opening a pair of wide brown eyes that he had to admit he found captivating. Porcelain-like skin, delicate features, and shoulder-length thick brown hair. She could have stepped out of a 19th century painting.

Focusing on him standing across the room and then down at her wrists that he'd tied down to the wooden arms of the chair, those already quite large eyes seemed to get larger. "You know this is kidnapping. You can't just do this without ramifications," she said softly.

He frowned. "Everything has ramifications, Madison. As does the attack in the French Quarter by your coven."

She took in another deep breath. He could see the rapid rise and fall of her chest. And more than that, he could feel it, feel much fear emanating from her.

"They were dark practitioners."

That took a moment to soak in. He opened to her now while still maintaining his guard. In truth, he still had no idea how dangerous she could be.

Her mind was clouded, tangled in its memories. Ah, yes, now he could see. Some true, some planted, truly she'd been tampered with.

"They were not."

Again, the dark eyes stared back at him, but with incredulity. "You lie. I saw the evidence with my eyes. Jayelle—" Then she stopped, suddenly seeming to be wary of giving him too much information.

Abruptly, he grabbed a straight chair from the small kitchen table and placed it directly in front of her.

"Madison, I know this is difficult to believe, but I am trying to help you."

At that, her face hardened. "Is that why you drugged me and kidnapped me? Is that why you destroyed Jayelle's mind?"

"That was not me, but Jayelle is not like you."

"Let me go."

"Tell me the truth, and I'll consider it."

She looked down, fidgeting in the chair. "Who are you?"

"My name is Lucas Allard, and I am a warlock."

🜨

Her mind swirled with a strange, disconnected reality. She should be afraid, terrified really, but instead she was floating on a distracted sea of acceptance, comfort, though that sounded markedly bizarre in her own ears.

Her arms were tied down, and she'd been kidnapped by a stranger intent on divesting her of her magical gifts. And she felt strangely comforted? As though she could relax and draw a quiet breath for the first time, and then she sighed, closing her eyes. Could it possibly be?

"What spell is this?" She asked, unable not to succumb.

"I wanted you to feel comfortable."

Madison drew another calming breath. "Then it's all false. There is no safety here."

"There is," the man who called himself Lucas Allard replied softly. "I mean you no harm, and the enchantment is rudimentary. You take of it what your soul craves."

She smiled deliberately, opening her eyes. "Why don't you get it over with, Lucas? You're here to divest me of my powers, and at present, there doesn't seem to be much I can do about it."

He frowned, looking at her oddly, but then again, what wasn't odd about this situation?

"You've been unhappy for a long time, Madison."

She looked at him with bewilderment. "I expected more from a witch hunter."

And then something like curiosity flickered in his eyes. "Is that what you believe I am, a witch hunter?"

She squirmed a bit, and a pain shot up her back in discomfort. "You're hunting witches."

"I studied with witches and warlocks."

"To what end?" she said, her back disrupting that peaceful feeling that had taken hold of her previously.

"Do you want a pillow behind your back, Madison? It's not my intent to have you in discomfort."

She wriggled again, muttering. "Then maybe you shouldn't have tied me down to a chair."

Rather fluidly, he was on his feet, grabbing a dark blue couch pillow, then lightly putting his hand on her shoulder. "Lean forward," he murmured.

It took a moment for his words to sink in, so dizzying was the energy she felt flowing through his touch. Slightly, she leaned forward and felt him rather gingerly push the pillow down behind her back. "That should help," he whispered, rather close to her.

"What do you want?" She couldn't help but ask but also noted that he hadn't removed his hand. The contact felt warming, fluid, as though some tangible intoxicant was slowly spreading throughout her body.

"I want to understand, Madison. When I touch you, it feels profoundly as though your spirit is in great pain. Whether you recognize it or not, you've been deceived and used."

"I don't—" It was hard to articulate. She was feeling so disconnected from herself, and the hand on her shoulder tightened. "I don't understand. What are you doing to me?"

"Trying to help. Serious bonds have been placed on you that are continuing to drain you."

"Bonds?"

"Yes, damaging energy bonds that have been placed deep and are compromising you. I need you to relax and feel peaceful because I'm going to attempt to remove them now."

Her head was spinning, and her vision blurred over as she found herself back home again, in her childhood bed. So soft, so inviting.

Distantly, she heard his voice still speaking to her and felt the pressure of his palms on her shoulders. But it was different somehow; they were on her bare shoulders.

He had unbuttoned her sweater and pushed it down.

"Relax now, Madison, and feel peace." She heard him. Then on the heels of that, she felt the palms of his hand warm, and then grow hot like fire scorching her, then actually melting through her skin and reaching inside.

She was still in her soft, comforting bed in her mother's house, safe and protected. But also, distantly, she could hear someone screaming.

✣

With shaking hands, he wrapped the blanket around her bare shoulders. He was dizzy, more than that, he felt sick.

There was a bucket beside them that he had placed the red coiling serpents inside, which he had ripped from inside Madison's body. Deeply exhausted, Madison had slumped forward, unconscious. He had no idea what state, mentally or physically, she would be in when she awoke.

Once he had uncoiled the bonds from her chakra systems, they manifested in the physical world as some kind of mutated snakes. He drowned them in the bucket, sealing them in with a containment spell. They would need to be destroyed once he had the strength.

He lightly touched the side of her face with his hand. Her breathing was shallow, but she was still within the protective bubble he had placed her in.

Slowly, he began to untie her arms and heaved her into his embrace. His arms went under her legs as he scooped her up. She'd sleep for a while, and then they'd talk.

✣

Madison awoke in her childhood bedroom, the light creeping through the translucent sheers behind her rose-colored drapes. Her eyes fluttered open, and she breathed in a delicate scent of violets that seemed to accompany her mother, Edira, whenever she was around. And indeed, she was sitting beside her bed in a small wooden chair she'd pulled up beside it.

"What are you doing here?" She murmured groggily, a heavy sort of drugged feeling still clung to her, and her mind seemed utterly incapable of separating what was actual and what was being dreamed. Everything was such a muddle.

Edira softly took her hand in hers and brought it to her lips to kiss lightly. Madison felt the surge of energy flow from her mother into her, stimulating her memory. She wasn't here, wasn't in her Memphis home. She was with that man, the one interrogating her, and then she remembered great rushes of pain, nearly unbearable pain.

"No," her mother had her hand clasped in both of her own now. "You must be calm, my girl."

She straightened up, her mind still spinning. "What did he do to me? Did he rip my power away?"

"No, he did not, Madison. He broke the bonds Jayelle had placed on you."

"What?" She whispered in a rasp. "Jayelle didn't—"

"Of course she did, Madison. Every time she performed a ritual with you, every ceremony, every time she put marks on you, every time your heart area was exposed in front of her, she created bonds, bonds to control you with, bonds to drain your energy."

"We were sisters."

Her mother's usually soft demeanor seemed to harden beneath her gaze. "Sisters don't use each other, don't implant false memories to manipulate."

She could feel panic setting in at her words. "I don't believe you. There are no false memories."

And then the grasp on her hands seemed to even tighten further if that was possible. "Have I ever lied to you, my child? Your mind has been filled with lies. Memories planted so that you would do what she wants. And be ready when she needs you ."

"Ready? What does that mean?"

"The snow moon, Madison. In only two days. It has always been her plan."

Her head throbbed with confusion. "I can't see, Mom. This man has done something to create all of this."

"No, Madison, he's trying to help you."

"Help? Why, why would he want to help me?" And then Edira looked at her squarely and with quiet determination and unfailing strength. "Because I asked him to."

🌱

Her eyes snapped open. Immediately, she knew the room was alien. Above her, a ceiling fan slowly turned, and beside her, still asleep on the double bed, was Lucas Allard, the man in question.

She looked around furtively. The door on the far side of the room, another door unopened, probably a bathroom, some maple-colored furniture, a dresser, an end table, and a rocking chair in the corner near a large window covered with mini blinds.

Gently, she made the move to sit up but found that every inch of her was aching with pain. Her skin felt chafed, and her bones hurt as though she had a fever.

With difficulty, she swung one foot off the bed onto the floor, then the other, again feeling the dizziness wash over her as she moved.

"You might want to rest before you try that." The voice behind her startled her so that she attempted to quickly come to her feet. Then, suddenly, strong and deliberate hands caught her shoulders in his grip. "You've lost a lot of energy, Madison. You are too vulnerable to leave here yet."

She took a breath, feeling her body tremble. "Let me go. Haven't you done enough?"

And then she heard him sigh, "I truly wish that was the case."

❦

"Are you hungry? I have some cans of soup here."

"Where are we?" She asked abruptly in a tone he couldn't help but interpret as slightly hostile.

He glanced at the cold fireplace across the den. Luckily, he picked up some wood and other groceries before, well, before he had intercepted Madison. "In the Village."

She was sitting at the table, staring at him stony-faced. He hadn't bothered to bind her again. In fact, he'd only done that for the operation of removing the energy bonds that Jayelle had entrenched inside her. Though he knew very well he had only been marginally successful. He'd broken the obvious ones and, in fact, had incinerated them out back not very long ago. His throat still felt singed and scraped by the acid smell from the disintegrating serpents.

As he'd been doing just that, he had looked up to find her watching him with no expression through the sliding glass door. However strong these energy bonds had once affected her, she now seemed untouched as he disposed of them.

The problem was now the bonds that were less accessible. The psychological ones, the dark witch had spent years erecting in her unwitting disciple.

"You really should eat something."

She turned her gaze away from him, staring off. "I'm not hungry. Did you really—" then she stopped.

"Ask me whatever you want, Madison."

"My mother, I saw her. She said she'd asked for your help."

He nodded slowly. "It was actually my uncle she first contacted. He was once an active part of our order."

"What order?" she said sharply. Her eyes look so wide and dark in that finely boned face. He had to admit she was quite beautiful, delicate in some ways. But that he suspected was deceptive because he could feel her mind even now reaching out to his, foraging for answers, for the truth. But he didn't trust, not yet, that something else or someone else wasn't eavesdropping through her.

He stared at her, wondering how much to disclose, but deciding for the moment that less might be more.

"Tomato or chicken noodle? Being upset with me takes a lot of energy, Madison, which at present you are lacking."

"Tomato," she said softly.

"Iced tea or water?"

"Why? Why would she approach your uncle?"

"She was worried, he said softly. "She sensed Jayelle's intentions were impure."

𝔛

*"Looks like they're programming someone who has been in the cult."*

*"A cult?"*

*"Well, a dark coven is rather a cult. A traditional cult also utilizes energy and sometimes dark magic to influence its members. Once clear thought is compromised, people can be manipulated into almost anything."*

*"So how does one begin to break such a hold?"*

*"First the cracks."*

*"The cracks?"*

*"There are always cracks. The stronger the mind of the one in question, the larger they are."*

Lucas remembered in that moment staring at his uncle and feeling in his heart how deadly serious he was. However, as it was, he was only sixteen at the time and would not put his advice into practical use for some time later.

✲

It was true. Madison hurt everywhere, and she was cognizant enough to know that it was a result of the ceremony that Lucas Allard had performed on her.

"Don't fight it." He murmured, almost as though he'd been reading her thoughts. "The energy bonds that have been draining you for some time are removed, but you've grown used to them. Your body, your spirit, needs time to adjust to the change."

"Am I supposed to thank you?" She said hastily, taking another bite of the soup that was actually reviving her a bit.

Lucas glanced up from across the round kitchen table that was situated in front of the sliding glass door. "Evidently not," he said flatly, then continued to eat his own soup.

"How long are you planning on keeping me here?"

And then he glanced up again, looking her squarely in the eyes. "Until after the moon, the full moon."

"The snow moon?" She murmured, remembering her mother mentioning it and then something else, something else she'd forgotten about it.

"Yes, once it passes, I believe you will have turned a corner."

"Jayelle is gone, essentially anyway."

135

"Essentially, as you say. But you're very weak, and there still is work to be done."

※

She had no idea what time it was. There was a clock on the wall, but oddly, it wasn't moving. She had spied one on the microwave as well, but she knew it wasn't right, reflecting 2:00 PM in the afternoon. Yet, she knew that couldn't be true because night had fallen outside.

Madison had decided somewhere along the way that silence was the answer. She had sat down on the well-stuffed, rust-colored sofa, grabbed one of its pillows, and watched him in stony silence.

This had been their afternoon together. Once or twice, she received an unreadable glance, but then he returned to busy work, coming and going from the room.

And she watched the door. There was one door she spied, other than the sliding glass doors, just to the side of the kitchen.

The floor plan was quite open, definitely in the style of a vacation home. The dining room and the kitchen were only separated by a peninsula, all flowing together. So, unless he took the stairwell downstairs to the bedrooms, he could always see her. She assumed there were multiple bedrooms, though she had only seen the one.

The only room on this floor that really afforded privacy, which Madison had checked out early on, was the bathroom. But there wasn't even an outside window within, so it was of little use.

She considered getting outside and running for help. She knew very well it was a gamble.

Some houses were quite isolated here, and even if she managed to reach another, there was no guarantee it would be occupied. All in all, it was a gamble, but something inside her was pushing her to try, to get out of his clutches, his influence, for a little while.

As she was contemplating her escape, Madison felt herself getting more and more drowsy and couldn't help but close her eyes for a few moments, just a few. Perhaps it wasn't wise, but in truth, it couldn't be helped.

※

A particular aroma permeated everything, a mix of smoke, ashes, and candles, and the scent unmistakably of coconut.

Gradually, she opened her eyes.

She was on a couch, but not in the den she remembered. Before her was a roaring fireplace and a cozy feeling that the stark room of the vacation house did not possess.

Slowly, with discrimination, Madison sat up. Lucas was seated across from her in a rocking chair, and before her, a white candle was set on a pristine white cloth, surrounded by ashes, and a goblet of water.

She breathed in deeply, feeling and actually smelling the fact that there was magic in the air. "This is a protection spell. My mother used to use these often," she murmured.

"Yes, mine as well. I was raised in a coven of witches, as were you."

She continued to breathe in deeply. There was pure cleansing to such a spell, soothing to the senses. Never had she experienced a spell or sensation like this in Jayelle's coven.

"There is a reason for that, Madison."

She looked at him, suddenly understanding. "You're reading my thoughts."

He leaned back in the rocker, seeming content with where he was at present.

"Yes, I have been for some time. Of course, it's easier here."

She looked away, "Then you know."

"Of your escape plan? Of course, but I wouldn't need to read your mind to pick up on that. Just to save you some wasted energy, we are quite isolated here. It would be very difficult to achieve your goals, or should I rather say hers."

She looked back at him with some confusion. "Hers?"

He nodded slowly. He seemed to be studying her somehow. "Yes," he said softly. "She can't affect you here as she can when you are in the physical."

"Here? Where are we?"

"My house, I have one in Natchitoches. Be still for a moment, Madison."

She frowned, taken aback by the firmness in his tone. "There is something, something physical she has bound you with." Breathing deeply, she felt the dizziness overwhelm her again. "What has she placed on you?"

"Placed? I don't know what—"

"It has to be permanent, an alteration of some kind." Then suddenly he was on his feet, approaching her, standing in front of her.

"Get up," he said quietly.

And she did so, almost feeling as though there was no choice. "I don't know—" he suddenly placed two fingers in front of her lips.

"Ssshh," he replied with determination. "Madison, there is something physical tethering you to Jayelle. Something that she is still using."

"She can't," she muttered, feeling a strange horror filling her. "She's gone."

"No, I'm afraid she's not. And she's looking for a body, a body she can house her disconnected spirit in."

Her eyes widened in dread at his pronouncement. "The snow moon," she'd always said. "It has the power of transformation."

"I feel as if she has put something on you. A cut would heal. It would have to be more permanent."

She drew her breath in with a gasp. They were all laughing. It was more like a party with food and wine. Jovially, Jayelle had taken it out of her pocket—small circles, two overlapping circles.

*"We'll be sisters,"* as she heated its metal with the flame of a black candle.

"It has to be on the torso, nearer the heart to bind fully," he murmured.

She looked up into his piercing eyes shakily. "I'm not sure."

"Show me," he compelled her almost hypnotically.

With shaking fingers, she unbuttoned her sweater, then lowered it, turning around. She felt his fingertips brush the small brand on her lower back. "I see. This was hidden from me," he said, almost to himself.

"It's permanent."

"Well, nothing is permanent. We'll just have to adapt it to our benefit."

❆

When Madison's eyes opened, the night had fallen outside. Lucas was in front of the fireplace, stoking a fire that had not been there when she'd fallen asleep.

She sat up as the intensity of her dream rushed back into her mind. "Lucas," she said impulsively as he straightened, then slowly turned around to face her. There was a panic in her chest, and it burned. The small brand on her back had become inflamed.

"Is it—" He held up a single finger in front of his lips to silence her.

"Eyes," he murmured, and she looked around in panic.

Slowly, he moved to her, extending his hand. Disorientation was flooding through her mind as though she simply couldn't think at all. She took his hand, and he pulled her to her feet, yanking her into an unexpected embrace in his arms.

"Follow my lead," she heard him distantly in her mind, and then suddenly he held her close and was kissing her. Instinctively, she tried to pull away, but his arms were like steel. Again, in her mind, "Follow along, Madison. Trust me."

So, she decided, and she let go, allowing and returning his passionate kisses.

He pushed her back to the sofa until they were both sitting. Then he was kissing her more, but on her neck, his hands going up under her sweater until he was brushing her bare flesh.

So odd, it felt languorous as though energy was flowing everywhere he touched and within her, stemming the fear and panic like an anesthesia.

Then, suddenly, he pulled her sweater directly over her head. She felt the chill surround her, but didn't mind as his mouth was on her flesh and his hands running along her back.

And then he kissed her once more, then spun her around unexpectedly so that her back was to him. Without warning, she felt it—something hot, so hot, connecting with her skin, then burning her right atop the tiny brand.

It startled her, and she cried out, not exactly in pain, because it didn't hurt as one might expect. But a great wash of pain did pass through her, on the inside, as though within some cord had painfully snapped.

"Easy," he whispered to her, holding her still tightly with one hand. "I'm sorry," he murmured. "That will leave a scar."

She was breathing heavily in his arms that were wrapped around her tightly, still pulling her against him. "It's broken, Madison. She has nothing left to anchor you with."

❦

It stung. She showered off with the coldest water she could stand.

"It will help your energy," he told her, which, given the temperature outside, in the lower twenties, was quite a hardship.

"I don't understand."

"It was a brand of sorts, small but not insignificant. I imagine she did the same to the others."

She struggled to remember. Everything in her mind felt like an odd shamble of images. "I-I can't be sure. Something's happened to my mind."

He was softly dabbing the spot on her back with a warm towel. "Don't fight it. It seems Jayelle has quite the gift for suggestion."

She looked at him oddly. "Suggestion? What does that even mean?"

"Placing of false memories. She would use her energy to plant strong suggestions in your mind when you were particularly vulnerable, and a false memory would be forged and reinforced with your belief in it. It can be quite damaging."

She took a quick breath, still feeling such waves of confusion. She was holding her sweater up in front of her as he ministered to the fresh wound that he had ostensibly created to diminish the effect of an old one.

"How did you do this?" Odd that Madison hadn't thought to ask before, but then again, maybe she didn't really want to know.

He stopped attending to her new wound, softly commenting. "I could bandage this, but I think it's best to leave it uncovered for now." And then he paused for a moment, adding, "My ring has an alchemical symbol on it. I heated it near a flame, then used it to alter the symbol on your back."

"Why didn't it burn your hand?"

"I used my energy to contain the heat as well as contain its impact on you." He flexed his hand a bit. "Unfortunately, I wasn't entirely successful." Then he glanced at her, "You should shower. Try not to let the water directly hit the burn and keep the temperature as cool as you can."

She took a deep breath. "I'm pretty tired."

"It's important. It will help clear some of the bad energy you still have clinging to you."

♃

He'd given her a gray sweatshirt with a picture of a snowy colored wolf on the front. Of course, all her clothes were still at the apartment near the marina.

As she pulled it on, then her jeans, she was comforted by the fact that it felt warm and freshly laundered. Her mind still felt in a tumult as though everything that she'd once known as real and concrete had somehow been stripped away from her.

A shakiness passed through her as she found a hair dryer on the cabinet and began to dry her wet hair. Her brush was in her purse, so she used her fingers to try to detangle her thick, shoulder-length, black hair. As she smudged the foggy mirror, she suddenly froze.

The figure stood behind her—red hair and brandy-colored eyes staring back accusingly at her.

"How could you do this, sister? Aid this defiler?"

She swung around sharply, finding in truth that she was alone in the room. But it didn't feel that way. Moments before, she was certain Jayelle had indeed been standing right behind to her.

⚜

It was panic, raw fear racing through her as she literally ran up the stairs to intercept Lucas in the kitchen, where he was evidently surveying dinner possibilities.

"She was here," Madison spat out uncontrollably. Immediately, he put his hands on her arms.

"Calm down," he said, entirely too passively.

"Did you hear me? I saw her here."

He was reacting oddly, breathing deeply while staring at her intently. Then, slowly, he closed his eyes as if focusing. "You've lost energy from this. It's essential you be calm."

She could feel it, overwhelming panic still pounding through her. "But how did she get here? What is she?"

His eyes opened, and he focused on her calmly. "Disembodied entity now, looking for a place to set up shop."

"You mean me?"

"Yes, that seems as though it might have always been the goal. She'd worn out her own shell with her dark magics. So, she wants a new one. But we've already taken great strides in

143

preventing that from happening. We just have to wait her out for a few more days, Madison."

"How can we do that?" Her voice was shaking. She could hear it as she spoke. How could someone she had recently viewed as a sister have become a threat to her so quickly?

"Don't try to puzzle everything out. Just anchor yourself to this moment."

"How exactly do we do that?"

And then his mouth quirked peculiarly, in an almost whimsical way she didn't remember seeing before. "Well, maybe we order a pizza. I'm famished, and it's difficult to strategize on an empty stomach."

"Pizza?" She repeated, feeling completely confused.

"Don't you like pizza?"

"Sure, why not?"

❅

He watched her carefully, though he did try to appear as if he wasn't doing so. *"This isn't who she is. Something has taken hold of her."*

Edira Angleterre had looked at him with eyes that reminded him so much of Madison's, exuding a palpable fear for her daughter.

"I'm not sure what I can do now. Madison has the right to join any coven she wishes and follow whatever path she chooses. Free will is sacred, as you know, Mrs. Angleterre. Unless, of course, they cross a line and do harm to innocents."

They were in his uncle's den. It was a small wood-frame house in New Orleans, right next to City Park. His Uncle Samuel had introduced him to Madison's mother, then had made himself scarce as they talked.

144

"I see," she said shakily. "But if that happens and this creature drags Madison with her into such damning territory, what happens to my daughter?"

He took in a deep breath. "Well, let's hope she doesn't."

He noticed she wasn't eating much, and though granted, it wasn't the most wonderful takeout pizza in the world, it was consumable.

"Not any good?" He asked, and her dark eyes returned to him from a place faraway and not a pleasant place from the look on her face.

"I feel like I'm crawling out of my skin. Do you have any wine or something like that here?"

"You shouldn't consume alcohol tonight. There could be ceremonies later."

She looked at him with confusion. "We would always drink in the coven when there were spells or ceremonies. Jayelle made it seem like a party."

He nodded slowly, getting a clearer picture of how things were conducted. "Yes, well, that made you vulnerable to her. No doubt she used your incapacitated senses to control and possibly drain you."

"Drain me?"

"Of energy, Madison. It's clear she's taken much from you." Eat, you're going to need your strength. No doubt it will be a difficult night."

She looked at him with fear in her eyes, and it disturbed him greatly. What a difficult thing when the foundation of your belief system is being torn away.

It is a painful process, particularly when that foundation is built on falsehood. He reached out a hand and put it on her arm. She did look surprised. "I am committed to helping you, Madison. You've already made great strides."

"It seems," she said hesitantly, "that I've been a fool in all of this." He could tell that this was a difficult admission for her.

"You've been used and taken advantage of. Now it's time to regain control of your life."

"How do we do that?" It was barely a whisper.

"Why, fight with everything we have."

⚹

He wasn't certain this would work, nor was he certain he could save Madison Angleterre. He wasn't even sure she was committed to being saved.

But all he knew was that he was committed to trying. He could feel her eyes on him, watching intently as they rearranged the furniture in the den, clearing a large space in the middle of the room.

"Why are you sure she'll come tonight?" she asked softly. There was a slight tremble in her voice that Lucas knew was fear.

"I don't, just a hunch."

"But the Snow Moon is tomorrow."

"Yes, but the energy begins tonight, and that's what she needs, its energy."

"You think she wants to possess me."

"I do," he said sharply, eying the space to see if it was adequate for his purposes.

And then she said something he did not expect. "I'm sorry. I'm sorry my stupidity dragged you into this."

He stopped, looking at her pale face and large eyes, reminding him a bit of a lost child. "We all make mistakes, Madison. That is how we grow. We learn, then we help others to learn."

"Is that what you're doing?"

"I am keeping a promise I made to your mother. The learning part we'll deal with once this is over."

"So, you think we'll pull through this?"

"I think we have a good chance," he said a bit more cheerfully than he felt. "What we'll do is give it our all. That is what I need from you. Can you do that?"

She nodded slowly, eying him with an expression he couldn't help but find intriguing. "Yes, Lucas, I can promise you I will give this fight every ounce of strength I have."

And with that, he smiled, feeling genuinely more optimistic about facing whatever was to come.

"What do we do first?"

"We build a protected circle and once we're inside, we seal it and wait."

She nodded, saying with determination, "All right. I'm ready."

# The Translator

There was a knock at the door.

It was early evening, so she didn't expect anyone, not at this time of night.

Of course, if she'd lived in the city, it would be a different matter. But not here, quarter till eight, her little house out in the forest, and all over pitch blackness. And, of course, she was all alone.

So, she decided not to answer. It seemed the best course. This was a gated community, and she had only rented this house over the winter. Rates were cheaper than in the summer months. That's when they made their bread and butter—this place, lakes and scenery, the resort end of things. Not with the other side— the full-time retirement end.

There were a lot of old people here, old people—some who seemed entitled, some who seemed to be barely making ends meet, holding on by their fingernails. She'd even seen some elderly reduced to taking post-retirement jobs as grocery store cashiers or baggers.

Surely that wasn't their dream, but the economy, by its fluctuating nature, didn't tend to stabilize dreams.

There was a deep inaudible sigh, right around her heart. Maybe this had been a bad idea to splatter her savings on this "vacation"—a three-month vacation to get her head on straight. Not that it had ever been quite that.

Another knock, a soft one—damn, couldn't they take a hint?

If she'd wanted to answer, well, clearly, she would have.

She pulled her black and white striped shawl more securely around her.

It wasn't unknown for there to be an occasional brown bear in this region of Arkansas but then again, it was winter. Weren't they supposed to be sleeping now?

Another soft tap, definitely not a brown bear.

She would ignore it. She wasn't in the mood for, well, much of anything. She took a sip of her hot tea laced with brandy. That was a danger, drinking alone. She followed the Village police reports. Yes, they had their own private "police force" although what miniscule crime they did have here mostly amounted to domestic squabbles often fueled by, yes, alcohol. A lot of drinking was going on in this largely winter retirement community. If these golden years were so happy, why so much drinking? Good question, and she made a note of it on the small pad of paper positioned beside her spiked tea. The irony was not lost on her.

Another tap, unfrickingbelievable. Who would be at the kitchen door at this time of night continuing to knock after they'd so clearly been ignored before?

Maybe some workaholic girl scout? Or someone who desperately wanted to clean out the gutters or mow the lawn. She lived in a forest for Pete's Sake.

Of course, she knew. Perhaps her angry reaction was a bit exaggerated. After all, there could be some distant neighbor desperately in need of assistance who had hiked for some time just to reach her door and beg a little help. Maybe they didn't have any stamina to make it to another house that actually was quite a bit further down the street.

As it was, this subdivision was less developed than some of the others. Her little winter rental was a good four well-forested lots away from anyone else. She had picked it for that reason. She didn't want to talk to people. She was tired of them. She'd wanted time, well, time—another knock.

She slammed her tea down on the end table and stalked over to the kitchen door.

On retrospect, she would have to say she wasn't being wise.

It would have been better to pack it in and go to bed, letting whoever was knocking, knock all the way until morning, until all she found outside was a pile of dust, a pile of dust in the bright morning light, all that was left of whoever the maniac was who wouldn't stop knocking.

Was this an overreaction on her part?

Perhaps, yes, she would have to say, perhaps yes.

It was true. She wasn't in a good place. Life hadn't been kind, and she felt like hitting someone hard, literally. But she might settle for verbally if that was indeed all she could hope for.

So, without caution, and not too gingerly she flung open the door.

And then, after a momentary pause, she drew in a deep breath. There was a man standing in the door frame, a tall, slender man, with brown hair and pale skin. He was all dressed in black, a black jacket, black jeans and a black turtleneck. And for some odd reason, seeing him felt like a bucket of cold water was thrown all over her, drowning all her built-up frustration and rage.

"Do you know what time it is?" She managed to get out albeit with much less force than she had originally intended.

And then he said calmly, "It's about eight, actually not that late if you think about it."

She waited, yes, a bit deflated. And then something on the heels of everything that had occurred up until now creeped in. He seemed tangentially familiar.

"Do I know you?" She murmured.

There was a slow smile that crept into that pale face. "I think so."

She waited, wondering if any nocturnal bugs had crept in. There were always bugs about here. "From?" She inquired shortly.

"The bookmobile," he stated without elaboration. Her mind quickly flipped back to about a week ago when she'd dropped in on that strange little bus just outside the Delightfully Brewed coffee shop. Oddly, the only coffee shop in the Village. She'd gotten a library card online, determined to catch up on some reading during her "vacation."

"Oh, yeah. The books aren't overdue yet, are they?" she muttered. Still at a total loss as to what this visit could possibly be concerning.

"It's awkward, isn't it?"

She frowned, "Sorry?"

"Having me turn up on your doorstep like this."

"I—" again, "sorry, not following."

He expelled a deep and somewhat unexpected sigh. "Yeah, I guess I was being impetuous. I'll try again."

❦

"There should be a number under K."

"K?" She glanced up from her crouching position in the back of the small and yes, somewhat claustrophobic bus.

"For King, you asked about Stephen King books." Her head swam a bit. Had she? She could of sworn, and then she straightened up because she could. She was only five four after all. Now, Stephen King, yes, vaguely, she recalled wanting to read, well something, so vague, all of this was vague.

"Did you find them?" He asked from the front. He was at a small sort of podium near the entrance, cramped though. Everything in here was cramped. She glanced over to the shelves of books on the sides of the bus, easy enough to find the K's with some great big fat volumes there.

"Oh yes, thanks," she replied, fingering the slick covered books, and realizing that she was living alone in a forest and maybe didn't want to be reading scary stories out in the woods.

"Ever read *The Stand*?"

"Oh, um, no. It's pretty long," she murmured. She didn't have much experience with a book mobile, but it seemed one didn't get much privacy to peruse like a regular library. Unfortunately, however, the closest brick and mortar variety was a good forty minutes away.

"Worth the effort though. When he's not being scary, he can be quite philosophical." She glanced back at him dubiously.

"You think?"

And then he smiled back at her, and she finally took him in, this person she was speaking to. Tall, slender, dark-haired, probably forties, near her age, with a welcoming face and odd, what was it? That's right, no accent. Everyone around here had an Arkansas drawl, but he didn't. "From time to time," he answered. Yes, no accent, she was right.

She grabbed the oversized volume of *The Stand*. A showdown between good and evil, how scary could that be? And then she

152

moved down quickly eyeballing the sparse Norah Roberts' offerings and grabbed something a bit frothier as a counterbalance.

She approached the odd little podium, handing him the library card that she'd fished out of her blue jeans. It was quite cold here in January, so she lived in jeans and sweatshirts. This one had Chicago on it. She'd made it a habit to get one in every city she visited. That of course was when she was moving around more.

Smoothly taking the card and the books from her, he started clicking in information on a small laptop as she waited.

"Been here long, in the Village?"

"Um, about a month I guess."

"So, how was your Christmas?" He asked, his dark eyes never leaving the computer screen.

"Quiet," she answered, feeling an odd sweep of dizziness.

He nodded, handing her back her card. "Would you like a book bag? They're free."

"Uh, sure," she was all in for free. He reached smoothly to the side grabbing from a box she hadn't taken in before. But then again, she wouldn't call herself a detail person, unless she was proactively focusing. A bright blue bag, stamped boldly with the moniker of Garland County Library. And before he gave it to her, he put the two oversized volumes that she now questioned if she'd ever read into it.

"Well, that's it, Mira," he said, and it jarred her a bit that he'd used her name. How did he—of course, the library card. She exhaled just a notch. For a moment, she'd thought something strange was going on here. "Unless of course, you'd like to have a cup of coffee with me."

She stared back at him a little blankly. "Coffee?"

"Yep, right here at *Delightfully Brewed*."

"Don't you have to stay with your bus?" She asked awkwardly, strange words coming out of her mouth.

And then he smiled, almost as though he appreciated the oddness of it. In about ten minutes, we're closing up here. So, I can take a break before I head back to the city. "Oh," she said. Of course, she could make an excuse and cut out. Socializing right now felt outside her wheelhouse, but then again, this bookmobile guy seemed nice, harmless. Though she didn't even know his name.

"My name is Edric."

She looked at him with confusion. Had she voiced that out loud? "Edric?" She repeated.

"Yeah, you might say my parents were fantasy buffs."

"Oh, that's nice." There seemed to be an awkward pause that uncomfortably she felt obliged to fill in. "My parents loved Star Trek, the original. They named me after Mira Romaine, The Lights of Zetar."

He nodded, smiling, nice comfortable smile. "Scotty's girlfriend."

"Yep," she nodded, amazed she'd actually stumbled across someone who knew the reference.

"So, coffee?"

"Coffee, okay I guess."

"You can read your books on that patio table while I finish out my time here." She glanced out the front windshield of the bus to the coffee shop. There was indeed several wrought iron tables outside. "Unless it's too cold for you."

"No, that's fine. I don't mind the cold. I'll just get my jacket out of the car."

❧

They ended up inside. By the time he closed up the bookmobile and rendezvoused with her by the coffee shop, her fingers felt numb flipping through the final chapters of *The Stand*. She'd seen the miniseries, in fact two versions of it, and all she was interested in was how King tied up loose threads in the book. Impatient, not willing to take the journey just get to the end, that was the flaw of modern Americans, not paying attention to the journey. Who'd said that? Some spiritualist or late-night talk show host? Crumbs of wisdom could come from any source really. Someone had said that one too.

"Inside?" He asked cheerfully. And again, she was struck with a wave of something, something unfinished or not begun.

"Maybe so," she answered softly.

❧

The almond croissant was really good. She hadn't remembered that she'd skipped breakfast until they were on the other side of the pastry counter, perusing its compelling contents.

Edric had an oversized blueberry muffin in front of him. It was three times the size of a normal one as if it had carnivorously consumed two little ones.

"So, you like living in the Village?" He asked just as she gulped her overly heated Café Mocha—sweets and sugary coffee with whipped cream, how she was indulging today.

"It's quiet," she murmured. She didn't want to talk about herself. It was depressing. But if she didn't want to—why again was she having coffee with a stranger?

He nodded, "Yes, true enough. But that's what you wanted."

Mira stared at him at the strange comment, then felt compelled to glance around. The coffee shop was virtually unoccupied, just one person in a far corner table on their computer and of course, a cheerful young redhead at the counter. It was amazing how many redheads she'd run into since she moved here. "What I wanted?" She repeated what he'd said. His version hadn't exactly sounded like a question but rather a statement of fact.

"Yes, let's see," he said lightly tapping his fingers on the table. "You wanted to get away from people, people you knew, to sort out your life."

Dizziness swept through again. She remembered a knock on the door that wouldn't stop. "How do you know that?" she whispered.

"Eat something. It will help," he said sedately.

More calmly than she felt, she brought the croissant up to her lips. It was a good-sized construction, and she should have torn off a piece first, but in retrospect it felt like she was in a bit of shock. So, she took a huge bite, and the sweetness exploded in her mouth. He was right. It helped. "I need to go home," she murmured.

And Edric smiled broadly. "Finish your breakfast, Mira. Then we'll talk."

✾

"This seems peculiar."

He glanced up. He'd been sorting through a stack of book returns while sitting in the driver's seat of the Garland County Bookmobile. The tall blond man dressed in a black turtleneck and black jeans was looking at him strangely. Edric had the books piled up on the passenger seat of the van. He could move them so his visitor could sit, but he didn't want to. He didn't want him to stay for a protracted amount of time.

"Not really, I just need to get these back on the shelves before another wave of patrons come in."

"Edric."

"Also some might be marked as holds, so I can't put those out."

"Edric," this time he'd said his name a little sterner, a little more emphatic, but not angrily. He stopped and looked up, ceasing his activity. "You know this isn't really your job."

"Yes, of course I know. And I've made all my visits. I'm not behind in anything."

He looked at him a bit dubiously. But then it seemed Fable was of that nature. "I don't doubt that, Edric. It's just that it's time, you know, to get some help with things."

He nodded slowly. Undeniably, he was tired. He shouldn't be as tired as he felt but the world, this earth, was a tumultuous place just now. "Yes, I am working on that as well."

Fable eyed him skeptically for just a moment, then seemed to relent. "Well, then carry on, Edric. And let me know if things get complicated."

※

She did enjoy the trails. That was what had made her decide to come. When she was a kid, her family had vacationed here for just a week, when she was twelve. She remembered running along the deep trails into the forest ahead of everyone. It felt like a fairy land—undeniably a place she could take one turn and disappear into an enchanted world.

"Is it too cold for you?" Edric was walking beside her. She glanced over off the trail down a short hill to a stream of rushing water on the side, so soothing. The trees were bare now, so the woods hid nothing.

"No, no it doesn't feel too cold." She canvassed her surroundings with contentment once more, then suddenly felt that very odd swirl of dizziness. She stopped. "We were eating in the coffee shop. How did we get here?"

He stopped short as well. She noticed he wore a long black trench coat over a black sweater and black cargo pants. That wasn't at all how he was dressed before. "Mira—"

"When did you change?"

He frowned, "Are you feeling all right?"

"No, confused, we were just at a coffee shop and then before that—" she halted abruptly.

"You might want to take a beat."

She closed her eyes shut.

�֍

She smelled firewood, burning firewood. Slowly opening her eyes, the surroundings were familiar. Back home again, and yes, now there was a fire in the fireplace that she hadn't lit since she moved in. Her cup of tea was in her hands and across from her, sitting in a rocking chair was Edric, Edric from the bookmobile.

She stared at him in disbelief. "What are you doing?"

He also had a mug in his hands, the other one. There were two she rotated with coffee and tea. "To be fair, the first two were me, but these last two shifts were all you. You might want to settle down so we can have a proper conversation."

"Conversation about what?" She muttered with a measure of panic.

"Don't be upset. Being upset will only complicate things."

"What do you want?" It sounded like a mere whisper, and yes, she was frightened.

"High emotions, cause these shifts, erratic, uncontrolled—"

"I asked a question."

He looked at her with concern or like she was a ticking time bomb. She wasn't sure which. "I actually, Mira, wanted to talk to you about a job."

❋

It was quiet, so quiet here, too quiet. She wandered the long hallway, her black boots echoing down the corridors. But at least the walls weren't white, they were softer, a blend between yellow and beige, soothing, and in some places lovely stripes of mint green.

*"It's all right. She's not in pain anymore."*

*"But she's not gone, she's just asleep."*

*"No Ma'am. It's a coma. Things are shutting down, you see."* She could hear through the doorway, voices floating outward into these long empty halls.

"It's not the best place to be now." She glanced over at Edric. He was leaning against one of those soft pastel-shade walls.

"What is this place?"

"You're very determined, aren't you Mira. Things could be easier, more subtle."

She crossed her arms in front of her defensively. "You're not really a bookmobile driver are you."

He shrugged, "No, I am and a librarian and well, a sort of a translator."

She wanted to be calm, but she could feel things on her skin, all sorts of things like fear, upset. "Translator? Of languages?"

"Not exactly."

159

"*She's too young.*"

"*Everyone has their time, Ma'am. It's in God's hands, not ours.*" Those voices wafting out.

"Who's in there?" She said with—what had he said—oh yes, determination.

"*I'll just give you some time with your daughter.*"

A tall dark-skinned woman dressed in a mint green pantsuit walked through the doorway. Her eyes widened upon seeing her and then flew to Edric. "This is a little out of the ordinary," she said serenely. She had a lovely voice, smooth, deep, but more than that it felt comforting. Mira distractedly realized she matched the stripes on the walls.

"Mira, I'd like you to meet Zinnia."

She frowned, looking from Edric then back to Zinnia. "Who's in a coma in that room?" she asked sharply.

Zinnia turned back to Edric. "Can you handle this?"

He nodded, "Of course, sorry to interject." And then Zinnia reached out, touching her arm. "You might need to rest."

※

She liked her little kitchen. It had a breakfast nook that looked outside into the forest. The small round table was made of a honey-colored wood, warm, inviting. But as she lightly tapped her fingers on its surface she couldn't remember if it had been furnished when she'd rented it for the winter or if—

"My memories aren't making much sense," she said aloud.

"Not unusual. Time, memories, spatial relations, all of it doesn't function the way we think they do."

She glanced across the room to where Edric was standing. He was staring at the now cold fireplace that had been flaming. Now—when was that again? "This is a nice place."

She stirred the cup in front of her with the long spoon that was sticking out of it, then brought it to her lips. Coffee, good, she didn't get to finish hers when, well, when they were in the coffee shop. Oh wow, this was getting just baffling. Outside it was bright, she glanced at a rustic looking clock on the wall, eight in the morning. How things did jump around.

"What does that mean translator?"

Edric turned to her. He was dressed in black again, black turtleneck, pants—frowning, wayward thought, just like the Grim Reaper.

"I know it seems overwhelming."

"Don't you ever give a straight answer?"

He sighed. "Sure," he said, aggressively pulling out one of the kitchen table chairs and sitting on it. "I make things easier for people who are having a difficult time of it."

She frowned, "Well, that's ambiguous as hell."

He stared at her as though he was trying to figure out how to deal with a porcupine. "What did you used to do, Mira?"

"Used to do?" She repeated his very non precise question.

"Before, before you came here."

She took in a breath, finally recalling with a bit of difficulty. "I was a psychologist."

"Really?"

"Yes, I had a small practice but worked with schools, hospitals, even police stations in St. Louis."

"For how long?"

161

She took another sip of coffee. It was strong. That was good. It might help her, because she was having real trouble remembering things. "For a while," she murmured.

"In your work, you tried to help people adjust to things."

She waited. He was expressionless, impossible to read or maybe she'd lost her knack. "I guess, I did."

He nodded as though he'd had a win. What kind of win? Didn't make sense then again, all of this, bizarreness didn't make sense. Some sort of hallucinations brought on by, what was she taking again, painkillers?

"Don't."

"Don't what Edric? Try to explain this?"

"Don't try to explain this away. It will make it harder, backsliding actually."

She took another deep sip of her coffee, but it wasn't good. It was getting tepid. "You know I'm getting sick of your vague non-explanations of things. It's really beginning to piss me off."

"You really got angry, didn't you?"

She could feel it now, anger, white hot anger. Everything was going just as she wanted it and then out of nowhere—"What does that mean, Edric? Translator? What do you have to translate?"

And then he looked at her pointedly. "The truth."

❧

She took a moment for his words to soak in before she asked, "Why do things keep flipping like this?"

"You mean, where we are."

"Yes."

"Things work differently than most people believe. Thought is powerful. If you think about something often enough you draw it to you. At the level we're on, that happens quicker."

She drew a deep breath. They were walking along the shore of one of the larger lakes in the Village. It was cool but not quite as cold as it had been before. It was comfortable. "Can you give me a for instance?"

"Yes, for instance you thought about walking by the lake and now we are."

"That seems quick."

"It is. We travel by thought, so, it's important to be more cognizant and in control of your thoughts than how you were before."

"Before what?"

❧

Long ribbons of mint-colored stripes. She stood just outside the door. She heard crying. No, it was sobbing inside. Should she go inside?

"Maybe not. She's in a delicate state. She feels you're gone. It might not due to confuse her now."

She turned to him. "Her? My Mom?"

He didn't say anything, just looked at her with compassion she would have to say. Those dark eyes definitely brimming with compassion. "I don't want to be here," she said.

❧

Quick this time, seamlessly, in a blink, back to that little breakfast nook in her bright sunny kitchen. Edric sat across from her, and he had a mug in front of him too. She took a sip, the coffee no longer tepid. "What else?"

"What else?"

"We can move with thought. What else can we do here?"

He smiled, but slowly as though he was oddly pleased. "Lots of things, Mira."

She nodded, "Is this place real? I mean the house. I don't think I ever actually rented it. I thought about getting away, wanted to, but now I think I got sick."

"Don't concentrate on it too hard. Yes, of course it's real. But it doesn't mean you didn't dream it, create it."

"A translator? Huh, do you like doing this?"

"I like helping people, teaching them, easing their pain."

"Tell me about it," she said softly.

# An Empath in the Woods

*I*t helped, at least sometimes, walking the trails.

"It's like being a bug born without its skin."

She couldn't help but glare at the analogy. "Really? So, I'm the bug in this scenario."

Dr. Crispin frowned, a curious woman originally from Romania, with short, curly, very reddish-brown hair, just into her sixties. At least that was what Allie surmised. She'd mentioned she'd be retiring in a few years, which wasn't good news.

Where exactly was Allie going to find another psychologist whose side specialty was paranormal phenomena? She doubted Health Grades would be helpful. With Crispin, she'd lucked out, a recommendation from a yoga teacher. Oh yes, she'd tried everything, from yoga to meditation, to the conventional routes of medication for depression, but nothing seemed to crack this puzzle. Her puzzle, her problems, that was.

But back to the point—

"Yes, I understand your reluctance to embrace the visual. But think about it. Our skin keeps us separate, separate from our environment, separate from one another. Without it, things are much more painful."

She did enjoy listening to Dr. Crispin's accent, even if she didn't always care for what she was saying. In a peculiar way, she found it soothing to her ragged nerves. Oh yes, back to the bug with no skin. "Could be messy, I mean, having no skin and dangerous, at least for the bug." Her voice sort of drifted off. Were they really discussing this?

She'd frowned at her, Dr. Crispin had, but then that might have been her resting face. She was actually a lovely woman, with her vibrant hair, trim figure, and just below-the-knee fitted pencil skirts.

It made Allie feel dumpy. She'd shown up at the appointment in jeans and a well-worn button-down. It wasn't as though she didn't have nicer clothes, but she was in a funk, a slump, worn out with all this. She hadn't even cracked thirty yet—no excuses there, except—

"So, how is your life going, Allison?"

"Oh, other than being a bug without my skin, just dandy." A reddish-brown eyebrow went up.

Too much sarcasm? Dr. Crispin was no-nonsense, for someone dealing with ghosts, goblins, and what was the terminology again?

"Don't forget, Allison, you are an extreme empath!"

That was it. No meds prescribed to dull the pesky awarenesses around her that did not belong to her.

"So, living in the Village, does the isolation help?"

Deep sigh, deeper than deep, soul-wrenching, good question. That's why Crispin got paid the big bucks, and she was scrambling to make ends meet. "I would have to say the jury is out, because there are always things to feel—and always people, people somewhere."

❦

The trails, the hiking trails around the Village, did seem to ease things, sometimes that is.

It was October, already late October, the Halloween season approaching. Her year here would be up come January. At that point, there was a decision to make, whether to spend another year virtually in isolation or back to the city, Little Rock, where at least she could see Dr. Crispin more often. That was until she retired, and one more column of support in her unstable existence just vanished.

*"Bad thoughts don't help."*

*"Bad thoughts?"* she'd questioned.

*"Negative, negativity lowers your energy vibration. Someone like you, Allison, can't afford that."*

Yep, she was right. She had to get hold, desperately trying to drive away these "bad thoughts." Everything around her was beautiful. Many of the trees were changing to their lovely autumn shades of gold, yellow, some orange, and the occasional red. But red was not one of her favorites – she'd seen it too often under other circumstances.

The fallen leaves crunched beneath her short hiking boots as she meandered down the winding pathway deeper into the woods.

She breathed in deeply. There was a scent, a curious scent of burning leaves. Foolish, everything was so dry right now, so foolish to be burning anything. She glanced around. This particular hiking trail she'd been on before. It was far away from any of the subdivisions, just woods and a creek a little further down the trail.

167

But she wondered if it would be dried up. It felt like it had been over a week since there had been any rain.

An unexpected dizziness swept through her so strongly that she had to stop for a moment. As she peered upward, she saw the tall trees all around her reaching toward a cloudy sky.

So strange, when she'd set out from the small parking lot near the dog park, it had been the clearest blue with a few puffy white clouds. But not like this.

Then, another substantial sweep of dizziness hit her, as if she were swirling while standing completely still. Maybe she shouldn't look upward. Maybe just head back now, but she didn't move, just rooted to the spot.

*"A bug with no skin."*

Something was definitely amiss, not the usual form of anxiety or bouts of depression that would spring on her inexplicably.

What she was feeling was different. She bent over, bending her knees, sort of awkwardly crouching down to the ground. It seemed silly, but then again, she felt desperate. Dr. Crispin called it grounding, putting her palms flat on the earth.

*"The earth is filled with powerful grounding energy. It seems odd, but this can help you stabilize."*

Yes, Allie agreed, it did seem odd. And if she wasn't alone, she'd never consider it. But desperate times—

She closed her eyes, breathing in deeply, indeed feeling a stabilization of the dizziness, at least momentarily. Deep breaths, deep breaths, she coached herself. So absorbed, that was the danger, she didn't even hear the crunching leaves behind her, but there was something—a shift, perceptible, and a heaviness accompanying it.

She opened her eyes, then slowly turned around, and a few yards away, she saw the figure—a man dressed in a windbreaker, a red one.

She straightened up, shakily standing, suddenly feeling the sweep of dizziness passing over her again. He wasn't moving, just staring at her—tall, brown-hair, tanned skin, beard, and mustache.

"I was trying not to disturb you." He finally spoke, kind of flat, unemotional, definitely no signature Arkansas accent, didn't move an inch, hands in his pockets.

"Oh, I had just dropped something, trying to find it," she murmured awkwardly.

"I thought you might be grounding yourself," he said rather casually.

What? That was an unexpected punch. She really didn't think this was a mainstream thing, *"grounding oneself."*

"Um, oh, well," she muttered in confusion.

"Did you find it?"

"Find it?"

"What you dropped."

A swirl of confusion swept over her. How did she get herself into these situations? "I was grounding."

Expressionless, "I know."

She drew in another deep, uncomfortable, awkward breath. "Yeah, well, it's late, I think I need to get back."

"It's only 10:00, 10:00 AM, here I mean."

Was this a bizarre conversation, or was it just her? "Here? You mean instead of in China?"

A strange sort of smile drifted across his face as though he appreciated the sarcasm. "No, I meant from where I came from, it was afternoon, around three."

Why did it feel acutely as though she was losing air out of her lungs? She really needed to shut up. "Where you came from? And where was that exactly?"

The smile was staying. Why was that? "Not far. You see, I was tracking."

"I don't think it's hunting season around here." She crossed her arms in front of her. Again, why was she still talking to him? He could very well be unhinged.

"No, no, I don't hunt animals."

And he was silent again, not elaborating. "Okay, well, as I said, regardless of the time. I need to get going. You have a nice day." And then she realized it. To get back, she'd have to walk right past him, the bizarre fellow in the red jacket. And it bothered her, worried her, but there seemed no help for it. Either walk past or make a beeline through the woods, which she was not going to do.

And it was true, she did need to get back. She worked online, several jobs online, one of which was freelance editing, a stack of articles she'd been putting off.

Allie steeled herself. She bent her head down and tried to give him a wide berth as she started to pass. Then it happened, the unthinkable. At least something she didn't see coming. His arm shot out, and he grabbed her forearm as she was passing.

Direct contact, not exactly direct because she was wearing a long-sleeved button-down, but close enough. Extreme, it felt sort of like a sizzling brand burning through her shirt. She twisted in reflex, trying to pull away, but it was like steel. He was immovable.

"Let me go," she rasped, because it was painful. She was feeling too many things, hot acid all over her. "Christ, where have you been!" she muttered frantically.

"Ssshhh," he said calmly. "Be still for a minute."

She didn't want to. She was outraged and horrified simultaneously. What the hell gave him the right?

And then she heard the words, loud and powerful in her mind. *"Stop."*

That silenced her, made her stop pulling every which way to get loose. Shocking, stunning, *"Quiet your mind."* Was the command on its heels.

Her vision began to blur, dizziness, such swirls of dizziness. "We need to talk," he murmured softly, before it all tipped into a gray blanket of mist.

⚜

*"Allie,"* whispers floating around her mind. *"Don't be so emotional. There's nothing to cry about."*

But there was, always so much pain around her.

*"Why can't you be like everyone else?"* Her father's pleas.

It wasn't always possible to pretend. Not always.

⚜

"Allie, wake up."

She opened her eyes and felt a chill instantly travel down her spine. And on top of that, she smelled smoke. Still dizzy and with a headache, she gingerly sat up and looked around. It was a room, a den, big rustic, larger than the one at her house, with a huge stone fireplace that was lit. "You can use the throw on the chair," a disembodied voice, though familiar masculine tones, floated in.

171

She glanced around. Beside her was indeed a wooden rocking chair with a beige woven blanket draped over it. She snatched it quickly. It was cold, much colder than it had been when she left her house.

And then the man in question made an appearance, the one from the woods, the one who'd grabbed her arm and now evidently had—"You know this is kidnapping," she voiced aloud, not sure if she should have thought that through more, given her unexplored predicament. But she did tend to be on the impulsive side.

"I made us some coffee, a teaspoon of sugar, and some milk, right?" He asked, bringing in two steaming mugs from around a corner, probably the kitchen, but who the hell knew.

She pulled the throw tightly around her that she'd wrapped up in seconds before. "I don't know if I want any."

He stopped in front of the sofa, then abruptly took a sip out of one mug and then the other. "See, not drugged."

"But now I have to drink after you," she spat out.

He nodded, unconcerned. "Okay, I'll go wash it down the sink."

"No," dang it. "I'll take it." She loved coffee, one of her few indulgences. She took it out of his hands, carefully, not wanting any direct physical contact. But taking the mug, she could feel an agitation passing into her fingertips, though not nearly as pronounced as when he'd grabbed her arm.

"I took a shower."

She looked up at him blankly. "Good for you."

Frowning, "To get rid of some of the gunk."

What a bizarre thing to say to a stranger, but then again, what about this wasn't bizarre? "Okay, not sure why I need to know that."

He frowned, "Energy, Allie, negative energy. That's what upset you when I took your arm."

"Took my arm? You mean when you grabbed my arm, and I couldn't get away."

"Yep, I can see why it would seem that way to you."

"Look, it didn't just seem that way—" then abruptly another disturbing thought filtered in. She straightened up further on the sofa. "Wait a minute, when did you have time to take a shower? How long have I been out?"

He sort of mumbled. "You didn't make the trip well."

Recoiling a bit, in fact backing up as much as physically possible into the corner of this rather large, overstuffed green sofa. "Trip? What trip? Did you put me in a car? Did you drug me?"

"No, this place is in the woods, the Village, just on a different plateau."

"Plateau? What gibberish is that?"

He frowned again, taking a sip out of his coffee mug. "Drink some. I put cinnamon in it. It's soothing."

She shouldn't just to spite him, but she did, take a huge sip, and it was good, strong with a fleeting taste of cinnamon. Well, her kidnapper makes a good cup of coffee. Wasn't that good news. "Look, whoever you are."

"My name is Ryland Gray."

"Okay, fine, Mr. Gray, I don't know who you are, but I really need to go home. I'm not like everyone else. I have complicated, um, medical issues."

"Yes, Miss Beckett. I am aware." Beckett, Beckett, she hadn't given him her name. Oh God, how did he know—"You really need to calm down, Allie."

She swallowed on a dry throat, even though she'd just had a mouthful of coffee. "How, how do you know my name?"

And then he looked down into his mug, "Yep." No elaboration.

"You won't find the answers in there," she snapped.

And then he looked up again. He had brown eyes, sort of brownish green and suddenly they didn't seem quite as hard and cold as they were a moment before. "It's complicated."

She swung her legs around, putting her feet solidly on the wooden floor. At least she was still wearing her hiking shoes. "Am I free to go?" She asked with feigned courage.

"Sure," he mumbled. "Be my guest."

Standing up while still feeling wobbly, she braced herself. She would simply walk out the front door, find her way back to the trail and her car, and put this insanity behind her.

He stepped back a bit, out of her way, and she noted for the first time he was wearing one of those heavy flannel button-downs, red and black like some kind of lumbar jack over jeans. Red, too much red, she detested that color.

As quickly as she could manage, she stalked across the den to the front door, turning a rather large bolt and then flinging it open. And then she just stood there on the threshold after a gasp. Distantly, she could hear him moving just behind her, "Yeah, it happened while you were asleep. We're about two months ahead of you."

"Ahead?" she whispered in shock because everywhere she looked outside was covered in a layer of freshly fallen snow.

"But the good news is it melts pretty quickly here. By the morning, we can get out again."

She stood there transfixed. It was so cold, but she was numb. "Have I lost my mind?"

"No, Allie Beckett. You've just traveled a bit."

She wandered aimlessly around the den of Ryland Gray's house in the woods, though exactly which woods and where was a pesky detail her mind couldn't seem to grasp just at the moment.

Had he somehow driven her—without her being aware, while she was unconscious—so far away from her Village rental that wherever they were now, it was actually snowing.

"No," he said emphatically.

She glanced across the room. Way across, because he was on one side, looking out a front window whose blinds he had opened, and she was way on the other side, staring out a sliding glass door that led onto a screen porch. She stared back at him. He wasn't even looking at her. "No, what?" She asked with irritation.

At that, he turned around, still holding a coffee cup in his hand. He couldn't possibly be sipping on that first cup of coffee still. "This is my second," he said out of the blue.

And then she got it. Allie might be slow to the race, but she did get there, well, eventually. "Are you—I mean are you really—"

"Reading your thoughts? Yeah, kind of. That's how I knew how you wanted your coffee, teaspoon of sugar and all that." He stated rather matter-of-factly.

Oh God, that was right. She hadn't even thought of that. "Wait a minute. I wasn't thinking about how I wanted my coffee fixed."

He frowned. Ryland Gray had a strange frown that kind of looked less like he was disappointed and more like the world was confounding. And he was a bit ticked off by it. At least, that was her take. "Yep, got me there, Allie Beckett. Just when I was starting to think you might not be too sharp, you get me in the side with a pocketknife."

"What the hell kind of analogy is that?"

"A serviceable one."

"The coffee, Mr. Gray."

Eyebrow went up a bit. They were kind of heavy dark eyebrows. Evidently, this face had a bit more malleability than she'd previously suspected. "You want another cup?"

"I want to know how you knew how I take my coffee," she nearly hissed back at him.

"Don't get so testy, Allie. It's best to be more laid back here. Things can be reactive."

She put her hands on her hips. She really felt like spitting at him, but spitting at a kidnapper might not be the best avenue to take just now. "I don't know what that means. I don't know what nonsense you're babbling about. Are you on some kind of meds?"

That frown again, definitely the resting face. "It's more permeable."

She let her hands drop from her hips, waiting for elaboration. But as she'd expected, none was forthcoming. "Oh well, thanks. That explains a lot."

"So," he said slowly. And it was a challenge to say such a short one-syllable word slowly. "You want some breakfast?"

Oh, God, this man was going to drive her bananas. "No, Mr. Gray, what I want is to go home."

He nodded, "Yeah, Miss Beckett. But as I explained, we're snowed in until tomorrow."

Hands instinctively flew back onto her hips. "Did you explain that? I don't remember you explaining shit to me about anything!"

Now there was a flicker of a smile. What the hell was wrong with this guy? "I think I told you not to be so upset, Allie," he said with a frustrating calmness.

"That's not explaining," she mumbled, because it suddenly felt as though she was losing breath, and on top of that, she was dizzy. "I feel funny."

At some point, he'd moved, moved quickly across the den, and grabbed her arm. She thought to pull away, but everything was spinning, colors spinning everywhere. "Take some deep breaths," he said with authority.

"I-I can't. I can't get my breath."

"You're acclimating. It will pass. That's why I wanted you to stay calm."

"Acclimating? What does that even mean?" She could barely get the words out. It was such a swirl, a swirl of colors all around her, then other things, things pulsating and writhing almost.

He took her other arm with his hand and began to shake her a bit. "Don't go there, Allie. Stay focused."

Vaguely, she wondered what he'd done with his coffee cup, then she could see it in her mind. So odd, like a freeze frame backup. She saw him on the other side of the room, talking to her just moments before. But it was different because now she could feel what he was feeling. He was talking to her, but also looking outside, and also seeing masses of colors slashing across the room. And he was elsewhere, inside her memories, standing next to her in her apartment, examining things, and in Dr. Crispin's office, sitting there listening closely to their private sessions.

"What the hell is this?" she whispered as she felt him scoop under her legs and lift her in his arms. Contact, so much contact. Usually, she couldn't bear it. But it was different, so different even from the first time he'd touched her.

177

"It's all right, Allie. I'm trying to help," he murmured. And then a drape of gray passed over her as she lost consciousness again.

❧

*"You might have prepared her a little better."*

*"I didn't think she'd fight it so much."*

*"That's why you picked her because she's a fighter."*

Her eyes opened slowly to the dim light of her bedside table. They hurt, her eyes, but she forced them to take in her surroundings. A white corner desk, an ash-wood tall dresser against the wall, and a bed surrounded by her light, fluffy, pastel-colored pillows. She drew in a deep breath that permeated throughout her—but not dizzying. She straightened up and glanced behind her. Yes, it was her ironwork sleigh bed. She was home, home, and profoundly, profoundly confused.

All a dream? Is that what he was trying to sell her? She glanced around, somewhat gratefully but equally confounded.

So, Mr. Ryland Gray was playing games with her.

She pulled her white faux fur bed pillow against her chest. It did feel good to be with her things, stability. And she could just let it be, let it be, and forget the insanity of the other stuff. It was like a gift, a parting gift, whatever he was after, whatever he wanted from her, just didn't work out.

She leaned back in the bed drowsily. Sure, path of least resistance. Sure, maybe, then she closed her eyes, feeling entirely too exhausted to figure any of this out.

❧

When she did finally get out of bed and checked the clock by her nightstand, it was early morning, just shy of seven, a little later

178

than she usually got up. But when she looked at her cellphone, she was stunned. Allie had found something utterly disturbing. She'd lost a day. She remembered clearly that it was Friday morning when she was walking the forest trail by the dog park. But this morning was Sunday. An entire day had just slipped away.

Her head was throbbing painfully, so she was determined to not deal with this until after coffee and something to eat. And then she noticed she was wearing the same clothes, blue jeans, and a sweater she'd been wearing when—

She shut her mind down emphatically. No, no, she would not deal with any of this insanity, coffee, food, then a shower. Exerting great control over her mind, the one that was literally bursting forth with fearsome questions and uncontrollable emotions, she began to move. She wouldn't backslide. Dr. Crispin had taught her how to maintain a degree of control. No matter what was happening, she wouldn't allow herself to slide back into that dark time again.

❧

Late morning, shuffling with distraction through the largely empty aisles of the only grocery right outside the gates of the Village, and by right outside, she meant a good six or seven miles away from her home. That was the rub of living in the secluded Village. It was indeed secluded and took a bit of time and driving to get anywhere.

It was a fact of life that one had to be a good planner here. It wasn't like you could just pop over to the grocery for something you'd forgotten. She yawned. A piece of toast, coffee, and a hot shower had not cleared the cobwebs. She usually did her shopping early Saturday morning, way before the crowds dribbled in. Sundays were dicier. The churchgoing group liked to hit the store early before the 10:00 a.m. service. And oddly enough, while no groceries, the large expanse of the Village, over 26,000 acres of the Ouachita Mountains, at least that was what the travel brochures purported, was dotted with so very many houses of Worship—every denomination to pick from, and some she'd never heard of.

But Allie wasn't a churchgoer. She'd had enough of that with a mother who'd brought her highly emotional child to a congregation that was only too happy to pray over her for exactly what she wasn't sure. Sadly, her well-meaning mother thought she was possessed by some aberrant evil of some capacity.

Another yawn, yes, this was going to be tough going, shopping the specials and buying for the week. Maybe she should have waited, waited, and done this tomorrow. But how she hated her inflexible schedule being interrupted, particularly after all those odd dreams.

Quite assuredly, the pieces did not fit together, not one bit, but the alternative seemed to be more than she could deal with just now. She pulled the grey hoodie that she'd pulled on over her black sweater more tightly about her as she moved her icy basket down the largely empty aisles. It was so cool this morning, a sudden chill in the air that had seemed to creep out of nowhere.

And then, abruptly, she stopped, stopped driving her basket past the pasta shelves. She had planned to make her grandmother's spaghetti sauce and portion it for four days, because after all, she was just one person. But then it happened again, like a stabbing pain darting up her spine, a pain that wasn't exactly a pain.

*"It's an awareness."*

*"What does that mean?"*

*"You have to accept the fact that you're like a radar for things other people can't feel."*

*"What kind of things?"*

"*Unfortunately, with you, I would suspect difficult things.*" Dr. Crispin had explained with the expected detachment of a professional.

Her eyes rose slowly, canvassing the aisles. She was situated at this point about in the middle. Forward, there was no one, and as she quickly glanced behind, she noted nothing there as well. She took in a quick breath. Well, either it would pass or, if it was too intense, she'd simply abandon the shopping cart and get out of there. Otherwise, as she'd found in the past, it could turn quite detrimental to her.

Allie steadied herself, drawing in a deep breath, closing her eyes, and attempting to center as she'd practiced during her sessions with Dr. Crispin. Once she felt steadier and had regained her mastery, she slowly opened her eyes and immediately saw a figure standing at the front of the aisle. It was jarring because, besides being positioned in the middle of what would be her exit and staring her down, there was the face. It was an old man with a bony, gaunt face—not one that looked naturally aged, but instead with pale, crinkled skin tightly stretched across his skull. His eyes were wide and unblinking, giving him a zombie-like expression, as if he'd walked out of *The Walking Dead*. Instinctively, she stepped back, then felt a decisive stab in her heart region.

"*Remember to see what is actually there, Allie. Not representative.*"

"*Representative? What does that mean?*"

"*Your brain and your eyes adjust to what you feel is the truth.*"

"*Could you be more opaque?*"

And then Dr. Crispin had frowned in her disgruntled/disapproving manner. "*Tell your mind to see what everyone else sees.*"

Okay, okay, fine, Dr. Crispin, she mentally acknowledged. Centering herself, she sent out a pure, crisp thought to her mind. ***See what everyone sees.***

It was blurry for a moment, as though her eyes were actively refocusing, and then she began to see the change. The old man's face sort of melted, molding into something else. It took her breath, for a moment, such a sharp, radical difference. Not only had the features softened, but they were no longer a man but instead a woman, a tall, statuesque blond, maybe early twenties, very pretty in a beachy sort of way. The woman was now smiling back at her in such a welcoming way. But Allie couldn't help but feel a lurch in her stomach, a lurch of nausea as the pain in her heart area only deepened. She was losing energy, clearly a drainer, but something else, something worse, somehow.

Without a thought, she flipped the direction of her basket around in the aisle, quickly moving toward the opposite end of the store. Once she was out of that thing's sight, she ditched the cart and rapidly headed out the front door.

Her breathing was shallow, panicked. It was so strong, the feeling of darkness, much more potent than she usually felt. When she reached the door of her yellow Jeep that she'd beeped open with her keys only seconds before, she was startled. In her panic, she hadn't noticed anyone approaching, and she actually jumped as a hand closed over her own. Her eyes jolted up, staring into a familiar bearded face, one she'd decided was a dream even though the pieces didn't add up.

"What are—" She started, not at all sure how to finish that question.

"Get in the car," Ryland Gray said with steel in his voice. "We need to talk."

✳

They were sitting in the front of her banana yellow Jeep in the parking lot of the Piggly Wiggly, she in the driver's seat and her uninvited guest, one Ryland Gray, who it was clear was no figment of her imagination, in the passenger seat. And oh yeah, he was saying nothing.

"Look, what is—"

"Sssshhh," he snapped impatiently.

"Hey, you were the one who said—"

"Be quiet, Allie. Don't you understand be quiet around here?"

"Around here?"

And then he gave her a glaring look that did indeed silence her. She tapped her fingers on the steering wheel, wondering if she should make a run for it because this guy was clearly a bit nuts.

"Look," he snapped out. "Is that *It*?"

Her eyes rose back to the front entrance of the grocery where that *Woman Thing*, whatever it was, had just exited the store. "Is that what?" she whispered.

"*It's* a shell."

Her eyes widened. "A what? A shell?"

He nodded slowly, his eyes fixed on the figure that had stopped a few rows over beside a bright red sports car. "Yep," he said slowly. "Good work, Allie. You're clearly raw at this, but excellent nonetheless."

Her eyes watched dubiously as the *woman/thing/shell,* as he called *It*, climbed in and started her car. "Excellent at what?"

"Being a diviner."

183

"A diviner, don't they predict the future?" She muttered in confusion.

"No, not that kind. Like the stick that finds water, a divining rod."

Now that image took a moment to soak in. "You're comparing me to a stick."

"Start the car," he said abruptly.

"Why?"

"Because we're going to follow *IT*."

🦋

"Don't get too close."

"I don't want to lose her or *It*," she grimaced. "Half the population around here own a red sports car." She was meandering down Desoto Road, pretty much the artery of the Village. It was the only road that really connected anything around here, at least one side to the other, the East and West gates.

"Just don't go so fast, lay back a bit. I don't want *IT* to mark your car."

Her heart clutched painfully at his words. "Why would *IT* mark my car?"

"Bright yellow, Allie, not too inconspicuous," he nearly growled.

"Sorry, I didn't know I would be doing surveillance when I purchased it. Why didn't we take your car?"

"My car is back home," he answered. She didn't question, just vaguely wondered if that was snowed in as well.

"I can't go too slow. Traffic backs up, and the retirees around here aren't, well, very retiring."

"A lot of impatience," he grumbled.

"A lot of dissatisfaction," she murmured. The truth was, she had nothing to back that up, just a feeling. And then two cars ahead, she noted the red car taking a turn. "That's one of the apartment complexes here."

"Yep, makes sense," he murmured. "Lots of people around, go ahead and turn in, but don't get too close."

"I—" She opened her mouth to protest but then didn't. What could she say? She had no idea what they were doing or why. Allie made a quick turn and then a curvy, well-forested bend right before the rows of condos appeared. She almost said she had no idea where the *It* had gone when she noticed the red car had indeed parked on a row that faced the descent down to the lake. And then, rather quickly, the door opened, and the blond stepped outside. Just the sight of her ran a quick chill of fear down her spine.

He put his hand on her. "Park somewhere as though you live here." Frowning, she pulled her car directly in front of one of the side rows of condos, then turned off the engine.

Her chest hurt, and her breathing felt strangely labored. "What now?"

"Just wait." His hand was still on hers, but she didn't push it away. The contact of this, yes, total stranger, felt strangely calming amid this bizarreness. Her eyes lifted again as she saw the woman standing beside her car, seeming as though she was looking for something. "*It* feels us," he murmured.

"I don't understand."

"Just be still and calm," he whispered. She bent her head down and tried to center herself, mentally erecting barriers as Dr. Crispin had taught her. "That's good," he said softly. And then she glanced up to see the tall blond unlocking the door on the unit on the end and going inside. As the door closed behind her, he said softly. "It's all right. I've marked her."

"You've marked her? What does that mean?" It was closing in, too much, too much external stimuli.

"It means when it's time. It will be easy to find her again."

Breathing deeply while trying to get hold, she looked over at him as though he'd lost his mind. "Time for what exactly?"

"Time to send ***It*** on its way," he said grimly.

She'd thought to tell him to get the hell out of her car, but she didn't. He suggested they go back to her house to talk. "It's my experience that when you say you want to talk, you don't do much of it."

"You're very hostile, you know," he said placidly.

"You think? I wonder why that could be?"

But that wasn't all that was going on. She tried hard to focus on driving, driving, and not driving off the road.

*"What do they feel like, these attacks?"*

*"I don't know. I guess like what someone else would think of as a panic attack."*

Dr. Crispin had looked down at her, tilting her head with her dark glasses in such a way that reminded her of her second-grade teacher, Miss Spell. And she was a pistol. *"You're not like anyone else, Allison. And you shouldn't keep trying to be so."*

*"I thought that was why I was here."*

*"Now describe them to me."*

It seemed to start with the breathing, quick, panicked breaths, and then that vice-like pressure in her chest. She was thoroughly checked out by a cardiologist, and, of course, the prognosis was nothing physical. It must be emotional, and her favorite, probably stress. Yes, yes, there was stress in being the way she was.

He'd put his hand on her again, pulling her out of the cage of her mind. "All right?"

"Not feeling well," she muttered.

"Pull over, I'll drive."

That probably wasn't a good idea. She didn't know if he had a license. She didn't know who or what he was. But her hands gripping the wheel were starting to tremble. So, crashing was indeed becoming a relevant possibility. "Maybe," she said.

He hadn't moved his hand from hers. Strange, but stranger yet that she hadn't asked him to.

*"It feels like fear."*

*"Fear?"* She'd repeated. And she wondered if a good chunk of your training at psychiatry school was just learning to echo your patients in order to eat up time.

*"Yes, fear like a blanket of it covering you, a living blanket covering, then suffocating you."*

She'd turned off onto a road, then pulled to the side, turning off the Jeep. She didn't speak, didn't move, just concentrated on getting air because now that fear had exploded out of control exponentially. Her vision was blotching with great black spots swirling around. "That thing drained your energy a great deal."

His hand tightened over hers. "I just need, just a minute," she managed to get out. Speaking was definitely a challenge when you were having trouble breathing.

"Close your eyes," he said calmly.

"Look—"

"Do it," he said firmly.

Without many options, she did, leaning back on the headrest. Colors, so many colors everywhere, and that fear, ugly fear, swallowing her up.

*"How long have you had these attacks?"* Dr. Crispin had asked.

*"Always, always, and never predictable."*

*"You know, you feel so much, Allison, from other people. It's not surprising your system just rebels against it all sometimes."*

"Try to relax," he said. "Don't force the breathing. It will straighten out."

How did he know? She stopped herself. How did he know so many things? She remembered him saying something about things being more permeable there, but that was somewhere else. Not here. "Try to let your mind quiet, not so much thinking."

"I can't help that," she whispered. So strange, she felt so sleepy all of a sudden, overwhelming, like she could barely keep her eyes open. And then he moved his hand away and got out of the Jeep, coming around to her side and opening her door.

"Come on, you need to rest," he said. She opened her eyes, thinking about refusing, thinking about resisting, but the truth was she didn't have it in her. Not at all.

❦

He was making a pot of coffee, Ryland Gray that was, in her house. And she noted distractedly that she was drinking a lot of coffee around him.

"What's a shell?" She called out in the direction of the galley kitchen.

"You should be resting," he called back. It was kind of gruff, like he was used to people following his orders.

"I want to understand what's going on." She snapped a little too hotly. What was it about this man's demeanor that seemed to aggravate her so? Besides all the strangeness surrounding him, and there was plenty of that to go around—plenty, plenty.

He rounded the wall separating the den from the kitchen and strode up to where she was reclining on the sofa. "You really don't like to listen, do you?"

"Not to strangers, generally."

"I thought we'd spent enough time lately not to quite be strangers."

She straightened up a bit, feeling generally vulnerable just lying here like this. "I know next to nothing about you. Except your name is Ryland Gray and you're some sort of hunter."

"Tracker," he said flatly.

"Oh well, that clears it up. Let's be besties."

That frown, that strange, curious frown he had, like he was looking at a disobedient child. "You're too tired to soak anything in right now, Allie Beckett."

"Tired?"

"Drained."

Her turn to frown. "Drained, yeah, you mentioned something about that."

He nodded slowly, looking at her oddly like he was surveying a chunk of farmland. "*It* drained your energy, pretty thoroughly."

She crossed her arms in front of her. "And you know that, how exactly?"

"Your aura, energy aura, is diminished. And there's quite a bit of yellow mixed in with everything."

"Yellow?" she repeated under her breath. "And that's about as clear as mud. So, what, you can see all this looking at me?"

"Yeah, you could too if you had a bit more discipline."

"Excuse me?"

"You've spent too much time treating the symptoms of your gift instead of working to understand it. You must let it run free enough so you can direct it to work for you."

Let it run free, indeed. He must be out of his mind. All that would do would let everything swallow her whole. Ridiculous. And then suddenly there was drowsiness, so maybe she would rest. One piece of advice that was actually useful.

✢

*"What does it feel like?"*

*"Being suffocated by fear."*

*"It's not your fear, you know."*

*"I know it in my mind but knowing it and feeling it are two different things."*

Her eyes opened slowly, adjusting and noting the ceiling fan casually spinning over the queen-sized bed. And then it slowly sank in. She didn't have a queen-sized bed. Hers was a double. She closed them again. She must be dreaming now.

"Not exactly." The voice came from the direction of the door-way that she'd noted just a few seconds before, on her last attempt at surfacing.

"This is your room," she murmured without even opening her eyes.

"Yes, from yesterday when you were at my house."

Without really wanting to, she allowed her eyes to flicker open again. There was a lot of light in here, streaming in from a sliding glass door on one wall of the room, leading out, well, somewhere.

"There's a porch out there and then a walkway down to a lake."

"Well, that sounds lovely," she mumbled, "but I don't remember this room from yesterday."

He'd dragged over a straight-back chair from behind a small pine-colored desk. Sitting beside the bed, he looked at her with concern. "I think there's much you don't remember from yesterday."

"So, you're saying this is a memory."

"An elaboration."

"A what?"

"It's complicated."

"No shit," she couldn't help it. These sharp comments just sort of flew out of her mouth. "Sorry," she murmured.

"As I mentioned before, things are more permeable here. Time isn't what you think it is, Allie."

She drew in a deep breath. And strangely, she felt better, lighter than she had at her house.

"That's why I tapped in here."

"Your words, Ryland, they have no meaning for me, *permeable, tapped in*. That doesn't correlate to what I know. It's nonsense."

He was looking at her oddly but not frowning. Was this progress? "When I say permeable, it means thoughts, your thoughts, are not as separate as where you live. Thoughts are energy forms, and energy here travels without as many impediments."

She sighed, "So, in a practical sense—"

"In a practical sense, it's easier to send energy, not as easy to steal it, and thoughts that you think are in your head are quite accessible."

"Oh," it felt like a fluttering in her chest.

"You're receiving energy, Allie."

"From you?"

"Some, and others. I put out a call for help. The thing, it hurt you."

She looked at him dubiously. "How could it do that? It didn't even touch me."

"It didn't need to. It was in proximity, very strong, built to be a parasite."

She straightened up on the pillows just a smidge. It was so comfortable here on this lovely bed with some kind of woven afghan spread over her. She could just drift off, so peaceful. "You called it a shell."

And there it was, the frown. "I didn't want to get into all this now."

"Might as well, Ry, do you mind if I call you Ry?"

"Yes." He said rather stoically.

"Okay then, Ryland, tell me about this shell."

"To tell you about that, I'd have to first tell you how people lose their spirits."

❀

A screen porch, rustic, odd, a screen porch just outside of his bedroom, or at least she thought it was his bedroom.

"Yes," he murmured from somewhere as of yet unseen.

Allie sipped the warm mug of mint tea that at some point had been placed in her hands. The crocheted white afghan that had not long ago been warming her on his bed was now neatly tucked around her, and she was sitting in a rocking chair watching the

192

snow coming down outside. "These transitions are confounding," she muttered.

"You'll get used to it," he said, sitting down in a similar chair right next to hers.

"Will I?" she asked.

"If you decide to spend any time in this place. Time moves differently, more connected to thought."

"So, I'm to gather that all of this took place a day ago."

"You're thinking too linear, Allie. It's difficult to understand unless you let go of some of your constructs."

"Gibberish again," she murmured. "Fine, you said something about people losing their spirits, or at least that is the last thing I remember."

"Okay, let's see. That is a spiritual matter."

"Clearly."

He smiled. She had no idea what had made him smile. "You're mind, your thoughts. They're muddled but quick, and I like the way they somersault about."

She took in a deep breath, trying desperately to convert this conversation into something she could work with. "Okay, so the spirit thing."

"Yes, well, in a nutshell, we all have a spirit."

She waited. Was she really going to drag everything out of him? "And?"

"And the spirit incarnates wherever it is with a plan, or rather, a path charted to learn from."

"What sort of path?"

"Things, events, relationships, illnesses, teachers along the way, ups, downs, all of it patterned for its evolution."

She chewed on this for a moment, a rather huge morsel to take in. "So, what, you're saying everyone has one of these paths?"

"Mostly, yes, but then there is free will."

Huge sip of mint tea that nearly scorched her mouth. "Free will?" she asked, because again, no elaboration.

"Yes, essentially choice. We all have a choice, or how could we evolve?"

Outside Ryland Gray's screen porch, the snow had stopped falling, and she just quietly looked at the blankets of white covering the forest around them. "So, what exactly does that have to do with—"

"With the thing you encountered in the grocery?"

"Yes, I guess," she murmured, feeling strangely as though threads were coming together.

"Well, let's say you were a teacher, a math teacher maybe, and your student completely ignored your lessons. And after a while, wouldn't even open their textbook, wouldn't even try to do a math problem, then stopped showing up to school."

Confounded a bit at the real-world analogy. "I'd be pissed."

"Yeah, you would, but you'd also begin feeling like you were wasting your time."

"I suppose. But other than report his butt, I'm not sure how I could force them to learn."

"Yes, well, a person, such as you, is composed of a spirit, a soul, and a body. If the soul and the body go too rogue for too long, the spirit gives up and just leaves."

"Leaves the soul and the body?"

"The body is left, the soul torn asunder, sort of ripped so to speak, not really wholly functional."

She straightened up, profoundly feeling disturbed by these images. "And if that happens, what happens to the person who's left?"

"They wander, aimlessly, a shadow of their former selves, until it is their time to die. And then their body dies and they with it."

"And that's it? That sounds terrible."

"It is. It is in extreme cases but does happen. But then, those it happens to, those living without that divine spark within, become a cavern."

"A shell," she whispered.

And then he put his hand over hers. "Yes, exactly. Allie, like a shell at the beach that has been abandoned by its living inhabitant, until something else crawls inside it and takes over."

*Something else crawls inside it and takes over.* His words sent chills throughout her as the visage of that zombie-like man in the grocery lashed treacherously across her mind. Panicked, she had to get out, away from here. Following a sudden impulse, she closed her eyes and concentrated intently on her own bedroom. Breathing deeply, when she opened them again, she was miraculously lying in her own bed, but this time Ryland Gray was standing in the doorway.

"That's good, Allie. You're beginning to get the hang of things. Now it's time to get down to business."

❦

*Like a shell at the beach that has been abandoned by its living inhabitant, until something else crawls inside it and takes over.*

Just turning over the words in her mind made a chill run down her spine. So, she didn't ask the obvious question.

"What has crawled inside?"

"That's not fair. I didn't ask you that. We're on my turf now, and you're not supposed to be able to read my mind here."

Ryland Gray didn't frown, not exactly—just kind of looked at her like he was indeed reading her mind and less interested in what words were coming out of her mouth. "Yep, well, the more time I spend with you, the more accessible I find you."

She stared back at him, "Great, so are we done with all this house-hopping business?"

"Sure," he said, making himself comfortable on her dark blue and beige plaid couch.

"Good, it's disorienting." She snapped back, now sitting in her grandmother's rocking chair that she had dragged around from rental to rental for probably too many years.

"You know, you were the one doing the hopping around for the last several."

"I can't do that," she muttered.

"You'd be surprised what you can do, Allie Beckett."

"You said we needed to get down to business. What does that mean exactly? You're not going to murder someone, are you?"

"I guess that depends on what you mean by murder."

"Can I get a straight answer out of you, Ryland?"

He shrugged. "Sure, if that's what you want." Silence again, she really wanted to kick him right in his plaid shirt right out of her house. "You don't like plaid? But your couch is plaid."

"Stop it. And I used to like it more than I do now."

Then he stood up and moved right in front of her. And she had to admit, with him sort of standing over her like that and glowering, or maybe he wasn't glowering, maybe this was just stoic, unruffled Ryland Gray. In any case, he wasn't really bad looking, sort of sexy in a lumberjack kind of way. "This thing that has crawled in that girl's spiritless shell is quite dangerous, quite old, and doesn't belong on this plane."

"Plane? What does that mean exactly, dimension? Is that what we're doing, some kind of dimension hopping? Your house, where time is different, where things are more permeable, where it's snowing? Are you telling me that's another dimension?"

"It's a bit of a simplistic explanation."

"Well, maybe I'm a simplistic kind of girl."

"I rather doubt that Allie Beckett." She thought she detected the slightest sparkle in his dark eyes, but maybe again that was just wishful thinking.

And then she sighed, sighed heavily, sighed audibly in a way that seemed to come from her very soul. "What do you want from me, Ryland Gray. I mean, really, what do you want?"

"I want to finish this job, and I need your help."

"Job? This is actually some kind of job?"

"I was hired to find this thing and send it on its merry way."

"Who the hell would hire you to do that?"

"No one from around here," he said flatly. "But everything's connected, and its presence is having reverberations every-where."

She frowned. "Could I get you some dry ice so you could be a bit more vague?"

There was a hesitation as she realized how poorly that remark had landed. "Dry ice?" A dark, heavy eyebrow shot up.

"Whatever! Look, you know where it is. You marked it. What do you need me for?"

"You have skills, Allie. You may not realize it, but you do. Why don't we take a ride in your Jeep?"

"A ride? Where?"

"To check out where that thing lives."

⁂

They were driving silently down Desota Blvd. again, and Ryland Gray sincerely wished there was more time, more time to prepare the woman next to him for all the changes happening in her life, more time to prepare her for what was to come in the future.

⁂

"What are you doing?"

His younger sister pulled her long ash-blond hair up into a disheveled ponytail, then unzipped her traveling bag. *"I'm leaving."*

"Leaving? Permanently?"

"Not sure," she answered, shoving a pile of t-shirts into the large duffel bag on her bed.

"Allegra, stop for a minute."

She did, looking at him strangely, but the way she usually did, as though she was peering. "I had a dream last night. It's time for me to move on."

It was not news to him that her dreams were not ordinary, but instead usually prophetic in some way. "Why? I need a diviner. I can't do this alone."

She nodded, "Well, other things are calling me now, and that girl will be here soon."

Now he frowned. His sister was indeed a very talented seer. The divining thing was a bit of a sideline for her. "That girl?"

"Yes, dear brother, the one who will help you. She'll be much better at it than I am. And you two, well, you won't want me around when things get going."

"Allegra, I don't know what you're talking about."

"Sure, you do, Ryland, you just don't want things to change. But whether you want it or not, change is coming." And then she laughed softly, "And from what I saw, she'll be a handful. But she's definitely the one."

"The one?"

"The one for you, Ryland."

⚘

He was driving this time, and the woman beside him had fallen silent. He wanted to reassure her, but language skills had never been his strong suit. He could send energy, was very, very good at hitting his target with that, but at present, that wasn't Allie Beckett's problem. Her problem was inflexibility. As Allegra had said, *"Whether you want it or not, change is coming."* That was the only constant in life.

"It's not so bad."

"What?" she said a little sharply.

"My life, the way I live. There's always something new happening."

"I don't like new. I like things to be predictable."

"Hmm," he considered. "So, do you really like it that way, or do you think you need it that way?"

Her arms were crossed in front of her protectively, and she was a bit slumped in the seat, reminding him very much of a stubborn child. "Is there a difference?"

"Well, are you happy, Allie Beckett?"

There was silence, silence he could feel. Because, well, because she'd become much easier for him to see lately. He could see her aura, how the colors would fluctuate when she was upset. He could see images that flew through her mind at lightning speed, because she did have a quick and active mind. And he could see when his thoughts reached her, and she had no idea what to do with that. Like right now, he left her befuddled and confused. And to be honest, he kind of liked that.

"I don't know, are you happy, Ryland Gray?"

He smiled, not so very surprised that she'd turned this around on him. So out of respect for who she was, he honestly thought about it. Lately, he'd felt content, content in his work, feeling as though he was contributing, being of service to the greater pool of humanity. But really happy? That was a consideration. Right now, right in this moment, driving down this long road with this particular woman at his side, filled with her inner conflicts, contradictions, the way she lashed out, the way she succumbed in her quieter moments. And he didn't really understand why someone would want a banana-yellow Jeep, but he appreciated the fact that she did. Yeah, right now, for reasons other than those myriad ones he'd just articulated in his mind, he was kind of happy.

"Yeah, Allie, I'm happy."

"You don't look happy," she smirked.

"Yep," he said, turning the Jeep into the apartment complex. "That's my resting face."

As they pulled into the parking lot and he turned off the car, he reflected.

"*She's the one, you know,*" Allegra had said. "*But you won't have an easy time of it.*"

"*I've never expected an easy time.*"

Then, she patted his shoulder. *"That's what I like about you, Ryland. You always persevere."*

"So, how do we deal with this thing?" she asked, straightening up in the seat and peering forward toward the thing's apartment.

"Well, Allie," he said a bit methodically. "I have a plan, but it will take some trust on your part."

"Trust, huh?"

"Yep, we're going to have to travel to another place to get at this thing," he said slowly.

"Another place?"

"One close, just a few fractions away, I think, but it won't see us coming."

She frowned, "Gibberish again, but okay, so then we'll kill it?"

"I don't think it can be killed, but if we're lucky, maybe we can coax it to evolve."

"Evolve?" she repeated, looking a bit confused.

"Yes," he said quietly. "That's not a small thing, and it's what it's all about."

It took a moment, but then, a slight smile flickered across her lips. She liked him. She really did. He could feel it. And that was no small thing. "What do we do?" she asked.

"Take my hand, Allie Beckett. Then I'll show you." It did take a second, but then she did.

# Unfinished Projects

"What does he look like?"

"Who?"

"The man, the one you met in the woods."

She smiled, wrinkling her nose a bit. It was a habit she had, or rather had cultivated since she was a teenager. She remembered staring at herself in the mirror of her mother's bathroom and deliberately developing the affectation. It took her about a month to settle on the technique. And even from time to time, she would revisit the process just to make sure she hadn't aged out of the expression. But for oh, these many years, it had served her well.

"It was only the once, and we only exchanged a few words in passing. I had just started the hike, and he was finishing.

Vicky smiled, "But you thought he was interesting."

She shrugged, "I did. Let's see, he was tall, dark blond hair, slender with a beard. His beard was darker than his hair. Is that strange?"

"No idea," she answered, bringing the oversized cup of coffee to her lips.

It was morning. Vicky had driven in from Little Rock. This was the ritual—these once-a-month catchups at the coffee shop inside the Village. It was usually Vicky who ventured her way, though it would unquestionably be more fun if she headed into the big city once in a while.

"So, he was good-looking?"

"Yeah, very and age appropriate—probably in his forties."

She nodded approvingly, "Maybe you should frequent that trail more often."

"I don't know. I really should be writing more. I have so many unfinished projects."

"And no personal life."

She frowned, didn't feel like wrinkling her nose just now. "Well, that's why I'm living here—so I can write, remove distractions."

Vicky eyed her a bit dubiously, "I worry about you, Maeve. You could move back to the city."

"I will. I just need a bit more time to finish some things."

❦

Maeve Silvershade—that was the pen name on her gothic romances, though it wasn't really her name, at least not Silvershade. Her name, at least her name prior to marriage, was Prescott—Maeve Harlow Prescott. She'd married at twenty-three and over the span of four years had been Maeve Prescott Galloway.

And when she'd begun writing, she'd thought about keeping it. But Asher Galloway wasn't in her life anymore. He was a historian, a writer, a researcher, intent on traveling.

So, she'd settled on something completely different, not her family name, not her married name. And just kept the Maeve.

203

"Have you heard from Asher lately?"

She looked up from her half-eaten scone on the small decorative plate.

"Asher?" A bit taken aback at the inquiry. She and Vicky had boundaries. No talking of Vicky's philandering husband that she refused to rid herself of, and no talking of Asher—the ex-husband who chose work over his wife one too many times.

She pursed her lips. This was not a developed affectation, just a natural quirk. "No, why do you ask?"

Vicky shrugged, her casually bunned up strawberry blond hair tendrilling in wisps about her heart-shaped face. "I don't know. Ted said last time he saw him, he asked about you."

Again, she pursed her lips, dismayed that the conversation had migrated into forbidden territory. "And what did Ted tell him?"

Her friend fidgeted a bit, moving the crumbly scone around on her plate. "He told him you'd taken a place here. I hadn't told him not to. Was it a secret?"

She rolled her eyes. "I guess it doesn't matter. I thought Asher had remarried a while back."

"Ted said he almost did but then broke it off. So, what are you working on?"

"A few things," she murmured, happy that once again they were veering from forbidden territory. Of all people, Asher Galloway! She didn't care if he veered off the face of the planet.

Maeve Nightshade was undeniably a different creature than young Maeve Prescott or heartbroken Maeve Galloway.

For one thing, she wasn't real, and for another, the isolation didn't bother her. There was plenty of company.

❀

It was cold, chilly really, not so unusual for late November. The leaves crunched beneath her boots. She'd taken the winding trail through the woods, stopping to watch a soothing creek's rushing water. And then she was forced to pause again because there he was. He just stood there right in the center of the path wearing his black hat and long black leather duster. And his hair, his shoulder-length blond hair, looked almost in shocking contrast to his dark attire.

She put the notebook down and watched the crackling flames in the fireplace. She hadn't lied to Vicky. She had met a man on her jaunt down the trail several days earlier. But it wasn't this man. He was older, well into his late seventies or even early eighties, she suspected, and out for some exercise, no doubt recommended by his doctor. Not at all the fellow she'd described to Vicky Burkhardt.

But now, upon reflection, she did, in all honesty, have to ask herself why she had done it.

"You didn't want her feeling sorry for you."

She frowned explicitly at the intrusive thought, or was it an intrusive voice? Hard to distinguish at this juncture.

The woman moved out of the darkness of the shadowed room and took a seat in the wing-backed chair closest to the fire-place—the gold one. She arranged her long velvet skirts—era far back, Gothic past, estimated the late 1800s perhaps. Her hair was lush and black and her eyes dark stormy blue, and skin—

"Yes, yes, fair like porcelain. I'm not here for more exposition, Maeve."

She smiled at her lovely creation. "Exposition is my bread and butter."

"No, dearest," she said in a clipped accent landing somewhere between Welsh and Scottish. "Imagination is."

She nodded in acknowledgment, "Touche," and took a sip of her hot tea, then placed it on the table next to her lounge chair.

"No wine?" Madeline Renourd asked her in a soft but silkily compelling voice.

"No, I gave it up."

"Completely?" She inquired with a mixture of amusement and incredulity.

"Too much drinking alone," she murmured, sipping her overly hot cinnamon tea.

There was a soft, lilting laughter that even she found compelling, and she was Madeline's creator. "I did have a question for you, my dear Maeve."

"Yes," she nearly whispered because she was losing interest in this game.

"Why are all your heroes blond?"

Maeve drew in a deep breath, and when she looked again, all was gone—Madeline, the gold chair, and even the fire in the fireplace.

She didn't question if she was losing her mind. There was always a touch of madness in the weavers of the imagination.

※

She was deep into her second draft of *Winsome Moon*. Maeve had pushed relentlessly into the narrative that morning, brushing away all other considerations other than sinking herself into the reality she was constructing.

It was a modern piece, not her usual historical fare in long-forgotten medieval castles. This one was set in a place not so dissimilar from where she was living. Setting the stage with a disillusioned woman just stepping out of her thirties, meeting a mysterious man on a winding mountain path.

It was the man with the black duster, black felt gambler hat, blond hair, and a beard that was a shade darker than his hair.

The chime of the front doorbell nearly made her jump out of her skin. She'd been sitting at a small round table situated in the middle of the large open kitchen.

She glanced at the clock on the wall, the one in the shape of a coffee cup, briefly reminding her that she hadn't had her second cup this morning. That was the self-imposed quota—two cups in the morning and if it was a particularly arduous day, one additional cup in the afternoon.

She rubbed her eyes, waiting to see if the intrusive ring continued, but it did not. Maybe it was a salesman of some sort—Girl Scout cookies or perhaps a Mormon looking to bring her to the light.

The truth was that she was quite isolated here and not the friendliest of neighbors.

She'd never been the most social of people. Even when there was a book signing, it felt like pulling teeth to get through the ordeal.

Starting to type again, she stopped in mid-thought. There was that Amazon order that was pending, but exactly what she'd ordered eluded her just at the moment. What a struggle, that other place, the winding mountain trail, beckoned her more strongly than her real life just at the moment.

Her fingers itched to type, but something else pulled her as well—curiosity of a sort. Closing the laptop lid and feeling the abrasive brush of her woven sandals that she wore indoors, she moved across the den.

The knob felt cool in her hands as she abruptly pulled open the front door—not checking the peephole as she might do in the city. Nothing ever happened around here. It was a gated community, and the house was nearly in the middle of a forest.

So, she acted without thought, without caution, with distraction, and found someone completely unanticipated, unexpected, and unwelcome on her doorstep.

If it were possible for her jaw to really drop, Maeve was more than sure it would be found lying on the wooden floor beneath her feet.

"Asher," she said with a mixture of astonishment and exasperation.

He smiled broadly in a way she recalled from long ago. "Happy to see me, love?" He asked lightly.

But she didn't answer because she had no idea what to say.

※

*"Why are all your heroes blond?"*

Madeleine's question hung in the air a bit like a great suspended sword ready to fall unceremoniously across the neck of an unsuspecting, foolish writer, or should she say foolish author.

He took a sip from the mug she'd handed him seconds ago. "Yeah, wow, I'd forgotten how strong you like your coffee," he said with a grimace.

"Yes, that's why we divorced," she responded flatly. "What are you doing here, Asher?"

He smiled, seemingly undaunted by her lack of enthusiasm at his presence. "You've been on my mind, Maeve."

She frowned. How bothersome that he was here. How bothersome that he felt he could drop in on her life after over a decade's absence, and lastly, but not insignificantly, how bothersome that her heart was beating rapidly in a way she couldn't remember it beating, well, since he left.

She sipped her coffee but stifled her own grimace. It was strong, stronger than she usually made it. Maybe she'd done it on purpose, unconsciously, or maybe his presence had her so rattled that she added too many grinds. Either possibility wasn't very comforting.

Rather abruptly, she put her coffee mug down hard on the surface of the round cherry wood dining table. "Asher, honestly, I don't have time for games. I haven't seen or heard from you in years. And frankly, I have work to do."

"Another book?" he asked dryly.

She frowned, remembering he didn't hold her genres of writing in high regard. "Yes, a new book."

He nodded, slowly, taking another sip of coffee. "That was wrong of me, you know. Belittling your endeavors. I apologize, Maeve. You've obviously been very successful."

A sudden breath stuck somewhere in the middle of her throat. An apology from Asher Galloway? That certainly wasn't the arrogant young man that she remembered. But then again, aging and the ruggedness of life's lessons did at times tend to beat the snobbery out of you.

At a loss of how to respond, she retrieved the coffee cup, bringing its bitterness again to her lips. "Well," murmuring, "I didn't expect that."

"Didn't expect me to learn from my mistakes?"

She looked at him sharply. "I thought you remarried or have a fiancé or something."

A slight smile touched the corners of his mouth. He was amused. How heart-warming. "Remarried? No, engaged for an interval. But that's over."

"By her or you?" Asking something that, upon reflection, she shouldn't have asked.

"Do you care, Maeve?"

"Idle curiosity. I don't really know you anymore, Asher. We've both changed."

"Hmm, I suppose. Though you look much as I imagined you would. Beautiful."

Frowning again, ah, yes, the charm was still there, though she didn't doubt his sincerity. Asher had always been a bit of a straight shooter. "I've changed, whether you see it or not. It's true," she said curtly.

He nodded slowly, looking at her steadily for an extended period as if trying to glean something.

"What?" she snapped out, unable to suppress her irritation at the scrutiny.

"I'm trying to see it," he said softly.

"See what?" She had to stop, stop engaging, stop falling into these obvious traps he was laying out for her. She sighed with exasperation. "Asher, you must stop. This is getting tiresome. What are you doing here? What do you want?"

"Well," he said, putting his coffee mug down, albeit a bit more softly than she had. "That hasn't changed. Very to the point, Maeve."

"As I said—"

"You have things to do," he broke in. "And my presence is an interruption."

"Your presence is confounding to me. So many years with no contact, no word from you. Nothing, Asher, and now here you are."

"I did," he said a bit sharply.

"You did? You did what?"

"You asked me who broke off the engagement. I did, you see."

She nodded, trying to soak that in. But the truth was she didn't see, couldn't see at all. "Why?" she asked. She shouldn't have because it was a door, and doors, once opened, allowed other things inside.

"Why?" he repeated. She noticed he wasn't smiling anymore. And the air around them had become, as she could only describe, tense. "Do you really want to know, Maeve?"

Her stomach flipped. Damn him, that ability he had to reach right inside her as it had always been. "No, no, perhaps, I don't. It really isn't any of my business."

"Because I couldn't imagine myself married to another woman."

She took a beat. "What does that even mean, Asher?" Because this didn't make a lick of sense to her.

And then staring at her rather solemnly. He proclaimed intently, "I want you back."

※

She decided to go to bed with him. That would get him out of her system once and for all.

"Do you really think that's a good idea?" Madeline again, Madeline's lovely lilting tones, trying to talk some sense into her.

"Why not? This is just an attraction. There's always been this overwhelming attraction between us."

Her expression was shrewd. One well-sculpted eyebrow went up. "And giving in to this attraction will make it go away?"

The reflection staring back at her from her dresser mirror was also skeptical. "I don't know," she whispered to herself as well as imaginary figures in the room. "I don't know what to do. I just—"

"Yes, it's obvious you want to sleep with him."

"But what does that mean? He wants me back."

"Perhaps you should ask him."

Her heart was pounding, her head spinning. Of course, it was getting close to lunchtime. Maybe she was hungry.

"Let him take you to lunch, then you can ask what it all means. At least you'll get a meal out of it," Madeleine said sweetly.

"Now that's a solution," she answered despondently.

"Small steps," her lovely creation murmured. "A lot of small steps, Maeve."

❦

His eyes were difficult to pinpoint—blue at times, at others green, changeable, inconsistent, unreliable—

"You seem preoccupied." The man in black voiced quite out of character, quite out of context.

"A bit," muttering with aggravation. This wasn't like her, not to be able to nail down the narration. Again, she looked into the character's eyes. But it wasn't his eyes that she took note of. It was the fact that he no longer had a beard. "Did you shave?"

"I'm your creation, my lady." My lady, that's a phrase Asher would use sarcastically at some moments and endearingly at others.

And son of a bitch, he had appeared on her doorstep with no beard.

She closed the top of her laptop abruptly, just short of slamming it. This was no good. He was invading her imagination now, her writing.

*"Why are your heroes always blond?"*

Or worse, he had always been there, just subdued, restrained enough not to cause her discomfort. But now he's not. He's back and not restrained.

He would be picking her up for lunch in a few minutes, so she was trying to do a little writing to calm her nerves. And what a great success that was.

※

There weren't a lot of restaurants in the Village, so she'd suggested a homey place where the food was reliably good and during lunchtime was well-populated.

"Oh, Ms. Prescott, table for two?" The young carrot-topped waitress asked with obvious interest. She came here occasionally, but usually for breakfast. Then, the word got out somehow that she was really Maeve Nightshade—a minor celebrity, and so she was celebrated and greeted with a tinge more graciousness than before. Once she brought Vicky with her but never had darkened their doorstep with a man in tow, much less her ex-husband. But, of course, they didn't know that.

"Well, this is cozy," Asher murmured, slowly surveying the menu. They'd been seated at a corner table, but *Esme's* lunchtime crowd was already beginning to filter in.

"Yes, it's quite good actually." Cozy was the term he used. Was that sarcasm or an acknowledgment of the warm homespun décor of the establishment? Hard to tell with Asher.

213

"I was hoping for a little privacy so we could talk."

Shrugging, "This is a small community. Not all that many choices, I'm afraid."

Frowning, he tapped her hand, "All right, tell me what's good here. I don't want to read through all this."

Great, like the old days, relying on her judgment. She should steer him toward something awful. He deserved that for trying to disrupt her life like this. "The catfish is good. You can order it with the lunch special with two sides."

"Hmm, two sides, and there are so many."

She smiled, couldn't help it. He sounded so out of his element. "Oh, I'm sure you can navigate it, Asher. You managed to get along in Thailand while you were doing research. This should be a piece of cake after that."

Thailand? Now, why had she brought that up? He took off the black reading glasses he'd been wearing and eyed her pointedly. "Mashed potatoes and coleslaw?"

"Sounds daring," quipping, then adding, "the home fries are better."

He nodded, "Good information. Now listen closely, I have a plan."

"Glad to hear it." She had to stop. She was getting absolutely snappy.

"Are you game?" He asked softly. He was staring at her in that naked, sincere way he had when he was trying to reach her.

"I am listening," answering quietly.

"Give me the name of two of your characters."

"Two? Haven't you read any of my books?"

"I have but as you know my memory is not—"

214

"Fine, Madeleine Renourd and Sophia Le Couer."

Sighing, "Male and female might be more suitable."

"Gregorie St. Marsh."

"Right, so we will talk, but will refer to ourselves as Madeleine and Gregory."

"Gregorie."

"Let's keep it simple for my sake."

"Is this really necessary, Asher?"

"Do you want our private business spread throughout this place? From the looks of things, it seems as though you're a bit of a celebrity here."

He had a point. How she hated that at this juncture. "Fine, I assume you want to be Gregory."

"If you don't mind."

"All right, Asher, since you've come all this way from Connecticut, I assume you're still ensconced there. I will indulge you, within reason."

"Thank you," he said softly. "So, I understand that Madeleine had some things to say about Thailand."

She blanched. She couldn't see her face, but she was more than sure her face had paled at the mention of Thailand. But she had been the one to broach it. Oh, why hadn't she just slept with him back at the house, and all of this would be done with? Maybe.

"No," haltingly, "as I recall, Madeleine didn't have much to say about Thailand, at least the last time I spoke to her." This was awkward and ploddingly difficult.

"That's not what Gregory believes," he said with sincerity. And then added in, "At least last time we spoke."

"So, what can I get you?" A small brunette waitress had snuck up on them when she was trying to muddle through this camouflage of a conversation.

Asher looked up with an affected smile. "Yes, how about two catfish lunch specials, with coleslaw, fries, and iced tea."

"And that's fried?" she asked.

His eyes migrated back to her. "Of course," Maeve answered.

❧

"So," he started, intently focusing on the plate before him.

"The tartar sauce is really good, homemade," she interjected, wondering why she even cared if he enjoyed his lunch or not.

"Ah," he stated, rather gingerly dipping a piece of fried catfish into the small cup of sauce. "I haven't talked to Madeleine in a spell, but Gregory did ask if I thought she was happy."

It took her a moment to untangle the convoluted mess of code he was weaving here.

Taking a bite of her catfish, she had to admit *Esme's* had this particular dish nailed—whether or not you appreciated the quaint atmosphere of red and white checked tablecloths and Coca-Cola memorabilia ad nauseum plastered on nearly every square inch. Though, she had to admit she did like the plastic statues of white cola bears, and the food was excellent.

"So, could you say?" He prodded.

Oh yes, back to the convoluted mess. "From what I can glean from her, Madeleine seems quite content. Her career is going well, and she has a comfortable home."

"Hmm," the sound she wasn't sure was in response to her answer or appreciation of *Esme's* culinary offerings. "Well and comfortable, sounds a bit tepid to me."

"Well, not all of us, particularly Madeleine," she emphasized, "aspire to be globetrotters like Gregory." Oddly, it felt as though she was choking on this play-acting dialogue.

"Gregory doesn't travel as much anymore," he stated. "He's affiliated with Yale, teaching and research. Working on a book."

"Yale? Well, good for Gregory. And I assume he's happy, overlooking his broken engagement."

He put down his fork, taking a sip of his rather large, iced tea. "I rented a house here for a week. You know one of these Airbnb's. But I have the summer off. I thought I'd travel."

"Oh, you or Gregory?"

He smiled. "Let's finish here and drive around a bit. I'm getting tired of this game."

She nodded, agreeing at least in this regard with him. She, too, was tired of this game.

᳘

They'd taken his car, a black Jeep. She tried to put herself back and remember what he was driving when he'd left.

"Where are you going?" she asked, suddenly aware that they hadn't taken the main artery back to her house.

"I thought you might like to see where I'm staying."

"Not especially," she grumbled.

Unexpectedly, he reached over and softly patted her hand. "Maeve, please, all I ask is that you keep an open mind."

"Because, why? For some reason, you decided your life wasn't going the way you wanted. You suddenly decided I was a necessity instead of someone you left in your back mirror."

"It wasn't sudden, Maeve. As much as I tried to put you behind me, I never could. You were always there with me in

217

glimpses, in whispers, in all the choices I ever made. All the women I knew, I couldn't help but compare to you."

It was painful, a stab to her heart.

*Why are all your heroes blond?*

"I can't trust that Asher. No, you, I can't trust you."

There was a sigh she heard from him, an audible sigh. "I know. It will take time."

�֍

It was a house, a small two-bedroom house nestled in the forest. But then again, everything was forest around here.

"Why did you get a house? They rent apartments and condos. There is even a hotel just outside the Village."

He opened the door, and she walked into a rustic but cozy den—stone fireplace, not much unlike hers. But then again, there did seem to be a bit of a repetitive element to these structures.

"I wanted some quiet. I told you I have a few weeks off."

She spun around on her heel. "Did you? A lot was said. I don't think I remember all the particulars."

He smiled a little sadly, she thought. He was worried now, worried all his efforts would be for naught. "Well, it's true, love. I have two weeks."

"Hmm, so you would really hang around here for two weeks, trying to convince me of what exactly?"

He reached out, taking her hand, then drawing her to sit next to him on the dark blue microfiber couch for a moment. "How about we resume our game just for a bit?"

"Really? That's what you want?"

"Just to get through a few things, Maeve—or I'll call you Madeleine."

A smile escaped her lips. She couldn't help it. "That wasn't exactly the game. You're changing the rules."

"Well, I made it up, so I'll change the rules."

She smirked, "If you can change the rules, you have to be Gregorie."

"Fine, Gregorie. I, Gregorie, would very much like Madeleine to tell me about Thailand."

She drew in a breath, right to the point. She felt in her skin that she shouldn't have to explain it to him. He knew, and she'd screamed it from the rooftops in her writing often enough, loudly enough.

"Why? Why is Gregorie being such a shithead?" She said flatly.

He didn't flinch. That was the thing about Asher Galloway. She believed even if he had a gun pointed at his skull, he wouldn't flinch, just deadpan face it with no compunction.

"Is he?" So devoid of emotion.

So, she plunged forward. "Of course, Gregorie knows very well what happened. He chose to leave Madeleine behind as he went to Thailand, an opportunity he couldn't turn down."

"It was only for three weeks."

"Yes, those pivotal, monumental weeks when he left Madeleine alone and the—" It caught in her throat, a bed of emotion that impeded speech.

"I know Maeve. You lost the baby. Our baby and you couldn't forgive me for that."

Her head was pounding, like her heart. "I couldn't, Asher. I was upset because you were leaving, couldn't change your plans.

I was angry, livid, and while you were gone, I lost our baby as well. It was my fault for being upset and yours for—for causing me to."

He shook his head slowly. "You know the Buddhist's believe one's lifespan is chosen before birth. That our baby was destined to only be here a short time to teach us something—help us to learn. It never intended to stay."

She was shocked to hear this from him. He had never struck her as a particularly philosophical or spiritual sort of individual. "I didn't know you were studying Buddhism."

He shrugged, tightening his grip on her hand. "After what happened, I felt the need to seek answers. It helped me."

She nodded. "Good, I'm glad you've found some peace with things."

And then there was that sharp smile she remembered so well. "Well, I didn't say that, my love. It's a work in progress. But regardless of what happens with us, my dear Madeleine, I would hate to think you were holding onto this pain."

"I'm not," she whispered. "Well, trying not to."

"I am so sorry that I left you. That I didn't fight harder to keep you. There have been mistakes, and I am asking for your forgiveness."

Forgiveness? With all her imagination, did she ever expect Asher Galloway to seek her forgiveness?

⚘

She'd taken that trail this morning because she didn't know what else to do. It wasn't one she usually walked, but she felt moved with a desperation born of longing, born of pain, born of craving to breathe in deeply again, something that was different.

The man she met was the same but altered. Not in black, not in a hat, just dressed in khaki cargo pants with a light tan jacket unzipped in case the weather changed.

"What brings you by?" he asked her in his soft, melting tones—the kind that turn your insides into marshmallow or something sticky of the like.

"Craving, I think," was the answer.

❧

"Can you?" he asked softly in that melting voice because, of course, it was his voice—truly and always his voice.

"I can," she murmured. "Forgiving myself is something else again."

"Okay," he was smiling, and her insides were turning to that soft sticky stuff. "Then if it were my choice, I would want you to forgive yourself, Maeve, my precious Maeve, and not forgive me."

❧

"Why are you crying?" The stranger on the path asked.

"Because words have fallen away."

❧

She nodded, choked up, so many tears. "I'll try. I'll try both maybe."

"We were young."

"Yes, yes, that's true," murmuring, feeling his hands pulling her closer. Of course, she'd already decided, maybe back at the restaurant, maybe when she first opened the door, maybe when she first saw the man in black on that long winding mountain trail.

221

Or maybe a long time ago, before they were born. It couldn't be explained, the two of them, you see. It just simply was.

# A Murder in the Village

Some things sit together easily, as though they are natural and integral to each other. And some things are discordant, and don't belong anywhere near one another.

So was the house on the hill on Perralena Way. It simply didn't fit easily into the forested landscape of the Village with its sharp white sandstone edges, and uncomfortable bay windows jutting outward on its second floor. To her, it looked like it should be plucked out of the woods and dropped somewhere near a beach where it would make sense. Modern, the realtor had described it. Was that a catch-all for this type of, and the only words she could come up with were, resentful sort of structure? Resentful, like someone who refuses to blend in, such was that house with its white shuttered windows and off-white sandstone, just sitting up on the hill, daring her to darken its doorstep.

She frowned, reluctantly coaxing her car up its nearly 45-degree angle driveway. Her little blue Pontiac compact was old and in need of replacement. But her salary from these odd jobs didn't afford such luxuries. She was coming to clean this house, one of her side gigs that paid the bills. It was between owners.

She mashed down on the emergency brake, hoping desperately that it would hold. The realtor called yesterday. Evidently, the relatives had just gotten the house cleared out of the last owner's possessions. He'd died. In fact, they'd found his body two weeks ago, an old man, living in that monolithic two-story structure all on his own. A grasscutter who came once a week became suspicious when he noticed the trash can wasn't out. Clearly, the body had been there a few days.

Sad, but not unusual around here. The Village was largely a retirement community. And this sort of thing happened. He had no children, and the heirs wanted this matter dealt with quickly, as not to interfere with, well, whatever it might interfere with. It gave her chills at how cold people could be. That was why she wasn't a nurse at present—simply couldn't take the upset and suffering anymore.

Her older sister, Caliste, said her skin was too thin. Well, that was one way of looking at it. So, back to it. In addition to cleaning houses for realtors in the area, she also delivered groceries from Walmart and performed some computer work for elderly residents, until she found a new career.

Of course, she understood she was still sitting in her car. "Use the entrance by the garage. It has the realtor box on it." That was Marilyn James, her boss. She would clean houses for her and get them ready for showings. She had the feeling that she kind of liked her, because this was the fifth house she had cleaned this month. But the others hadn't been deaths like this one, just people moving.

She clicked her unmanicured nails on the steering wheel. That was another thing that she couldn't afford and rarely bothered to do herself.

It was acknowledged. She really, really didn't want to go into that house. Her feet felt like cement. Oppressive was one word. Scary, that was another.

"Stop being so sensitive. You have to be practical." That was her younger sister, Isaline. She called her the no-nonsense sister. She worked in Hot Springs as a records clerk at the police station. Caliste worked as a lab technician in a doctor's office in the Village. And she, Medora, presently cleaned houses or was trying to anyway.

Closing her eyes, Medora took in a deep breath and stilled herself within. Around her, she visualized a protective shield of white. It was probably just scavengers anyway. Once she was around for a bit, they would move on.

Slowly opening her eyes again, she reluctantly eyed the sandstone edifice before her. Unless, of course, if there was a concentration of negative energy, then they would be hellbent on sticking around, their favorite food and such.

She stepped out onto the pavement. It was a hot August day, and without question, she would rather be any other place in the world.

❦

"So, what was the man's name again?" Caliste asked, handing her a hot cup of mint tea. Hot tea didn't seem like a great choice on such a balmy August day, but then again, her nerves were more than rattled after what she'd been through.

"Albert, Albert Farwell," she mumbled, settling into one of Caliste's wicker lounge chairs on her screen porch overlooking Lake Balboa.

"Hmm," Caliste murmured, lightly tapping her white teacup with freshly manicured rose-colored nails. It was Saturday. Her sister's day off, and she was lucky to intercept her right after her appointment. Caliste was a tall, slender woman, just forty-five, very attractive with short, cropped auburn hair. That was a thing, all the Crais sisters had red hair. Caliste was the dark red, she, Medora, was a carrot top, and the youngest, Isaline had a strawberry blond curly mop. "Albert Farwell, Albert Farwell," Caliste kept repeating to herself and lightly tapping the porcelain mug. "He was an old man?"

"Not when I saw him."

It all happened while she was in the front room, vacuuming the great expanse of beige plush carpet spreading across the den. She would do a preliminary vacuum, then tomorrow return with a steam cleaner for all the carpets. As Medora was forcing pure concentration on the task at hand, that was when it happened.

"I thought you said he was an old man."

"He was ninety-three when he died."

"But when you saw him—"

One minute her eyes were cast down, her ears tuned into the classic Heart album, *Dreamboat Annie*, courtesy of earbuds, when she looked up to see the man standing in the doorway. He was in glasses, full beard, and mustache, not much older than her, just maybe into his forties, she surmised.

She stopped the vacuum, staring back at him in a bit of shock. "I-I didn't know anyone was here."

"So, he looked young?"

"Yes, fortiesh I guess."

"What else?" Caliste murmured. Medora had enough experience with her sister's gifts that she knew she was trying to see.

"Um, he had a long-sleeved shirt on, button down with khaki pants."

"Dated?"

"Excuse me?"

"His clothes, Medora. Did they look dated?"

"Oh, I don't know," she muttered. "Do men's clothes really change all that much?"

Caliste shrugged, "Fair point, but you're sure he said he was Albert Farwell."

"Yes, absolutely, that's what he said."


"Yes, I'm here." The man standing before her commented as he took off his dark-rimmed glasses. His hair was thick, sort of longish, below his collar, and a lovely chestnut shade.

"I'm cleaning the house for Marilyn, the realtor. They're putting it on the market soon."

"You clean houses?" He said blandly.

She frowned, wondering if this was some kind of snobbery. "I do a lot of things."

"Your hair," he murmured. "It's very orange."

She touched it self-consciously. It was undeniably a vibrant shade. "Um, should you be in here? As I said, this house is going up for sale. How did you get inside?"

It seemed like an easy question, but then she noticed his eyebrows sort of darted together angrily. "So, they're selling this house," he said in almost a low growl, and it was at that point she began to realize something was very off.


"What exactly did he say?" Caliste quizzed her with focus, seeming to hang onto every word.

"Who are you?" Maybe she shouldn't have asked. Yes, she definitely shouldn't have asked him anything.

"I'm the owner."

"The owner? You mean you're a relative of Albert Farwell?"

"No, Miss, to whom am I speaking?"

"Medora, Medora Crais."

"Miss Crais, I am Albert Farwell, the owner."

At that point, she was pretty sure she just let go of the stand-up vacuum cleaner as it fell over with a clunk. "Oh," she said somewhat breathlessly.

"You didn't know he was a ghost?"

"No, I, well, I wasn't expecting that. And he was so solid, just like you sitting there in front of me."

"Hmm, that is curious. But then again, you don't usually see them, ghosts, spirits, I mean, do you, Medora?"

She took a deep breath in, reflecting on her time working as a hospice nurse in the Village. "Not really," she replied, not precisely the truth but close enough.

"Well, maybe I should clear out of here for now," she said hesitantly. Either this guy was nuts or the alternative—

"Am I scaring you?" he said placidly.

"I-no, I just am surprised you're here."

He nodded slowly as though really concentrating on what she was saying. "What does it look like to you, this house?"

"The house?"

"Yes, Miss Crais, what do you see when you look around?"

Her heart was really racing now. "I-uh, just an empty house, empty rooms."

There was a pause and then, "Hmm." He made that sound in the process of sort of nibbling on the end of his glasses in contemplation. "Well, you see, Miss Crais, I see something quite different. I see a house full of furniture, just like it was when I lived here."

She glanced around, having no idea what to make of that. "How long, I mean, how long did you live here, Mr. Farwell?"

"Here? Only about ten years."

"Ten years? Is that all, but you look so—" then she stopped, sensing a bit of a quagmire.

"Young?" He asked with little emotion.

"I should go," she murmured anxiously, abruptly pulling the cord out of the wall for the vacuum and beginning to wind it up.

"So, you would expect an old man." He spoke as though he was piecing things together, sort of having a professor quality to his demeanor, she thought.

"Oh, well, I don't know about that," she laughed nervously, glancing around for her things so that she could gather them quickly and get the hell out.

"Not old then, what exactly, Medora?" Albert Farwell quizzed her rather sternly.

So, she stopped and looked up, looked up into a very nice pair of deep blue eyes. "I would expect you to be dead, Albert."


"You told him he was dead?" Caliste asked her in surprise.

"Well, I didn't intend to. It just came out."

"You know, you need to proceed delicately when attempting to get the departed to cross over."

"Well, I didn't know that. It's not something I really do. You and Isaline have had more experience in that area. But honestly, it just came out."

Caliste quietly sipped her tea as though considering, then shot her a curious glance. "So, what happened next?"

"I see," he said softly. Then, rather smoothly, he moved over to the mantle of the fireplace, where he sat down on the black hearth of that smooth off-white sandstone construction. "So, you believe I'm dead?"

Medora was standing in the center of the den, still grasping the handle of her upright vacuum cleaner. How did one answer such a question? "Well, I'm pretty sure Albert Farwell is dead. But he was ninety-three and you look, well, so much—"

"Younger," he filled in with a tired voice.

"Maybe you're not really Albert. Maybe you're a son."

"I had no children."

"A nephew."

"Miss Crais."

She hesitated, "Yes."

"I do recall being ill, very ill, and after that seeing quite a bright and compelling light in my room. But you see, I do remember that I deliberately decided to remain here."

"Oh," she said softly. Then, it did sink in. "Remain? Um, why was that, Mr. Farwell?"

And then he looked at her oddly, inscrutable might be the word she was searching for. But not really like a professor, but instead a scientist, as though he was trying to see something. "I believe that I had something left to do here."

"Something?" she echoed a little hesitantly.

He spoke slowly, almost distractedly, as though putting together some puzzle in his mind. "Yes, Medora Crais. You see, I believe I was murdered."

Caliste stared back at her a little blankly. "He said he was murdered."

"He said he believed he was murdered."

"Believed? How very peculiar."

"You think so?"

"Don't you?" Well, she couldn't argue with that. "And how did you leave it?"

"I said I had to leave, but I'd come back, with some help." And then her sister's eyes narrowed.

"You know, Medora, those who refuse to cross over are usually a problematic lot."

"Yes, but he seemed pretty coherent. And young, that was very odd."

"Very," her sister murmured.

"So, what should we do now?"

"We? You want me involved."

"That's why I came here. I want help."

Caliste tapped her longish rose-colored fingernails on the glass patio table in front of her. "I think we should call Isaline. If it's really murder, she has connections."

Medora leaned back in the uncomfortable chair and breathed out a deep sigh of relief. Ideally, the two of them would simply take this out of her hands. But then again, she was the only one with access to that house. She recalled Albert Farwell silently watching her as she headed out the door to leave.

"You are returning Medora Crais, are you not?"

"Yes, I will come back with some help."

He nodded silently. "Good, I believe our meeting was fortuitous."

And then she'd smiled, having no idea how to respond to that.

✼

Isaline had opted for a very short, pixie-style haircut. More serviceable was her explanation, but her strawberry blond locks still refused not to curl femininely around her round face, and her choice of baby blue jogging pants and matching shirt did nothing to dispel that effect. This was a woman who could not look tough, regardless of the façade she attempted to adopt.

She was sitting on one of the three camp chairs they'd brought, as Albert Farwell's house had no furniture, regardless of how he might see it. Isaline was bending forward and staring at him intently, because Medora could clearly see him standing by the fireplace, as he had initially been, arms crossed, dark-rimmed glasses on, staring right back at them.

"Are you seeing him?" Medora asked in almost a whisper because she knew better than to interfere with her sisters when they were in the zone.

"Yep," Isaline murmured.

"Me too," Caliste said less softly from nearer the kitchen. "But he's not at all as you described him, Dora." Caliste was loud, even when she wasn't trying to be. She was floating behind them in one of her silky, kaftan-style shirts, which she always seemed to wear. And Medora was the odd duck, dressed in an old black T-shirt and well-worn blue jeans.

232

"She's not wrong," Isaline said less loudly, straightening up. "I'd say late eighties, early nineties."

Now that was strange, because here he was, looking at all of them as though they'd lost their minds just as she'd seen him the first time, forties at most. "Then why am I seeing him young?" She asked to anyone who might care to answer.

"Ladies, I would appreciate it if you addressed me directly, not like some bug under your microscope."

Isaline glanced over to Medora with surprise on her face. "Apologies, Mr. Farwell. But it has been my experience that ghosts who refuse to cross over aren't usually open to interaction."

He grimaced, now looking at the three of them somewhat as though they were now the bugs under a microscope. "So very odd, all redheads of a differing shade." He shook his head as though confounded. "So, you've decided I'm a ghost."

"What do you think you are?" Caliste asked rather abruptly from somewhere behind them.

"A person who has clearly died but has not completed their purpose."

"Purpose?" Isaline muttered.

"He thinks he was murdered," Medora whispered loudly to her sister sitting beside her. But she didn't really know why exactly she was whispering. Everyone could clearly hear her.

"Oh yes, Caliste mentioned that, Mr. Farwell," Isaline's voice increased in volume. "I have checked your records with the coroner's office. You are listed as having died of natural causes. Some heart complications. Did you have heart problems, sir?" Isaline was very business-like and to the point, no doubt a demeanor adopted at the police station.

"I was on heart medication, high blood pressure, and a blood thinner for heart failure." Isaline caught her eye at his answer and then plunged forward.

"Well, it is possible, don't you think, that you did indeed pass on from natural causes."

And then he looked at Medora with a bit of frustration. "Is this the help that you've brought me? These women to only contradict what I've said?"

"No, Albert. Of course not."

And then Caliste circled around and chirped in. "Mr. Farwell, why don't you tell us why you think you were murdered."

"Because I was asleep upstairs when I felt someone put a pillow over my head until I couldn't breathe."

Medora turned to look at both Isaline and Caliste, who were staring back at her with question in their eyes. Was it really possible that he was indeed murdered?

❦

"Why am I seeing him as a younger man?"

They were standing outside on the back patio of Albert Farwell's sandstone residence. "Why are you seeing him at all?" Isaline said flatly. "I thought you didn't see spirits."

"Well, I don't. I mean, I haven't really, since I started working in hospice. I sort of shut all of that down, just to cope."

Isaline was eying her a little too suspiciously. "Right, but then you quit that too."

"Do you think we could stay on target here and keep my life choices out of the line of fire?"

"Smothering, the symptoms of that aren't the same as having a heart attack, Dora."

She frowned, wishing she had a cigarette in her hands just now to help with the tension. But then again, she'd given that up years ago. "But maybe he had a heart attack while being smothered and the coroner got it wrong."

"Maybe," Isaline murmured unconvincingly. "I'm not an expert. But think about it, Dora, even if he was murdered, how exactly could you prove such a thing?"

Caliste was frowning, not speaking much, but frowning. "She has a point. There isn't a whole lot that can be done here."

Medora stared back at her sisters with disappointment. She knew the signs. They were throwing in the towel. But what about Albert? She had promised she'd help, and she hated to go back on a promise.

❧

"So, the help wasn't much help at all."

Isaline had left with Caliste in her car, leaving Medora to deliver the news. And Albert was watching her with those eyes that, if he weren't a ghost, she might consider quite sexy. "They think it's unlikely there's much we can do even if you were murdered, Albert."

"You know, I think you're the prettiest, if I had to choose out of the three of you. You're very bright hair is unique and goes well with your fair skin and green eyes."

"They're hazel, but thanks, Albert." A bit surprised at the comment, she sat down awkwardly in the only remaining camp chair. They'd taken the other two with them. And it crossed her mind for pretty much the first time that she needed to finish cleaning this sandstone monolith. "I was wondering if you might consider moving on, Albert. I mean, it would be more pleasant for you."

"I'm not unhappy. I have my books. I used to teach, you know, at a university."

She smiled, "What did you teach?"

"Psychology," he answered a bit despondently.

"Oh," she said softly. "So, psychologically thinking, why do you think someone might want to murder you?"

He crossed his arms and sort of leaned against the wall, eyeing her oddly. "I wasn't a very nice person."

"You weren't?"

"No, I was gruff, exacting, not very nice to people."

"Why were you like that?" she asked, not meaning to pry but somehow feeling compelled to pry.

"I suppose I was disillusioned by life."

She drew in a deep, painful breath. It hurt because she could feel the sad feelings emanating from him. "So, where can we start with this, Albert?"

❧

"You're not very happy."

She sat rocking slowly in her grandmother's rocking chair. Granny Annie, they'd laughingly called silver-haired Annabelle Crais. She had left it to her in her will, remembering something about Medora as a little girl crawling up into the oversized hickory wood well-cushioned chair next to her Granny to listen to tales from her childhood. And she remembered vividly three days after she'd died, awakening to find the old woman standing in the corner of her room. Of course, she never told anyone. That was Caliste and Isaline's thing.

"Why didn't you tell anyone?" He asked from across her den. He was staring out of her apartment's picture window into the darkness.

"What?"

And then he turned around, pulling off his glasses. He really was actually very handsome she'd have to say. "I was wondering why you didn't tell anyone you'd seen your grandmother's spirit."

She took a sip of mint tea. "How do you know that?"

"Your thoughts are loud and vivid. I could see the old woman standing in your room. You seemed shook."

"I was nine. And it's none of your business why, well, why I didn't say anything."

"Those sisters seem a bit pushy."

"We're here to talk about you, Albert."

He shrugged, turning back to the window. "It's so dark here. I remember thinking that. I should have retired in the city. I don't know why I came here."

She took another sip of tea. She didn't believe him when he said he could go home with her. But, sure enough, once she got into the car, he was sitting right beside her. Peculiar behavior for a ghost, not that she'd had that much exposure to them.

"You're as sensitive and gifted as they are, but you're content to fade into the background while they hog the limelight."

"I wouldn't call being able to see ghosts much limelight."

"Being psychics, clairvoyants, mediums, soothsayers, all that hogwash."

"We wouldn't be conversing if it were really hogwash."

And then he turned around again, frowning. "It might strengthen our trust in this matter if you answer some of my questions."

"About the limelight?" Another sip of warm tea to soothe her very mangled nerves. "They're not so bad, really. Just rather emphatic about who they are, what they believe they deserve. And I'm just quieter, that's all."

"Not to rain on your parade, Medora Crais, but all of that sounds like weak tea."

"Nice pun, Albert. Fine, I don't like to talk about it because it hurts."

"Hurts? What hurts?"

She shrugged. "Dealing with your kind, ghosts. It hurts. It feels painful to me, so I try not to."

He was staring at her intently as though trying to see something. "So, the hospice work."

"Intolerable," she murmured.

"Before or after?"

Her eyebrow rose, "Before or after what?"

He walked closer, settling into an overstuffed armchair near her. "Before or after they died, Medora? When was it painful?"

She suddenly realized for the first time that she hadn't mentioned her hospice work to the handsome ghost in front of her. Reading her mind didn't seem to be the only thing he was doing. He appeared to be rummaging around in her mind. "Both Albert. Many of them were afraid, afraid of dying, and then confused once they did."

"No comfort from their religion?"

"Anticipating jumping off a cliff and doing so are two different matters."

He smiled, and he had dimples. Why in the world did he have dimples? "Point taken," he said with a touch of humor in his voice that felt inappropriate given what they were discussing.

"Were you afraid, Albert? Before you crossed over?"

"Well, Medora Crais, I have to say I was very afraid when someone shoved a pillow on my face."

⚜

"Yes, of course, I remember Mr. Farwell. I did checks on him once a week for the last few months of his life."

Violet Jakes was a nurse who worked in the Village and outlying areas. In Medora's estimation, she seemed in her late fifties, was rather plump with short blond hair, and had a dour expression as though she really didn't want to be bothered.

"So, was he in good health?"

"Are you a relative of Mr. Farwell's?"

She smiled, trying to appear non-threatening. "A family friend."

"I didn't know Albert had any family. He seemed to be quite the loner." She took a bite of what appeared to be some kind of chicken salad, not too appetizing from what Medora could ascertain. Violet Jakes clearly didn't seem too pleased when she tracked her down and asked for this little chat. But finally, after a bit of coaxing, she acquiesced and agreed to meet on her lunch hour at St. Vincent's Hospital cafeteria. Apparently, she moonlighted there on Mondays and Tuesdays, leaving the rest of the week for mobile visits.

"I really never saw any family of his or much of anyone."

"Really, no one?"

She took a sip out of a diet Coke can. "Well, there was that fellow who cut the grass, Joe, hmm, Joe something. I came in one

239

day and they were having coffee. Of course, I told Mr. Farwell to watch his caffeine intake, but I don't think he listened to me."

"Yeah, so his death. Were you surprised?"

She shrugged, continuing to move her salad around with a fork as if she was none too thrilled with it as well. "Surprised? No, not really. The Village is largely a retirement community after all. People die all the time."

"Hmm, I suppose that's true," wondering exactly where to go with this now. "So, Mr. Farwell, did you like him?"

And then she looked up, meeting Medora's gaze directly with dark brown eyes and a glimmer of a smile. "Like him? Not to speak ill of the dead, but he wasn't a very pleasant man. One of those intellectual types who thought they were better than everyone else and looked down their nose at people working for a living. Not much to like there, if you ask me."

"Unpleasant woman."

"Hmm," she murmured, filling her mouth quickly with a sandwich she had made when she got home. So much cheaper than fast food, and she really had to get back to the sandstone monolith to finish cleaning before an upcoming open house. "She said the same of you."

"You know if you keep eating that quickly, you'll be the one ending up on the mortician's slab."

She frowned, taking a sip of iced tea. "That's harsh, Albert. So, she said there was a grasscutter named Joe."

He frowned, "Joe Hartly, nice chap. Likes poetry."

They were both standing in Medora's small galley kitchen. It seemed Albert was confined to her house and his, for some odd reason, unable to travel with her to her interview with Nurse

240

Jakes. Apparently, there were odd rules for the afterlife that she was not privy to. "Hmm, that's different."

"What, you don't think blue collar workers have a soul, Medora?"

"I'm blue-collar, Albert. I just meant I haven't encountered many men who have a penchant for poetry."

"I have volumes of it on the shelves in my study, or rather, I did."

Again, she frowned, feeling as if they were making zero progress. "So, anyone else besides this Joe Hartly used to visit you?"

"UPS, Amazon drivers, and an occasional Walmart delivery."

"So, you really were a recluse."

And she saw something odd pass across his face. "Don't feel too bad for me, Medora. We all make our own prisons."

✹

It was nearly two by the time she pulled back into the steep driveway of Albert Farwell's sandstone mausoleum, or how she'd come to designate it in her mind. As much as she hadn't liked the place when she first saw it, she really didn't like it now after spending time with Albert. This really couldn't be the way it was supposed to be at the culmination of one's life, alone, isolated, ostensibly waiting for things to end. Where's the meaning or purpose in that? Surely there must be more.

It was with a heavy heart that she stepped out onto the impossibly steep driveway and watched as a well-worn pick-up truck pulled up in front of the house. She waited as a man stepped out, neither young nor old, probably around her age or maybe a tinge older. She thought to go inside, but her feet felt cemented to the pavement. She could see clearly the lawn equipment sticking out of his truck. What was his name again?

He suddenly noticed her, standing there in the driveway, staring at him. So, he waved. She walked forward a bit, plastering on a smile. "Mr. Hartley, do you have a few minutes?"

⚜

It vaguely crossed her mind that she had made very little progress in cleaning this monstrosity of a house. And it also crossed her very cluttered mind that Albert Farwell was nowhere to be seen. So odd, he'd made himself scarce after lunch, but she'd fully expected to see him wandering about once she and Joe Hartly came inside. But as it was, it was just the two of them, perched on the fireplace mantle, drinking two bottles of cold water he'd retrieved from an ice chest in his truck.

"Thanks for the water," she said. "I usually bring something with me when I'm working on houses, but I was rushed today."

"No problem, Miss Crais, is it?"

She smiled, suddenly feeling extremely awkward. How did one launch into an interrogation with no reasonable reason why? "Medora, please."

He smiled. Nice smile, actually, up close, Joe Hartly was pretty good-looking. Sandy blond hair, a short beard, sparkling blue eyes, dressed in an orange T-shirt and well-worn blue jeans—the appropriate wardrobe for someone getting ready to cut the grass. Nothing to complain about there. "Now that's an unusual name."

"Old family name, great-grandmother, I think," she murmured awkwardly. "So, I was just wondering, did you know Albert well?"

"Mr. Farwell? I don't know if I could say well. I've been working his yard for about four years. He was a nice old man, a

242

generous tipper. We shared a few meals. He liked chess, so I'd come by after work sometimes and play him, order a pizza, or bring something I'd cooked. He seemed to like that."

She paused, taken a bit aback by his description of their relationship. "So, seems like you liked him."

"Sure, he liked to read, and so do I. We talked about books, world events. He was a picker."

Her eyes widened. "A picker?"

He shrugged, "That's what I call someone who likes to pick things apart and analyze them."

"And you, Mr. Hartley, are you a picker?" Wow, once that came out of her mouth, she was hit with how bizarre it sounded.

"Joe, please. No, Medora, I am an observer, I suppose, but I tend to let things be. Maybe it comes with working with the earth so much, nature and all has its process."

She nodded, wondering where in the world to take this now. Because she was feeling good, kind of soothed by Mr. Joe Hartley's no-nonsense but kind attitude. "So, do you think other people liked Albert?"

At that, she saw an odd expression cross his face. "Can I ask you something, Medora?"

She took a quick gulp out of the water bottle, suddenly feeling like some table somewhere was turning. "Yeah, sure."

"Did you know Mr. Farwell?"

She thought quickly—how to answer that. Of course, she could lie as she had done to Violet Jakes. But Joe here, and she was suddenly wondering if his full name was Joseph because she did like Joseph, she really didn't want to lie to him. "No, not really. My first exposure to him was when I came here to clean the house. I work for the realtor who is selling the property and, well, I just tend to get feelings about places, people—" Her voice drifted off as she wondered if he thought she was a loon.

He paused for a second, looking at her, well, as if he knew something about her. "Have you seen Mr. Farwell here, Medora?"

She tilted her head a bit. Had he really asked her that? "Seen?"

"Yes," he said slowly. "His spirit? You seem like someone who might see spirits."

Awkward pause that felt like a massive hole of strangeness opening up right down to the bowels of the earth. "I-I seem like someone who sees ghosts?"

"We always called them spirits, my mom and I."

She just sat there, kind of transfixed, really, really not expecting this. "Sometimes they're ghosts," she murmured.

And then he smiled. "Yeah, but that's kind of a tainted term. I prefer to call them spirits who haven't crossed over yet."

"Yeah, semantics. So, um, you and your mom see spirits?"

"Mostly my mom and grandmother. I do, but rarely, but I do feel things and see auras. You had a pink one around you, lots of confusion right now."

"Yeah, well, that's true enough," she muttered. But in that very moment, she decided to go for broke. "All right, Joe, since you brought it up. I have seen Albert a number of times. He won't cross over because, well, because he believes he was murdered."

His eyes widened a bit. Not so laid back now, are you, sexy grasscutter? "Murdered?"

"That's what he claims. The problem is, there wasn't a whole lot of opportunity for that. Albert Farwell seemed like a bit of a recluse. Except for you and his nurse, who didn't like him nearly as much as you did, well, there's not much there."

244

And then he looked at her oddly and took a rather large gulp of his water. "Murdered? I just don't know if I can see that, Medora. It doesn't feel quite right."

She frowned, "Well honestly, I don't know where to take this now. Albert, well, he did say he resisted crossing over because he felt he still had something to do here."

He nodded slowly, "Well, old Mr. Farwell, as I remembered, wasn't always straightforward. He liked things complicated, layers."

"Layers, what does that mean?"

"The easiest thing I could say is that he didn't always play his cards right away."

She nodded, considering, "Hmm, okay."

❧

Joe Hartley stayed another half hour, half an hour that she should have spent cleaning the house, and he should have spent cutting the grass. Apparently, this was a side gig for him while he was building up his landscaping service. She didn't learn a whole lot about Albert Farwell but did learn that Joe was divorced. And, he very much wanted to take her out to dinner sometime. So, they exchanged phone numbers.

And by the time he left, she felt better, better about life, about herself, just a bit happier. "He's a special chap, isn't he?"

She'd seen Joe to the door and found Albert waiting for her by the fireplace in the den. When in the world was she ever going to clean this house? "Joe, yes, he's very nice."

He took off his glasses, quietly rubbing them clean with a handkerchief he'd pulled from his shirt pocket. "I thought you two might hit it off."

She looked at him curiously. "You did?"

"Joe's an intuitive guy. You two could help each other."

She stood in the middle of the den, wondering for possibly the first time if Albert Farwell was playing some kind of a game with her. "What's going on, Albert?"

He glanced up at her, putting his glasses on again. "That light is back. I think I can move on now, my dear."

"Now? But you said you were murdered."

He nodded, "Yes, yes, I did. But now it doesn't seem all that important. Maybe I was, maybe it was a hallucination of some sort when I was crossing over. Maybe Violet was having a really bad day."

"But if that's true, she would just get away with it."

He smiled softly, at least softly for Albert Farwell. "No one gets away with anything. Don't you know that, Medora? The worst things are the ones we do to ourselves. If she did kill me, she has her own consequences to face. If she didn't, well, then we had a nice interlude, you and me. You should be kinder to yourself, Medora Crais. Take some of that limelight, enjoy it, and enjoy the blessings. I missed a bit of that. Thanks for reminding me."

She stood there in Albert Farwell's den, now recognizing that she was alone there. She walked across the room and looked out the blinds, watching Joe Hartley cutting the grass. Maybe she'd text him tonight and tell him that Albert was gone. Or maybe she'd phone. That might be better.

## The Alchemist's Bride
6 x 9 Softcover 230 pages
ISBN 978-1-61342-454-4
ISBN (Hardcover) 978-1-61342-455-1

From a young age, Emmeline Lescale has been raised as an outsider by her aunt's family on the lavish estate of Belle Coeur in Vacherie, Louisiana. Ostensibly an orphan, she is treated as an unpaid servant. But in her twenty-fifth year, with her eyes on a dismal future, something radically changes.

Her father, a renowned physician who has ignored her existence most of her life, suddenly insists that she come to live with him. And New Orleans in the 1880s seems like no place for a proper young lady, especially when her father is embroiled with a mysterious young doctor whose interests venture deeply and dangerously into the world of the supernatural.

Jack Fallon, the protege of Emmeline's father, lives a life filled with secrets. His home, deep in the French Quarter on Bienville Street, is much more than meets the eye. And before too long, he draws Emma into the crosshairs of an existence that questions the nature of reality itself.

## The Story of Enid
*Vol. 2 of The Clandestine Exploits of a Werewolf*
6 x 9 Softcover 254 pages
ISBN 978-1-61342-453-7

What happens when your one true love reincarnates, and you just happen to be a werewolf?

Ethan Garraint is an old soul. He has been alive for hundreds of years, battling countless challenges and foes along the way—not the least of which was living through the genocide of the Cathar people at Montsegur, a society that wholly embraced him despite his lycanthropic nature. But in Volume 2 of The Clandestine Exploits of a Werewolf, he faces a dilemma that brings his past and present full circle, merging them both.

## The Broken Vow
*Vol. 1 of The Clandestine Exploits of a Werewolf*
6 x 9 Softcover & Hardcover 204 pages
ISBN 978-1-61342-133-8
ISBN (Hardcover) 978-1-61342-420-9

In the heart of every man, there is a history. In the heart of every monster, there is a story. In this first installment of The Clandestine Exploits of a Werewolf, Ethan Garraint is on a vendetta that begins in the heart of the Pyrenees with the fall of Montségur and leads him to the streets of New Orleans nearly five hundred years later. But the person he chases isn't really a man anymore, and Ethan has been a werewolf for almost a millennium. With the aid of a gifted seer, he is on a blood hunt that will culminate in a journey that crosses the line between heaven and earth and ends somewhere in between.

## The Lady in the Blue Dress
6 x 9 Softcover & Hardcover 214 pages
ISBN 978-1-61342-600-5
ISBN (Hardcover) 978-1-61342-418-6

When she was a child, Mika Devalieur was introduced to her grandmother's most precious possession—a priceless and mysterious painting that she simply called The Lady in the Blue Dress. Upon Adele St. Clair's death, the painting is left in the care of her granddaughter with only one stipulation. Mika must hand over the family heirloom to a total stranger. Mika Devalieur desperately wants to deny her beloved grandmother's last request, but she can't. Torn between her Gran's last wishes and her desire to hold onto the Lady, she ultimately journeys to rural

Virginia, where an enigmatic man shows her that this painting is only the beginning.

What quickly becomes clear is that James Clairmont knows much more about her and the Lady than he is letting on. He begins to slowly unravel a powerful supernatural connection that spans three generations of her family. Mika finds herself desperate to uncover the entire truth before she falls in love with a man filled with so many secrets—secrets about him, about her, and most especially about The Lady in the Blue Dress. (First published on Kindle Vella, episodes 1-23.)

### Dumaine Street
6 x 9 Softcover & Hardcover 306 pages
ISBN 978-1-61342-902-0
ISBN (Hardcover) 978-1-61342-416-2

Voices in her head, catastrophic emotions, hallucinations—Rebecca Wells is more than convinced that she is losing her mind. And as a last-ditch effort, she contacts a self-professed counselor who seems convinced he can help.

Gabriel Sutton has abandoned the world of medicine to navigate a realm filled with psychic phenomena. Diagnosing Becca with extreme empathic abilities, he struggles to help her stabilize her gifts while trying desperately not to fall in love with his patient.

From the realm of vulnerability into a crusade to use their profound gifts to rescue others from peril on the other side of death, these two follow an astonishing and unpredictable path into each other's hearts.

**The Tethering**
*A Portent of Crows*
6 x 9 Softcover & Hardcover 201 pages
ISBN 978-1-61342-599-2
ISBN (Hardcover) 978-1-61342-419-3

Deborah Brandt's beloved Aunt Gena always told her that she was special, a bit different, and would have to live her life, unlike other people. Of course, this she disregarded as the ramblings of her lovely but notably eccentric aunt. Although there were the things that Aunt Gena said that seemed true—like Deborah being sensitive to energy shifts, having potentially psychic impressions, and dreaming of a spirit guide—none of it could be real. But the most ridiculous thing that her Aunt Gena told her before she died was that someone special was out there for her. She said that he was an extraordinary man who was not only her perfect match but someone who she would learn from so that they could help the world in difficult times. How ridiculous! It sounds like a fairy tale, and no such person exists.

Daniel Wren is unique. He has been raised and trained from a young age to hone his psychic gifts. He lives in a world unimagined by most. And he has been waiting for years to contact his counterpart, soulmate, if you will. But the problem is that she is painfully unaware of the type of life that he lives and the life she would be entering into if they came together.

His dilemma becomes how best to proceed. How can he win her over and move forward before outside forces take that decision away from him?

More Books by Evelyn Klebert

**Travels into the Breach**
*Accounts of a Reluctant Mystic*
6 x 9 Softcover & Hardcover 171 pages
ISBN 978-1-61342-323-3
ISBN (Hardcover) 978-1-61342-417-9

At first glance, his life seems quiet, serene, and even un-eventful. Malachi McKellan, a 65-year-old widower and author of esoteric books, lives largely as a recluse in a house situated just off the banks of Bayou St. John in New Orleans. But unbeknownst to most, he is also a bit of a detective, a specific kind of detective whose specialty is psychic attacks. Alongside his lifelong companion and spirit guide Simon Tull, a 19th-century, 20-something English gent, Malachi battles the unseen, and is an unacknowledged hero to the most vulnerable. Most of the population have no idea what is really happening beneath the surface of the world in which they live.

In this collection of adventures, Malachi McKellan and Simon Tull wage war against the most insidious elements of the paranormal. In *The Three*, Malachi and Simon come to the aid of a young woman being victimized by a group of dark witches. An old apartment building is the scene of an unimaginable battle against monstrous forces in *The Lost Soul*. Malachi and Simon find themselves strategizing against a psychic vampire in *Obsession*, and *The Hotel* turns back time to the 1980s where Malachi confronts a demonic spirit. In *Between*, a past life is revisited as Malachi attempts to rescue a beloved sister from committing her existence to vengeance, and *The Wedding* takes a personal turn when Malachi must confront painful truths while endeavoring to protect his niece from a potentially devastating union.

Travel into the breach with a pair of paranormal warriors who choose to confront overwhelming forces on a battlefield unsuspected by most.

**Gravier's Bookshop**
*A New Orleans Paranormal Mystery (#1)*
6 x 9 Softcover & Hardcover 172 pages
ISBN 978-1-61342-288-5
ISBN (Hardcover) 978-1-61342-411-7

Max Gravier had no intention of becoming a recluse, but after his wife's death it seems his life is heading in that direction. He spends his time running Gravier's Bookshop on Magazine Street and occasionally on the quiet helps the police solve a crime with his psychic sensitivities. That is until he answers Caroline Breslin's call, a cry for help out of his dreams that draws him into a fierce battle for a young woman's soul.

In this first installment of The New Orleans Paranormal Mystery series, Caroline Breslin, an amazingly gifted empath, is determined to strike out on her own and has moved out from the protection of her family home. All is going extremely well until, of course, she comes under siege from a devastating supernatural attack. The last thing Caroline wants is to run back to her family for help, even though she is painfully in over her head. What she really needs is a knight in shining armor—or maybe just that guy that keeps haunting her dreams.

Join them and the whole Breslin family psychic clan in this first installment of The New Orleans Paranormal Mystery Series where you'll travel into a new world just a few steps into the turbulent realm of the unseen.

## The Hotel Mandolin
*A New Orleans Paranormal Mystery (#2)*
6 x 9 Softcover & Hardcover 146 pages
ISBN 978-1-61342-290-8
ISBN (Hardcover) 978-1-61342-412-4

Peril is wrapped up in the most enticing of disguises in *The Hotel Mandolin*, the second installment of The New Orleans Paranormal Mystery series. It's opulent, classic, and one of the most renowned hotels nestled deep in New Orleans' famous business district, but something is amiss at The Hotel Mandolin.

PI Peter Norfleet is calling out the big guns to help him investigate a recent suicide at the famous establishment—his good friend Max Gravier, a formidable psychic, and his girlfriend, Caroline Breslin, a talented empath. But none of them can seem to scratch the surface of this puzzle, no one except Cassie Breslin, Caroline's clairvoyant mother, who has somehow tapped into an unexpected connection with a tragic ghost from the turn of the century. And the more she uncovers, the more dangerous and malevolent the mystery becomes

## The House at Pritchard Place
*A New Orleans Paranormal Mystery (#3)*
6 x 9 Softcover & Hardcover 138 pages
ISBN 978-1-61342-292-2
ISBN (Hardcover) 978-1-61342-413-1

Nothing is really wrong with the old Warrick House on Dante St. except that there most certainly is. Nothing is exactly wrong with its new mysterious owner except that Elise is sure that something doesn't add up. It isn't obvious, but sometimes the most dangerous things aren't.

In the third installment of The New Orleans Paranormal Mystery series, with the help of her very psychic sister and her children, the Breslin clan, Elise Ashford is about to embark on a wild rescue mission straight into another dimension that will land her squarely somewhere she doesn't expect, right back into her past. She'll land full circle; in a childhood home whose memory still haunts her to this day -- *The House at Pritchard Place.*

## Treading on Borrowed Time
6 x 9 Softcover & Hardcover 223 pages
ISBN 978-1-61342-214-4
ISBN (Hardcover) 978-1-61342-436-0

For Julia Moreau, life seems complicated. Emerging from a failed marriage and managing a lifetime of diabetes, she lives alone in her childhood home where she communicates with the spirit of her Great Aunt Lilia. But Julia doesn't have a clue what complicated is until she is thrust into being the key chess piece in a match between two powerful men of extraordinary abilities on the wild hunt for a mystical creature hidden in the heart of New Orleans' French Quarter. Will Julia lose her soul to the karma of a devastating past life or her heart to the love of a man driven by dark forces? What is clear is that whichever way she turns she is *Treading on Borrowed Time.*

More Books by Evelyn Klebert

## Sanctuary of Echoes
6 x 9 Softcover & Hardcover 371 pages
ISBN 978-1-61342-211-3
ISBN (Hardcover) 978-1-61342-409-4

Ghosts unacknowledged do not sleep.

Corey Knight has resigned herself to a quiet, reclusive life spent living out the rest of her days in her childhood home on the fringes of New Orleans' French Quarter. But the unexpected specter of her deceased father plunges her into a mad quest for a missing supernatural weapon unearthed long ago. And unfortunately, her only ally is a lost love she once betrayed.

Iain Shaw returns to New Orleans, a city he abandoned a decade before while fleeing a devastating past. Here, he is forced to confront it again in the visage of the woman he once adored - one that he is now determined to get back at any cost.

Follow them both in a wild paranormal tale of discovery and redemption as they confront and unearth the echoes of a buried and unyielding truth that once tore them irreparably apart.

## A Quiet Moment
6 x 9 Softcover & Hardcover 273 pages
ISBN 978-1-61342-326-4
ISBN (Hardcover) 978-1-61342-435-3

Jacob Wyss is caught in a rut, in fact on the verge of being engulfed by it. After an excruciating and disillusioning divorce, his life as an artist in a sleepy-college town at the foot of the Appalachian Mountains has become quiet, routine, and maddening in its predictability. One wintry day, his deep restlessness drives him out in precarious conditions to a largely empty bookstore nearly devoid of another living soul, nearly.

Aimee Marston isn't like everyone else. On the surface, she lives a sedate life working as a feature writer for a small local newspaper in addition to several other editorial jobs to help make ends meet. But just beneath, her existence is largely not her own. She is a sensitive, an empathetic psychic, guided by her calling to use her gifts to help others. Unfortunately, as a result, her secretiveness has made her defensive, protective of herself, and prevented her from having much of a life.

A psychic call for help sends Aimee out on a freezing January morning where her destiny and Jacob's collide sending both their lives spiraling onto an unexpected and often disturbing track. Two lonely souls connect, not by accident, but by design. Theirs is the intersection of two spiritual paths, two lovers who must struggle to overcome the phantoms of a past life, as well as the challenges of their own inner demons to carve out an extraordinary future together.

### A Ghost of a Chance
6 x 9 Softcover & Hardcover 230 pages
ISBN 978-1-61342-162-8
ISBN (Hardcover) 978-1-61342-440-7

You never know what's coming next.

Jack Brennan, an ambitious high-powered attorney, dies. But that's not the end, rather only the beginning. He finds himself constrained to an inexplicable afterlife as an earth-bound spirit trapped in an old Virginia farmhouse. His only companion is a very much living, reclusive writer of campy vampire novels. The maddening problem is that Hallie does not know he is there, nor that he is somewhat reluctantly falling in love with her.

Hallie Barkly is recovering from a painful and disillusioning divorce. Out of the ashes of her former life, she has managed to somehow forge a career and exorcise her demons by writing under the pseudonym of Sebastian Winters. Slowly, she is awakening to the fact that she is not alone.

Their lives intersect, and two unconventional lovers are brought together under insurmountable circumstances. Together they must battle an unseen force hell-bent on possessing Hallie's life and bridge death itself to make possible what cannot be—to find a chance.

### Dragonflies - Journeys into the Paranormal
6 x 9 Softcover & Hardcover 176 pages
ISBN 978-1-88756-072-6
ISBN (Hardcover) 979-8-32548-418-6

In every form of creation, there is a blueprint for living, for experience, for interpretation. In flight, they can twist, turn, alter direction, pause in midair, and even fly backward. The dragonfly is the master of adaptability. They are a living prism, refracting light, and color, seemingly shifting their essence.

The lesson the dragonfly gives is that life is never what it appears to be.

In "The Wizard," as a novice practitioner of magic, Aurora Finn finds herself battling against the illusions of a powerful wizard intent on separating her from the world she knows. "The Sojourners" is a gentle story of a mother and daughter whose tenancy in an old Virginia farmhouse uncovers the trials and sorrows of its former occupants. A bookstore clerk gets an extraordinary customer on Halloween night in "Late One Night at Berstrums Books." In "The Tear," a woman coping with her fatal illness unknowingly begins a track on a mystical journey that will entirely restructure her vision of the world.

These stories follow the path of the dragonfly imbued with the momentum and energy of change, taking a winding and treacherous journey that ultimately leads to truth buried beneath perception.

## Breaking Through the Pale
6 x 9 Softcover 134 pages
ISBN 978-1-88756-045-0

Journey with metaphysical author Evelyn Klebert into a collection of short stories that travel beyond the pale into the unpredictable realm of the paranormal.

In "A Grey Mourning," a disillusioned man encounters a mysterious being on the foggy streets of New Orleans. "Contact" is a tale of automatic writing, when a young artist establishes communication with a spirit guide, and the victim of a car crash unravels the true nature of her existence in "Dancing on the Threshold." The final tale is called "Isolation," in which a confused and disoriented woman finds herself in an old, quaint house where she must piece together the mystical implications surrounding her predicament.

## The Witches' Own
6 x 9 Softcover & Hardcover 140 pages
ISBN 978-1-61342-058-4
ISBN (Hardcover) 978-1-61342-428-5

On the surface things seem quiet and serene in the picturesque coastal village of Kilmarnock, Virginia. But something unseen roams its lush forests as the past and present collide and the unthinkable begins to wreak its vengeance. Young Lucy Bonner is executed for witchcraft in the town's distant and brutal past. Her death triggers an unholy chain of events which grasp at the restless heart of novelist Peter McQuade, spurring him towards a quest to uncover the dark and terrifying truth.

### The Left Palm
*And Other Halloween Tales of the Supernatural*
6 x 9 Softcover & Hardcover 122 pages
ISBN 978-1-93493-556-9
ISBN (Hardcover) 978-1-61342-442-1

Halloween is the time of year when that veil between worlds is thinned, and you can just catch a quick glimpse into the realm of the unknowable. In this collection of short stories, Evelyn Klebert takes you to a place where ordinary life splinters into the sphere of the paranormal.

The journey begins with one woman's unstoppable quest for vengeance against a supernatural creature in "Wolves" and continues in an old historical graveyard where a horrifying discovery is uncovered in "Emma Fallon." In "The Soul Shredder," a psychiatrist's unusual patient opens his eyes to a disturbing new view of reality, while in "Wildflowers," a woman strikes up a supernatural friendship with impossible implications. And in "The Left Palm," a fortuneteller in the French Quarter receives a most unexpected and terrifying customer.

### White Harbor Road
*And Other Tales of Paranormal Romance*
6 x 9 Softcover & Hardcover 152 pages
ISBN 978-1-61342-066-9
ISBN (Hardcover) 978-1-61342-441-4

A psychic soul mate, a time traveler, a horror writer, and an enigmatic stranger take a selection of resilient, life-battered heroines to a place of paranormal healing and transformation. In this collection of short stories, *White Harbor Road* is the last stop where life's burdens and hardships evolve into something unexpected.

## Explanations
6 x 9 Softcover 82 pages
ISBN 978-1-93493-515-6

In this, her second poetry collection, Evelyn Klebert takes us down the intricate path of a personal journey. Life with its particular struggles, pitfalls, and ultimately triumphs clearly begins to mirror a universal path, the quest for answers that we all ultimately pursue. In this reflective, esoteric collection we can all explore and seek some of life's elemental mysteries and hopefully when all is said and done emerge with some *Explanations*.

## Considerations
6 x 9 Softcover 84 pages
ISBN 978-1-88756-062-7

Sometimes the struggle to understand the meaning and complexities of living comes down to a single moment of introspection or a fleeting yet meaningful reflection. This collection of poetry by Evelyn Klebert takes you down a winding path of self-discovery where the resolution may not always be absolute, but the journey is indeed unforgettable. It a wide and varied map of inspired poetry for your examination and consideration.

**Appointment with the Unknown**
*The Hotel Stories*
6 x 9 Softcover & Hardcover 155 pages
ISBN 978-1-61342-360-8
ISBN (Hardcover) 978-1-61342-421-6

A hotel, for most, represents a normal place, a predictable realm of commonality. One might even go as far to say a safe space, the reliable where nothing particularly unusual is expected to happen. Or is it? Dimensional traveling, spirit guides, mystical storms, and soul mates separated by time are only a few elements dotting this supernatural landscape. Drop into a collection of romantic paranormal stories where that place of commonality is only the threshold, the jumping-off point, for extraordinary adventures into the unknown.

Visit Evelyn's website at:
www.evelynklebert.com

Cornerstone Book Publishers
www.cornerstonepublishers.com

www.ingramcontent.com/pod-product-compliance
Lightning Source LLC
Chambersburg PA
CBHW030103260626
47156CB00008B/2497